THE ODYSSEY
—HOMER—

TO ANDREA, WHO SHOWS ME EVERY DAY THAT WE CAN BE WHO WE WANT TO BE
- TIM

TO MY MOM, WHO LET ME READ THE WEIRDEST BOOKS AS A KID
- BEN

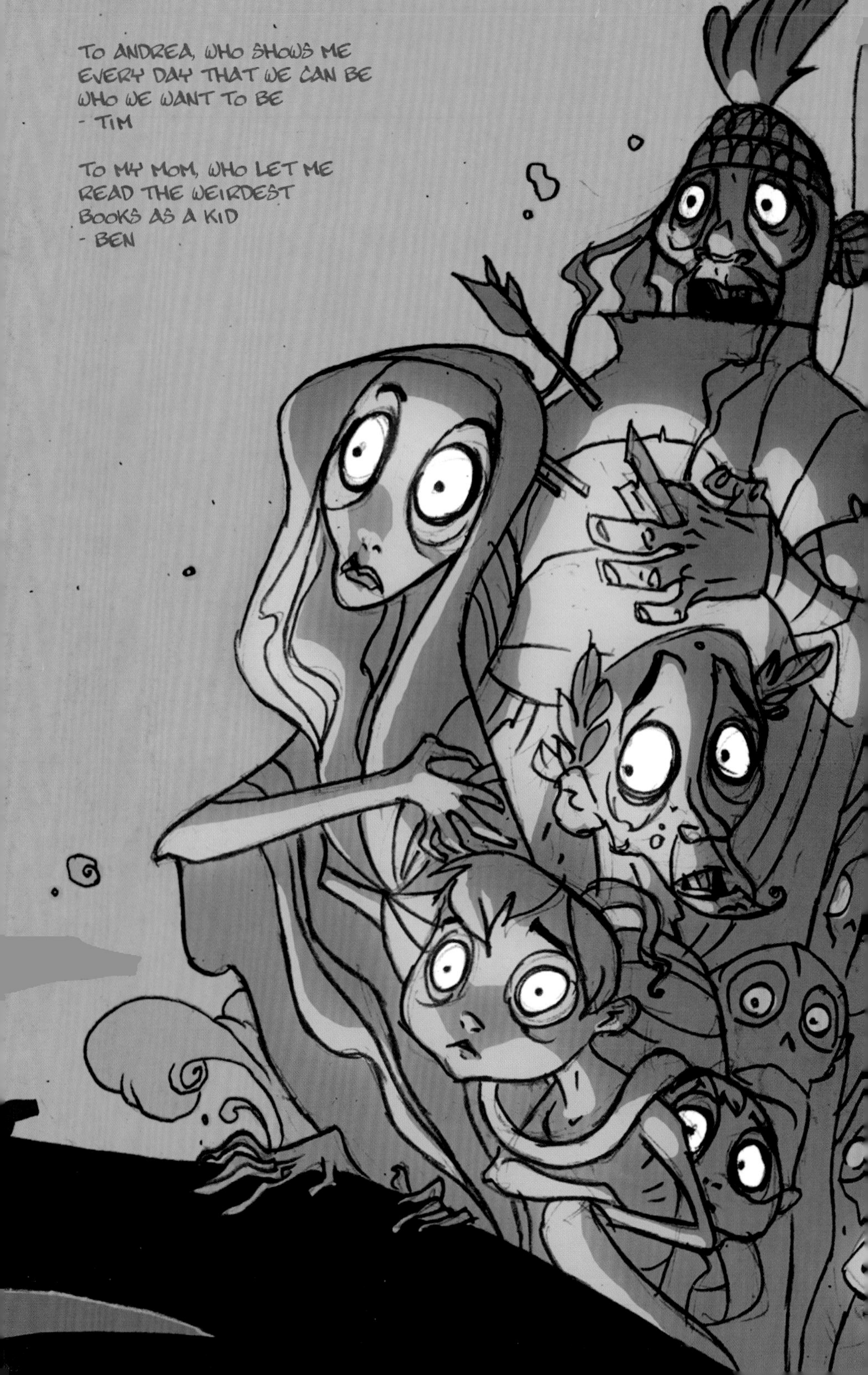

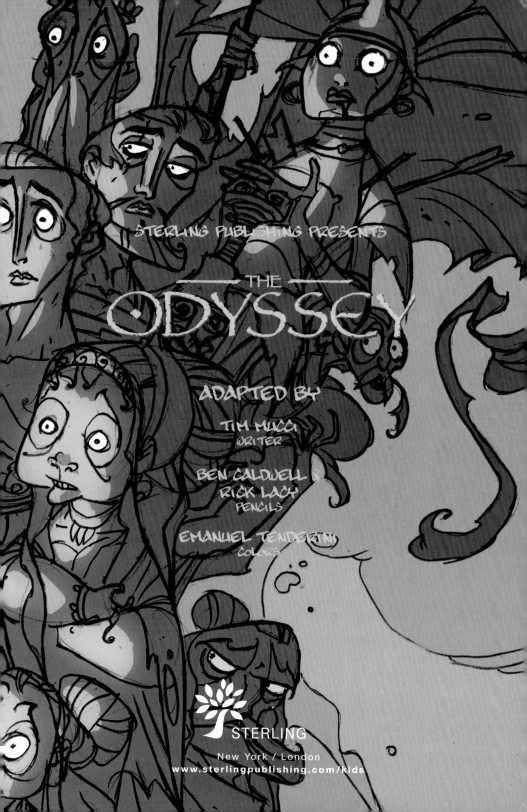

STERLING PUBLISHING PRESENTS

THE
ODYSSEY

ADAPTED BY

TIM MUCCI
WRITER

BEN CALDWELL &
RICK LACY
PENCILS

EMANUEL TENDERINI
COLORS

STERLING

New York / London
www.sterlingpublishing.com/kids

STERLING AND THE DISTINCTIVE
STERLING LOGO ARE REGISTERED TRADEMARKS OF
STERLING PUBLISHING CO., INC.
LOT # =
2   4   6   8   10   9   7   5   3   1
02/10
PUBLISHED BY STERLING PUBLISHING CO., INC.
387 PARK AVENUE SOUTH, NEW YORK, NY 10016
© 2009 BY BEN CALDWELL
DISTRIBUTED IN CANADA BY STERLING PUBLISHING
C/O CANADIAN MANDA GROUP, 165 DUFFERIN STREET
TORONTO, ONTARIO, CANADA M6K 3H6
DISTRIBUTED IN THE UNITED KINGDOM BY GMC DISTRIBUTION SERVICES
CASTLE PLACE, 166 HIGH STREET, LEWES, EAST SUSSEX, ENGLAND BN7 1XU
DISTRIBUTED IN AUSTRALIA BY CAPRICORN LINK (AUSTRALIA) PTY. LTD.
P.O. BOX 704, WINDSOR, NSW 2756, AUSTRALIA

STERLING ISBN 978-1-4027-3155-6

FOR INFORMATION ABOUT CUSTOM EDITIONS,
SPECIAL SALES, PREMIUM AND CORPORATE PURCHASES,
PLEASE CONTACT STERLING SPECIAL SALES DEPARTMENT
AT 800-805-5489 OR
SPECIALSALES@STERLINGPUBLISHING.COM.

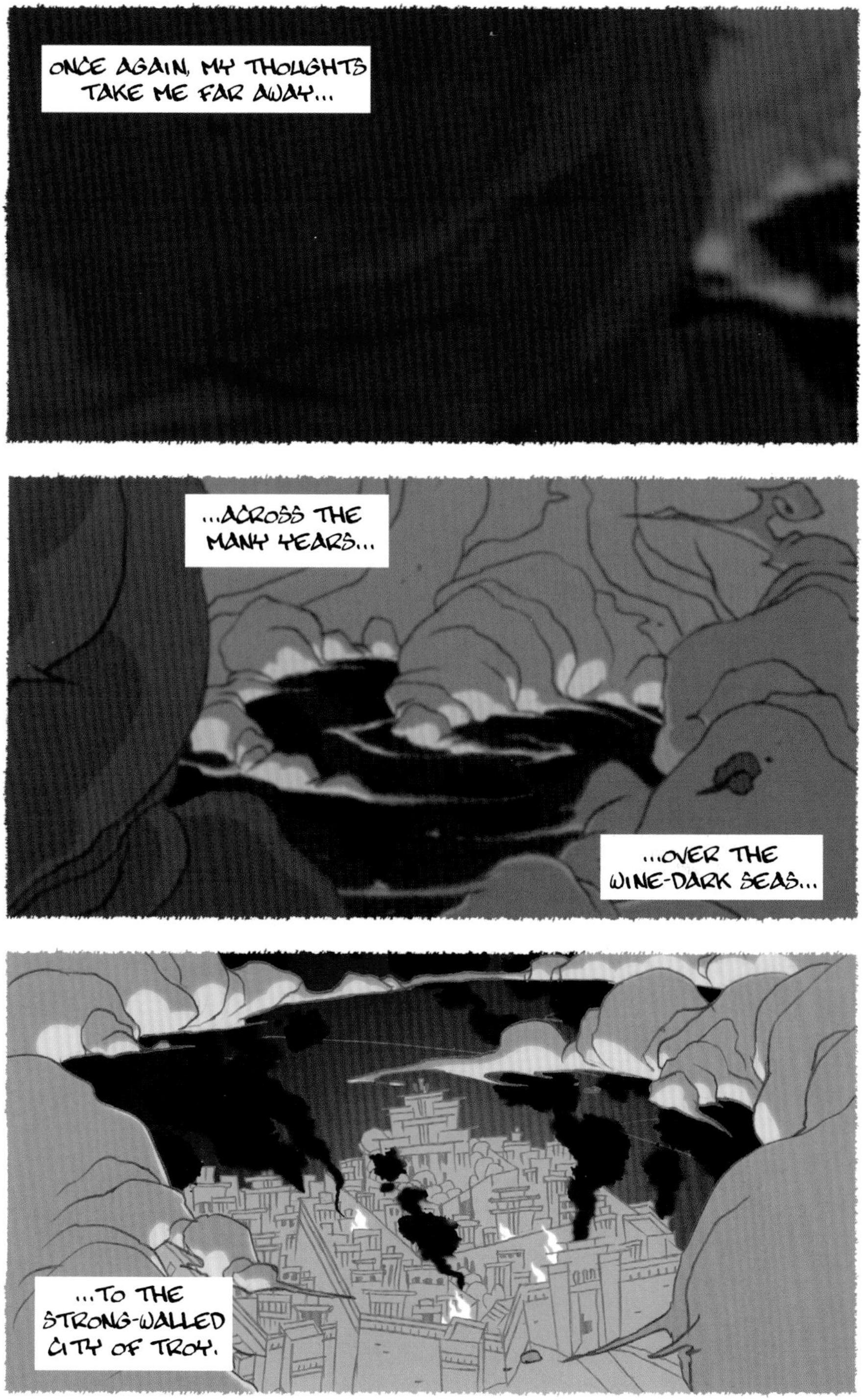
ONCE AGAIN, MY THOUGHTS TAKE ME FAR AWAY...
...ACROSS THE MANY YEARS...
...OVER THE WINE-DARK SEAS...
...TO THE STRONG-WALLED CITY OF TROY.

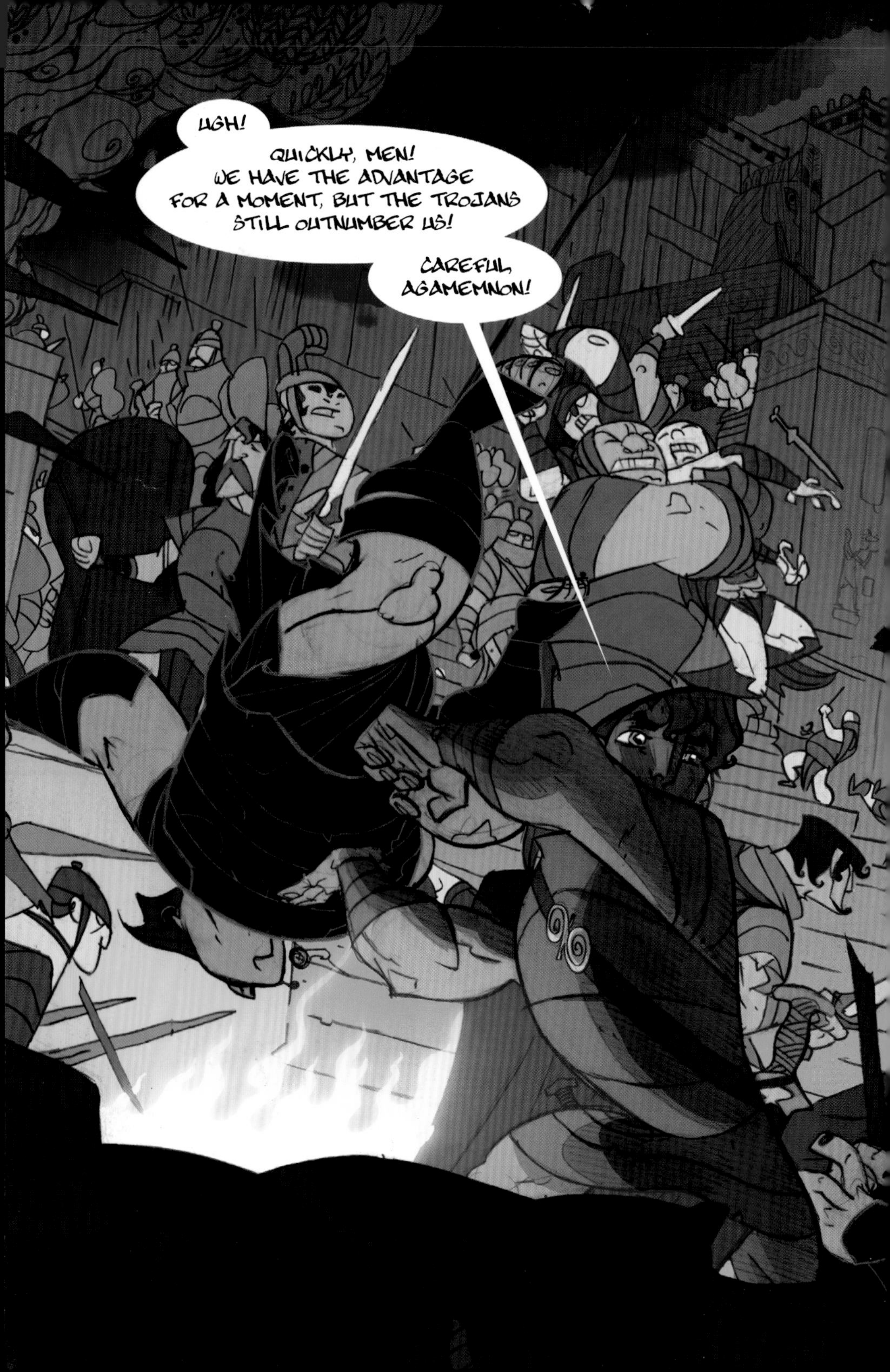
UGH!
QUICKLY, MEN! WE HAVE THE ADVANTAGE FOR A MOMENT, BUT THE TROJANS STILL OUTNUMBER US!
CAREFUL, AGAMEMNON!

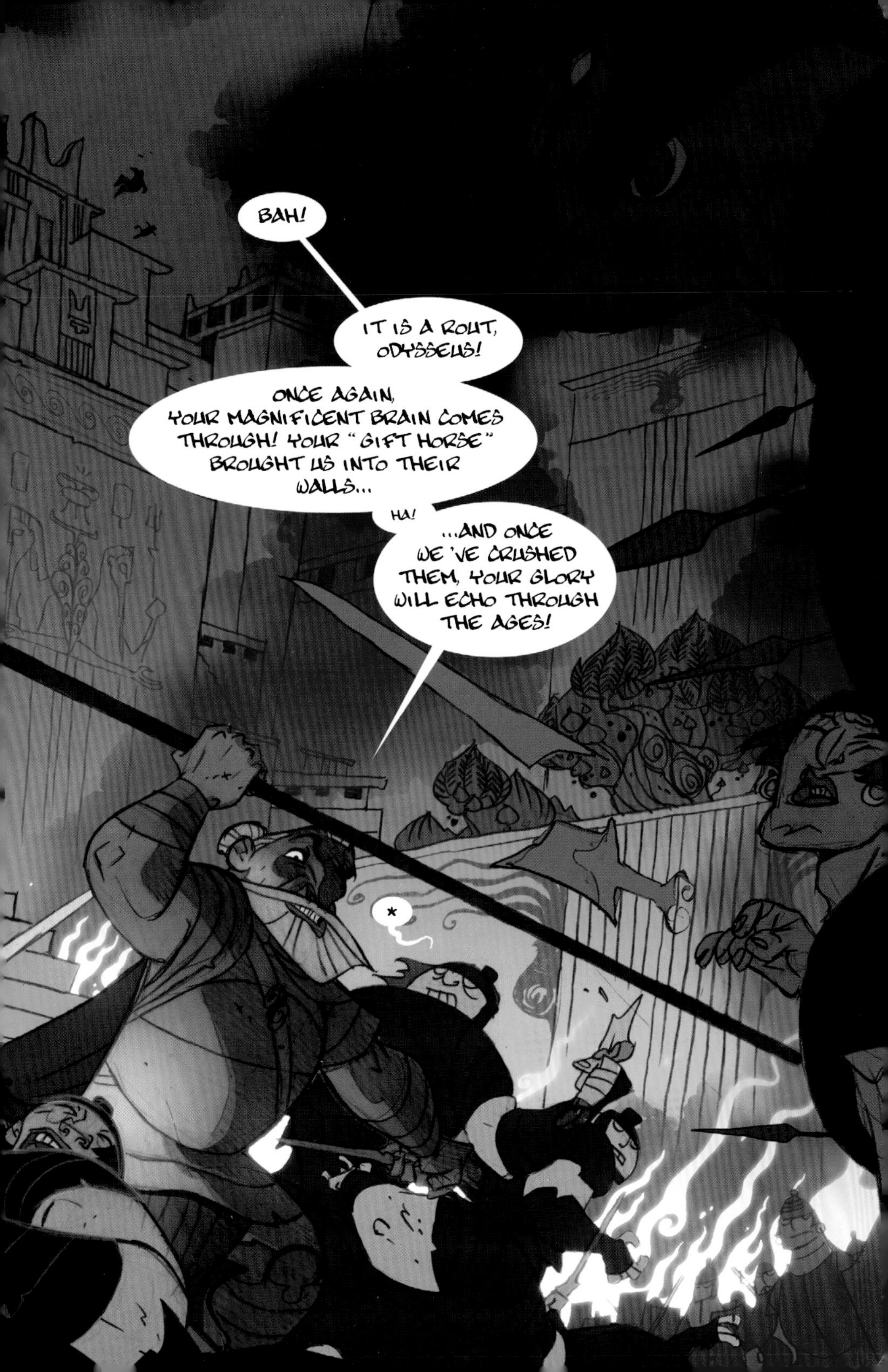
BAH!
IT IS A ROUT, ODYSSEUS!
ONCE AGAIN, YOUR MAGNIFICENT BRAIN COMES THROUGH! YOUR "GIFT HORSE" BROUGHT US INTO THEIR WALLS...
HA!
...AND ONCE WE'VE CRUSHED THEM, YOUR GLORY WILL ECHO THROUGH THE AGES!
*

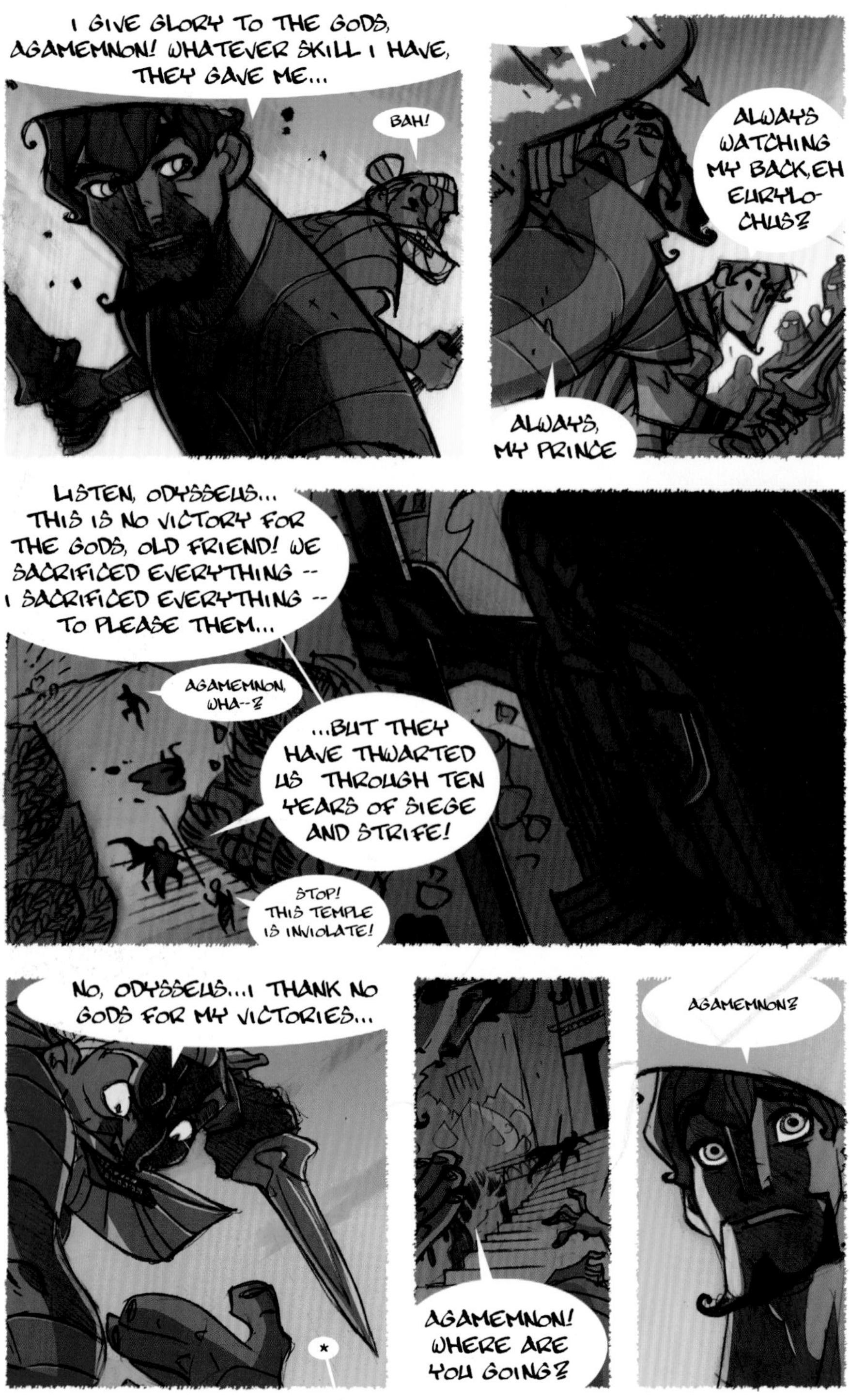
I GIVE GLORY TO THE GODS, AGAMEMNON! WHATEVER SKILL I HAVE, THEY GAVE ME...
BAH!
ALWAYS WATCHING MY BACK, EH EURYLOCHUS?
ALWAYS, MY PRINCE
LISTEN, ODYSSEUS... THIS IS NO VICTORY FOR THE GODS, OLD FRIEND! WE SACRIFICED EVERYTHING -- I SACRIFICED EVERYTHING -- TO PLEASE THEM...
AGAMEMNON, WHA--?
...BUT THEY HAVE THWARTED US THROUGH TEN YEARS OF SIEGE AND STRIFE!
STOP! THIS TEMPLE IS INVIOLATE!
NO, ODYSSEUS...I THANK NO GODS FOR MY VICTORIES...
*
AGAMEMNON! WHERE ARE YOU GOING?
AGAMEMNON?

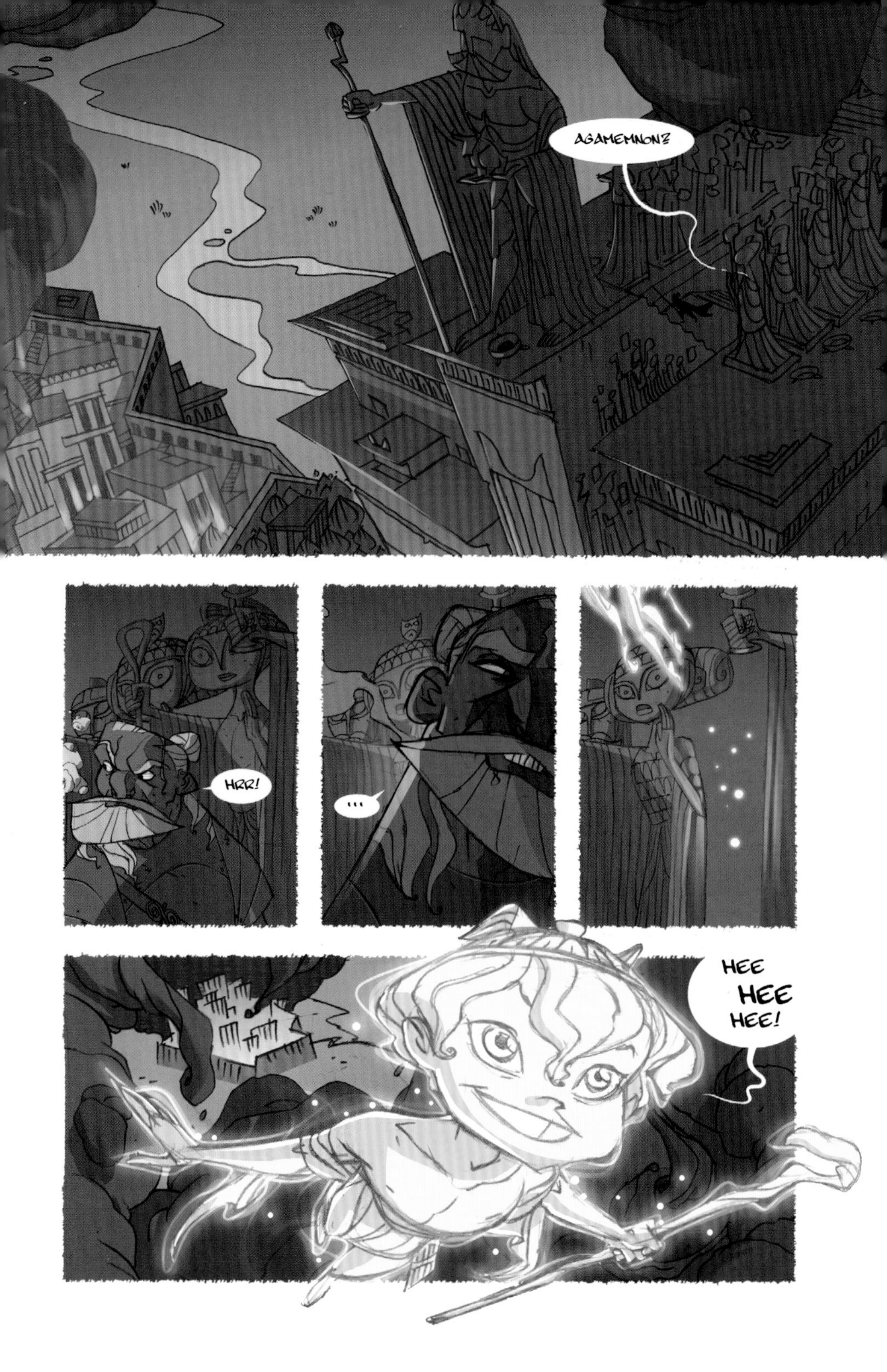
AGAMEMNON?
HRR!
...
HEE HEE HEE!

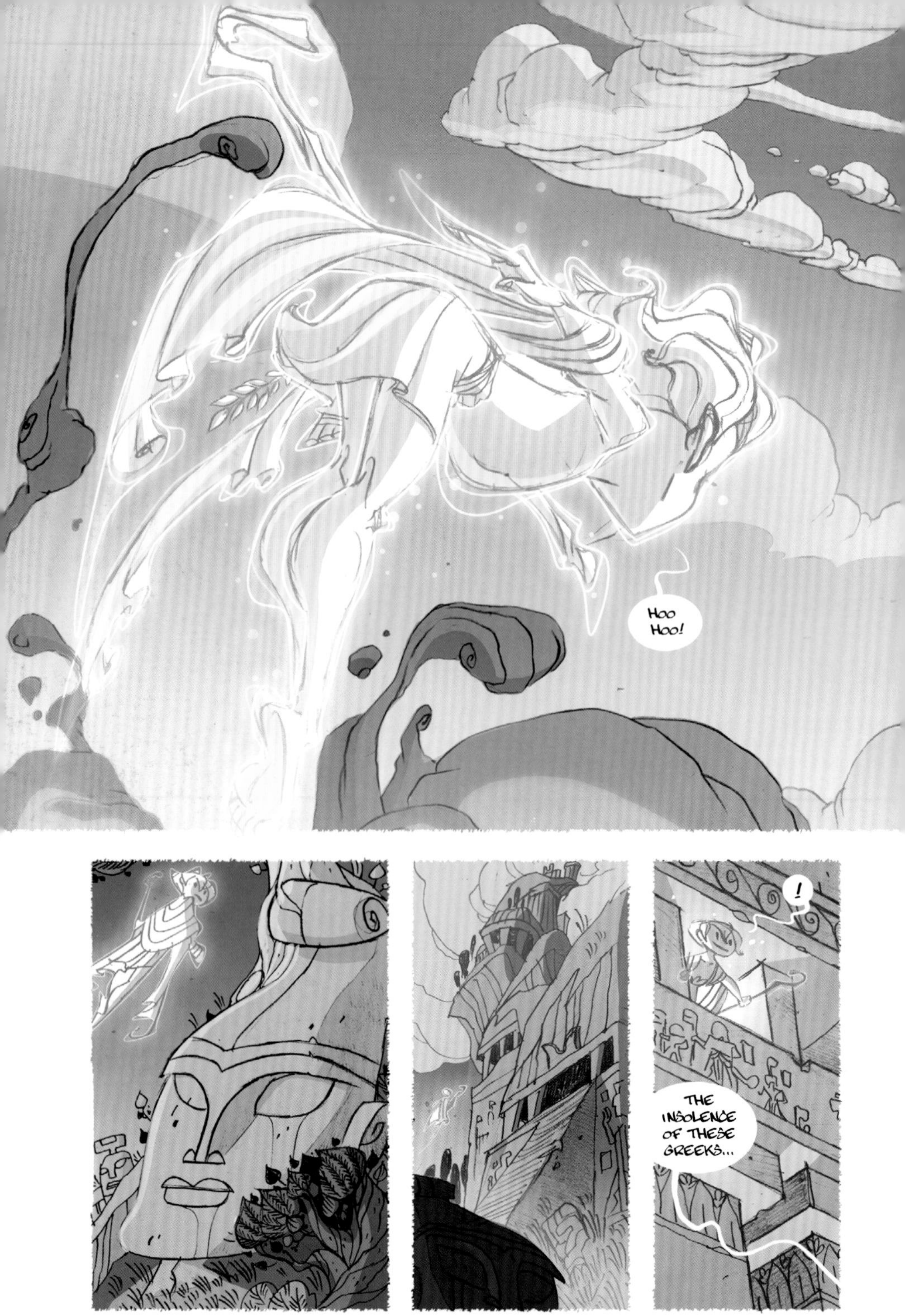
HOO HOO!
!
THE INSOLENCE OF THESE GREEKS...

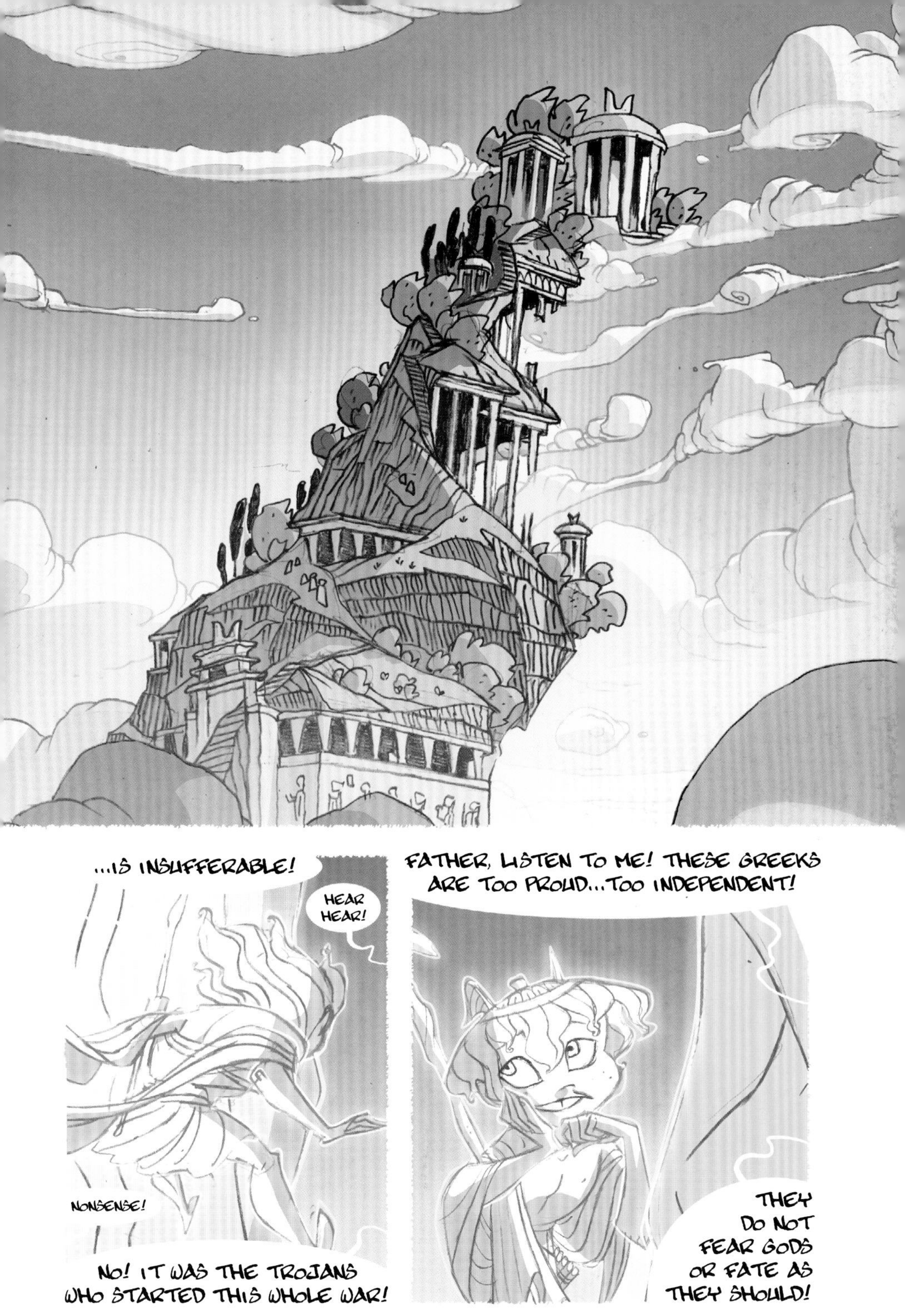
...IS INSUFFERABLE!
HEAR HEAR!
NONSENSE!
NO! IT WAS THE TROJANS WHO STARTED THIS WHOLE WAR!
FATHER, LISTEN TO ME! THESE GREEKS ARE TOO PROUD...TOO INDEPENDENT!
THEY DO NOT FEAR GODS OR FATE AS THEY SHOULD!

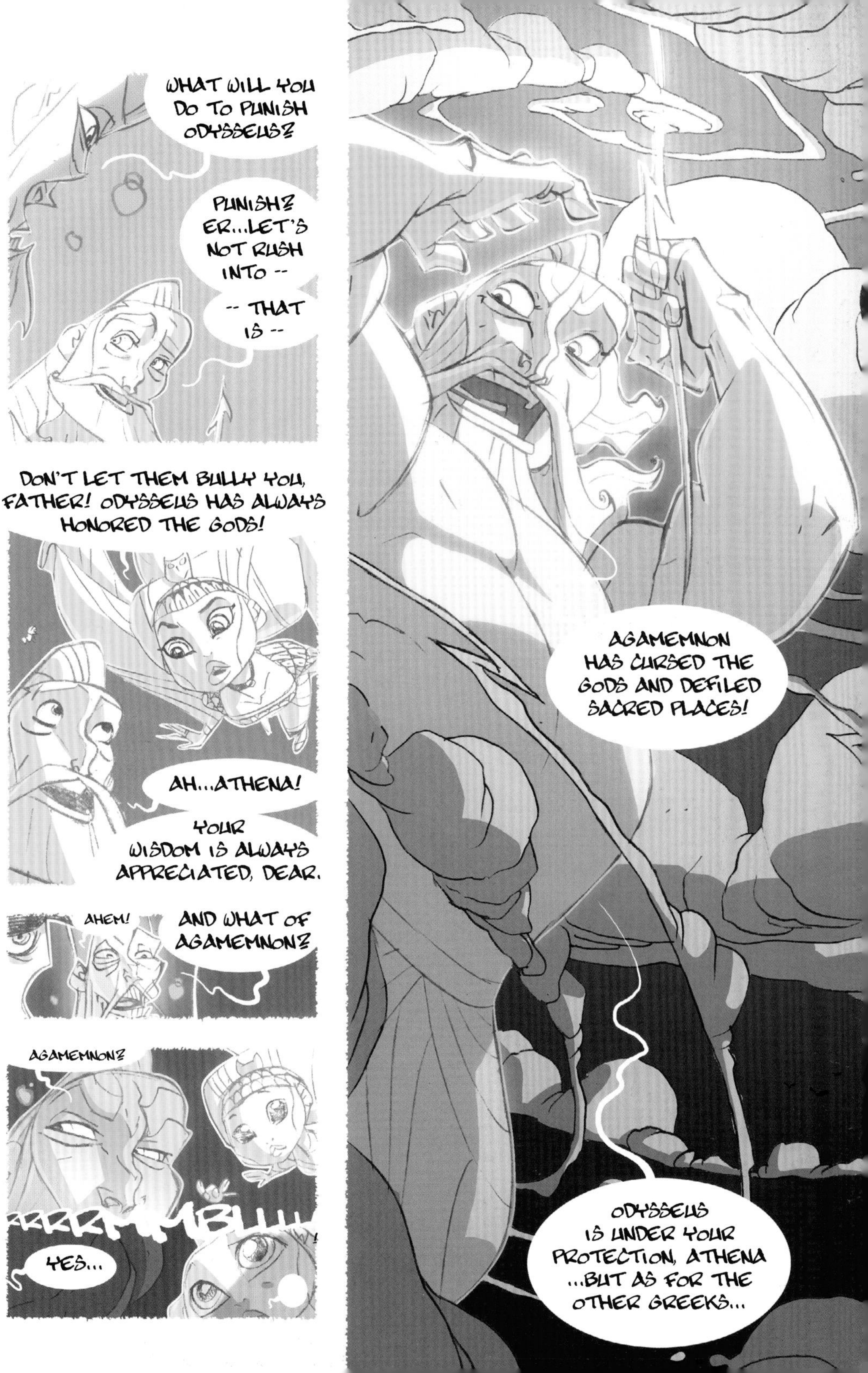
WHAT WILL YOU DO TO PUNISH ODYSSEUS?
PUNISH? ER...LET'S NOT RUSH INTO --
-- THAT IS --
DON'T LET THEM BULLY YOU, FATHER! ODYSSEUS HAS ALWAYS HONORED THE GODS!
AH...ATHENA!
YOUR WISDOM IS ALWAYS APPRECIATED, DEAR.
AHEM!
AND WHAT OF AGAMEMNON?
AGAMEMNON?
RRRRMMMBLLL
YES...
AGAMEMNON HAS CURSED THE GODS AND DEFILED SACRED PLACES!
ODYSSEUS IS UNDER YOUR PROTECTION, ATHENA ...BUT AS FOR THE OTHER GREEKS...

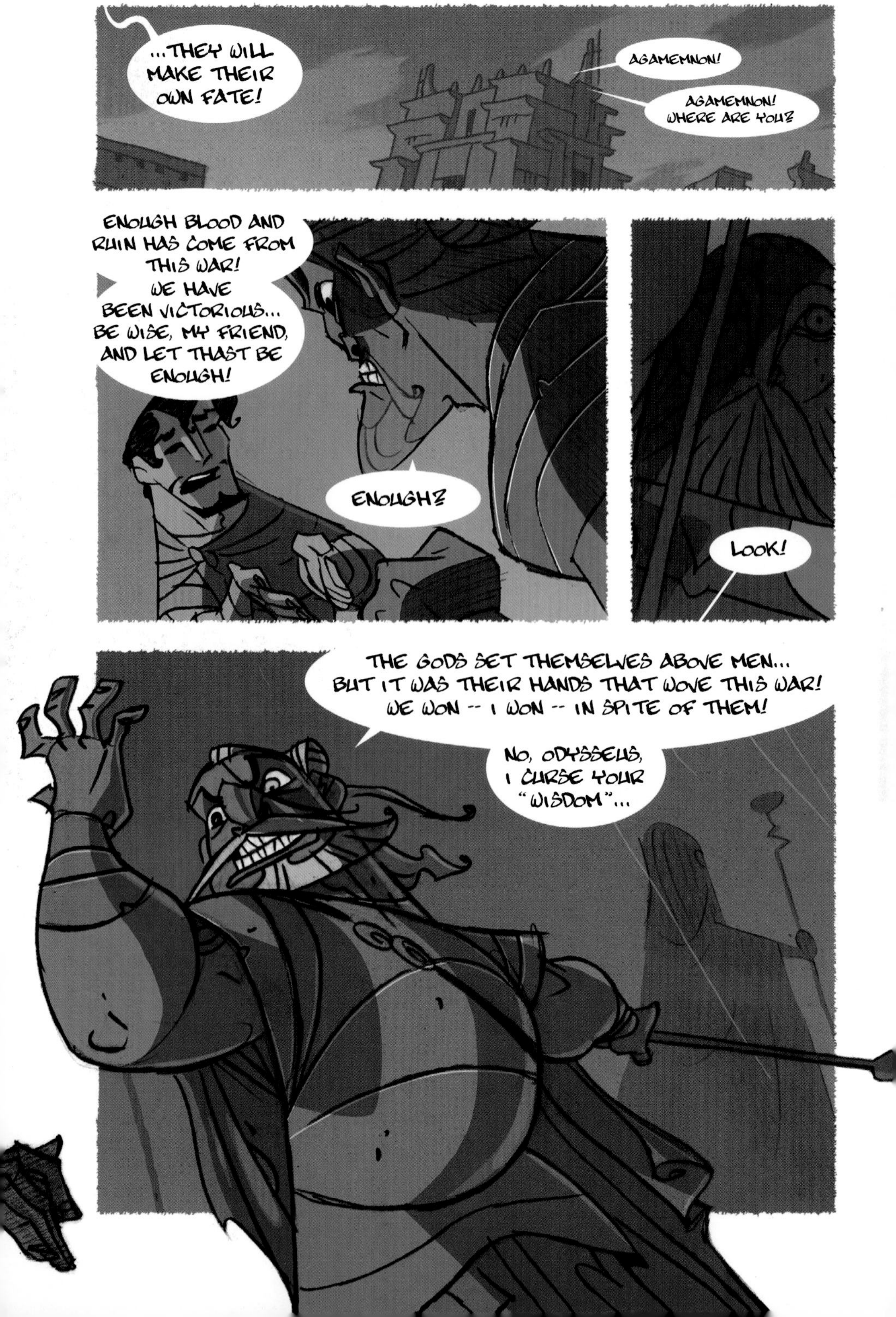
...THEY WILL MAKE THEIR OWN FATE!
AGAMEMNON!
AGAMEMNON! WHERE ARE YOU?
ENOUGH BLOOD AND RUIN HAS COME FROM THIS WAR! WE HAVE BEEN VICTORIOUS... BE WISE, MY FRIEND, AND LET THAST BE ENOUGH!
ENOUGH?
LOOK!
THE GODS SET THEMSELVES ABOVE MEN... BUT IT WAS THEIR HANDS THAT WOVE THIS WAR! WE WON -- I WON -- IN SPITE OF THEM!
NO, ODYSSEUS, I CURSE YOUR "WISDOM"...

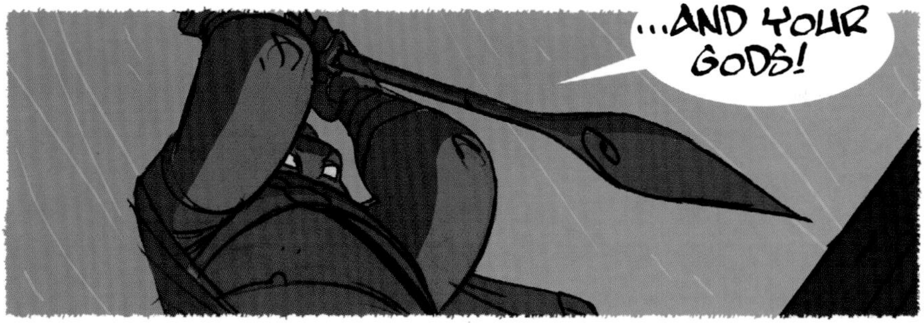
...AND YOUR GODS!

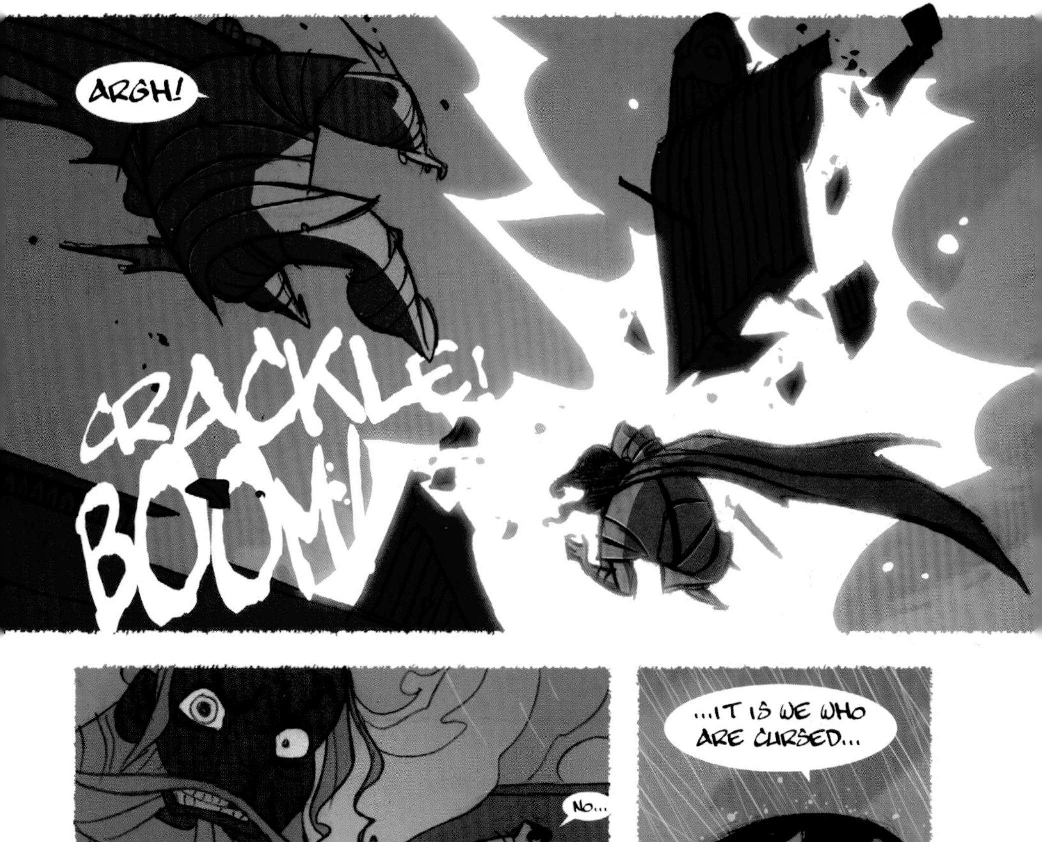
ARGH!
CRACKLE!
BOOM!

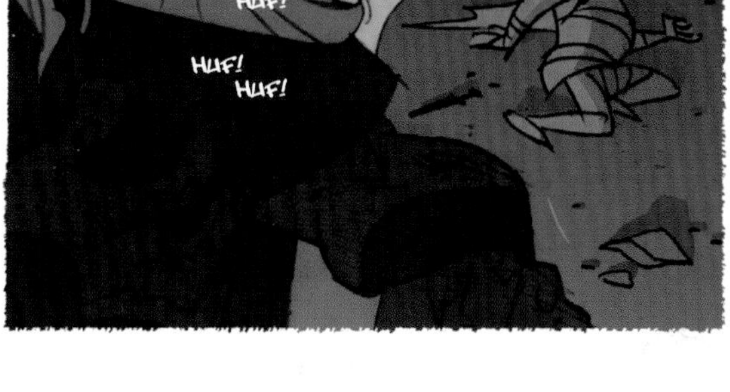
NO...
HUF!
HUF!
HUF!

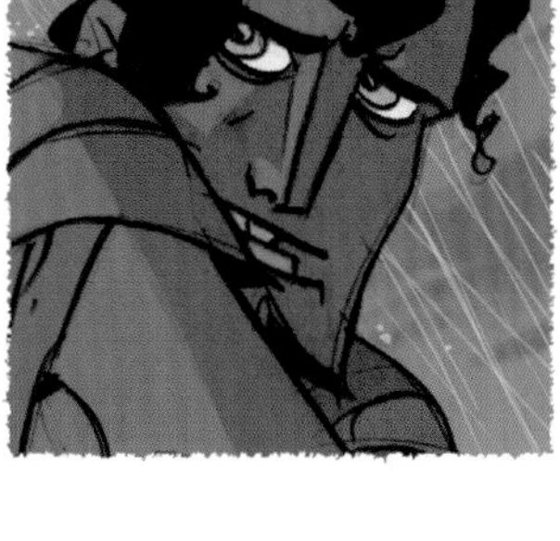
...IT IS WE WHO ARE CURSED...

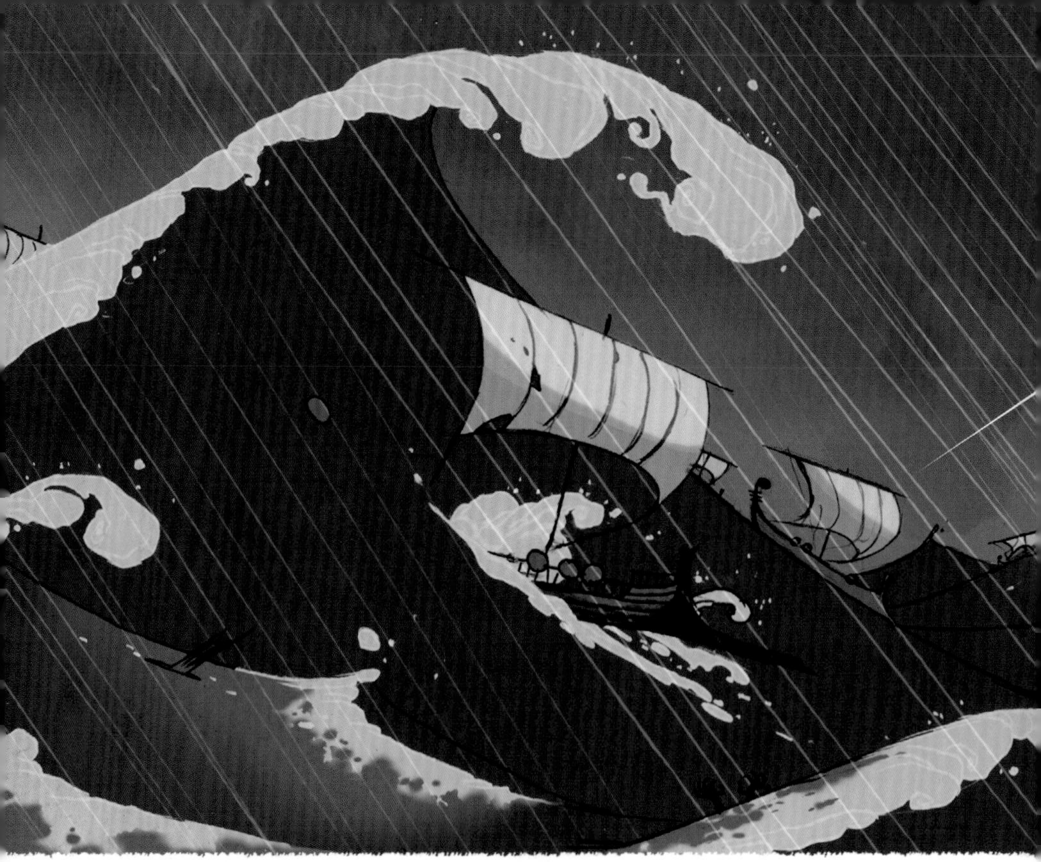

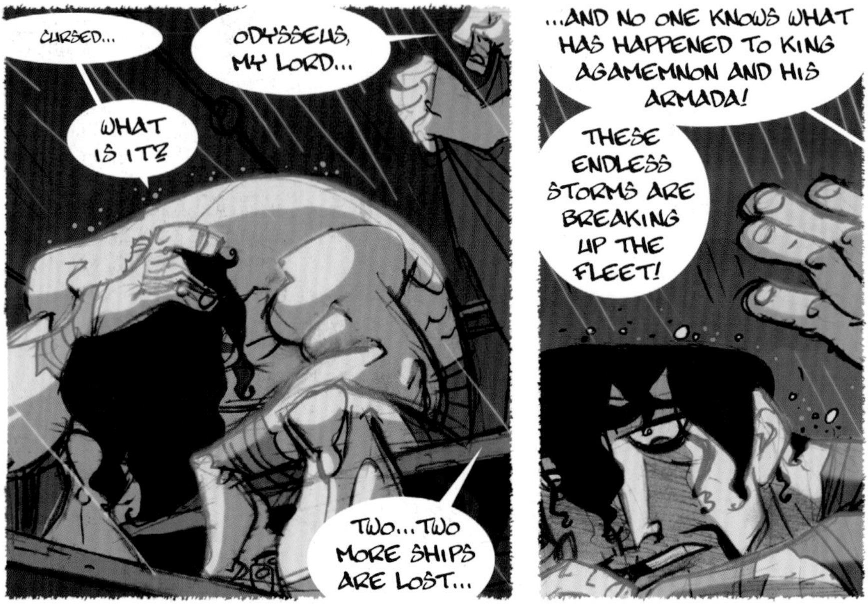
CURSED...
ODYSSEUS, MY LORD...
WHAT IS IT?
TWO...TWO MORE SHIPS ARE LOST...
...AND NO ONE KNOWS WHAT HAS HAPPENED TO KING AGAMEMNON AND HIS ARMADA!
THESE ENDLESS STORMS ARE BREAKING UP THE FLEET!

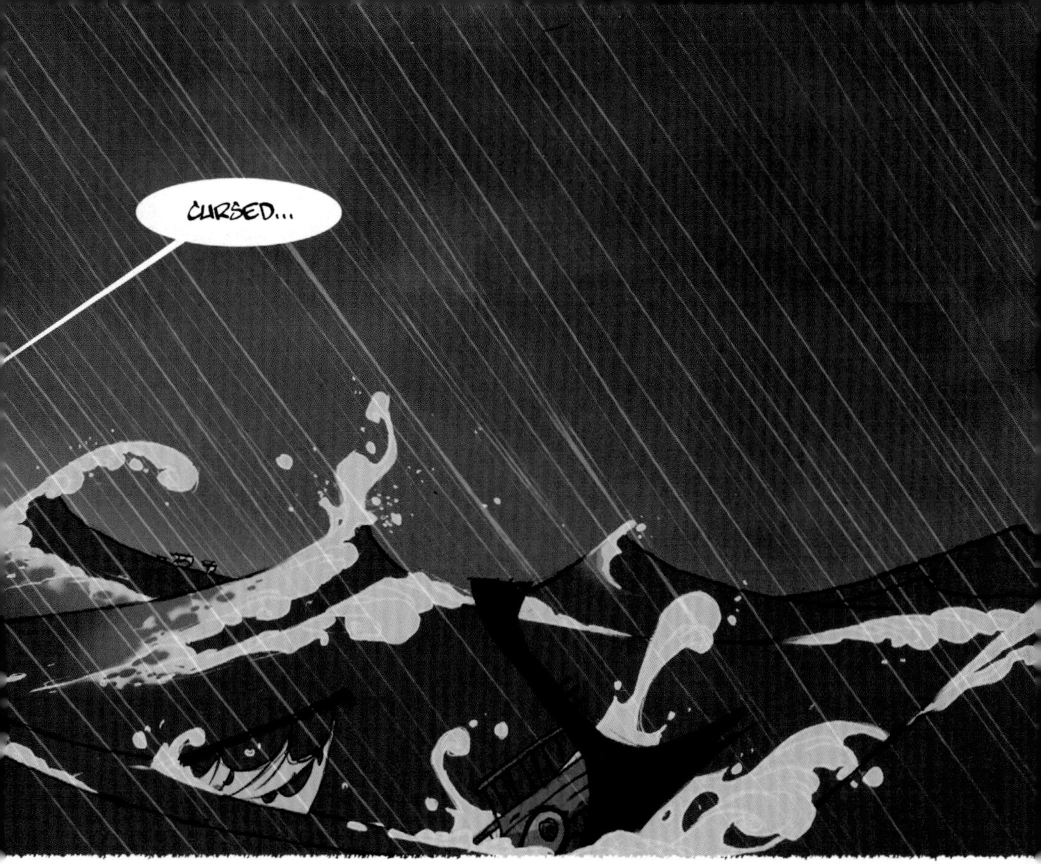
CURSED...

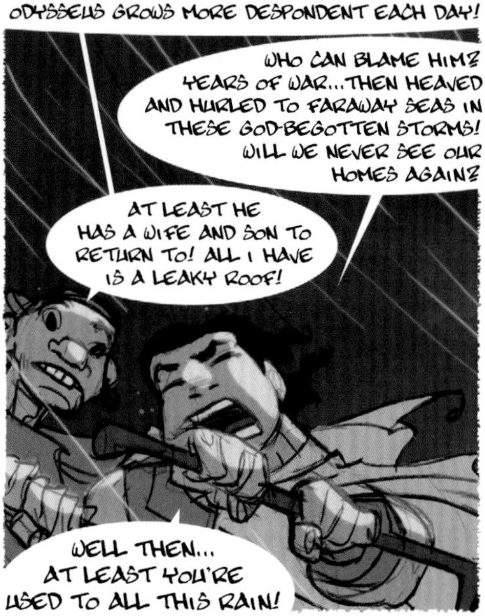
ODYSSEUS GROWS MORE DESPONDENT EACH DAY!
WHO CAN BLAME HIM? YEARS OF WAR...THEN HEAVED AND HURLED TO FARAWAY SEAS IN THESE GOD-BEGOTTEN STORMS! WILL WE NEVER SEE OUR HOMES AGAIN?
AT LEAST HE HAS A WIFE AND SON TO RETURN TO! ALL I HAVE IS A LEAKY ROOF!
WELL THEN... AT LEAST YOU'RE USED TO ALL THIS RAIN!

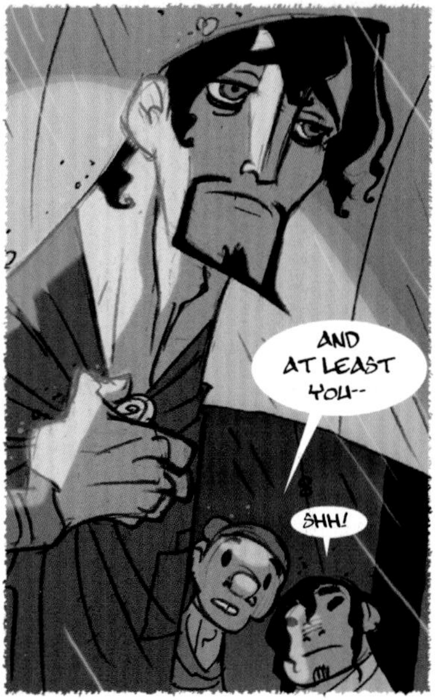
AND AT LEAST YOU--
SHH!

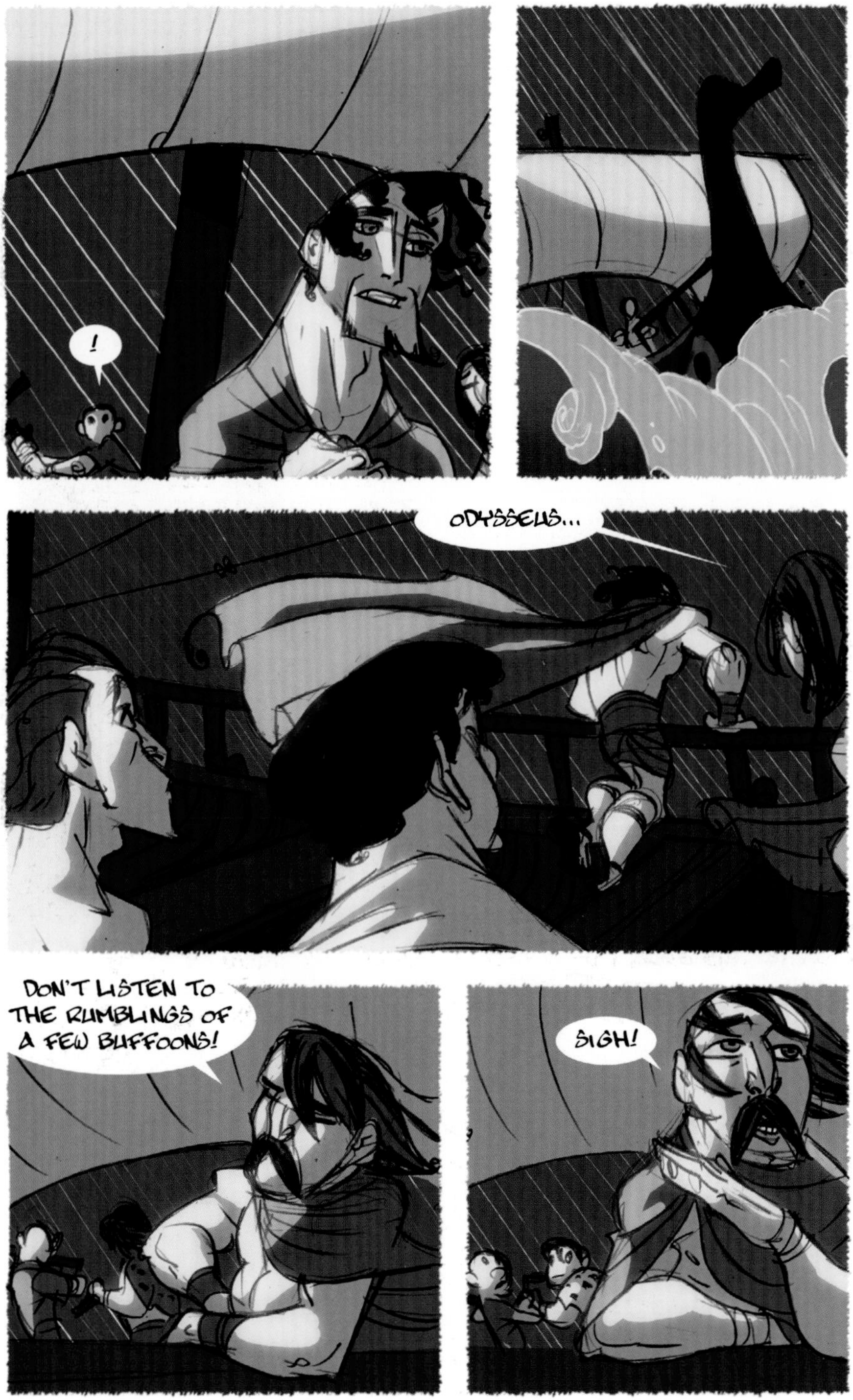
!
ODYSSEUS...
DON'T LISTEN TO THE RUMBLINGS OF A FEW BUFFOONS!
SIGH!

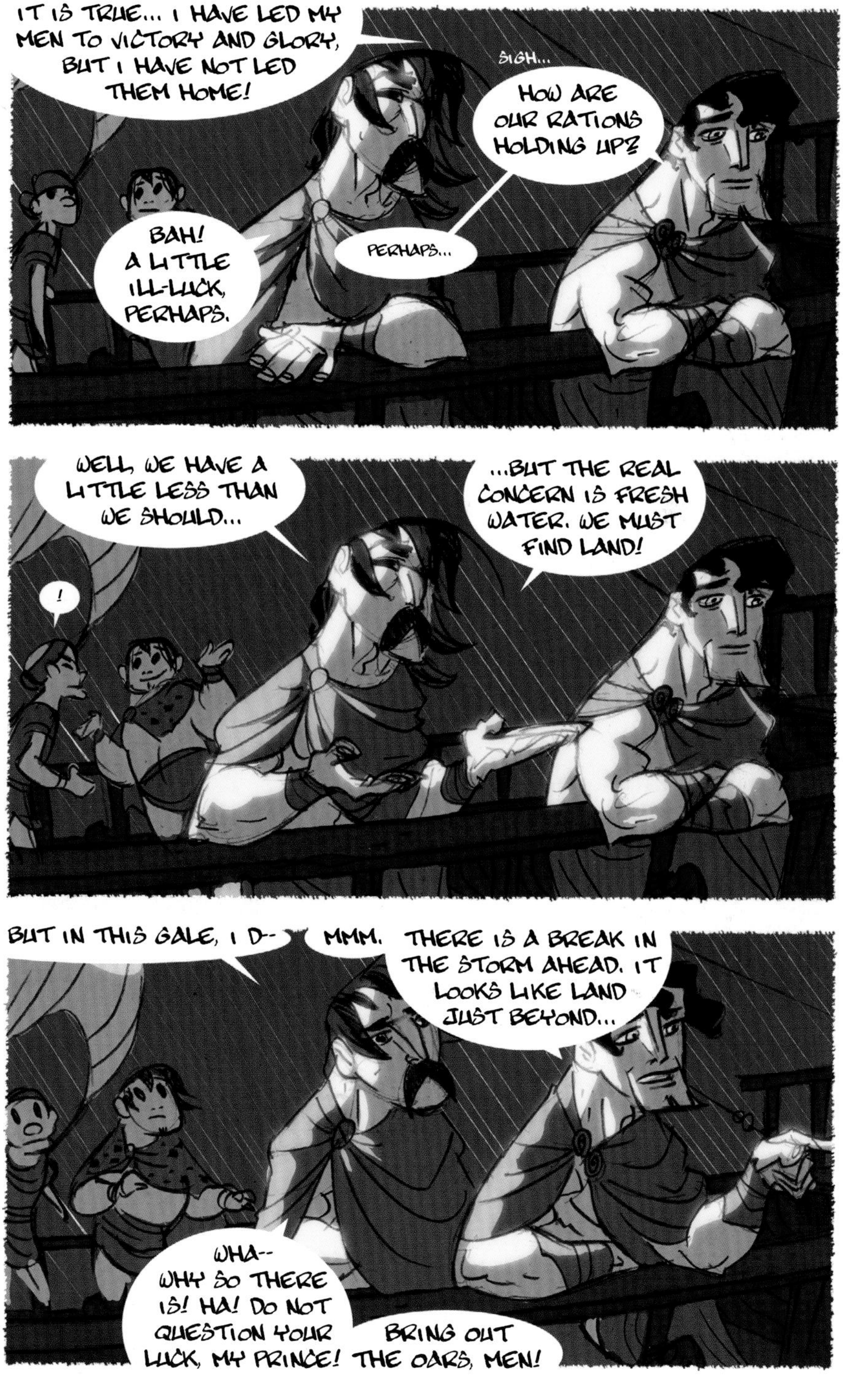
IT IS TRUE... I HAVE LED MY MEN TO VICTORY AND GLORY, BUT I HAVE NOT LED THEM HOME!
BAH! A LITTLE ILL-LUCK, PERHAPS.
PERHAPS...
SIGH...
HOW ARE OUR RATIONS HOLDING UP?
WELL, WE HAVE A LITTLE LESS THAN WE SHOULD...
!
...BUT THE REAL CONCERN IS FRESH WATER. WE MUST FIND LAND!
BUT IN THIS GALE, I D--
MMM.
THERE IS A BREAK IN THE STORM AHEAD. IT LOOKS LIKE LAND JUST BEYOND...
WHA-- WHY SO THERE IS! HA! DO NOT QUESTION YOUR LUCK, MY PRINCE!
BRING OUT THE OARS, MEN!

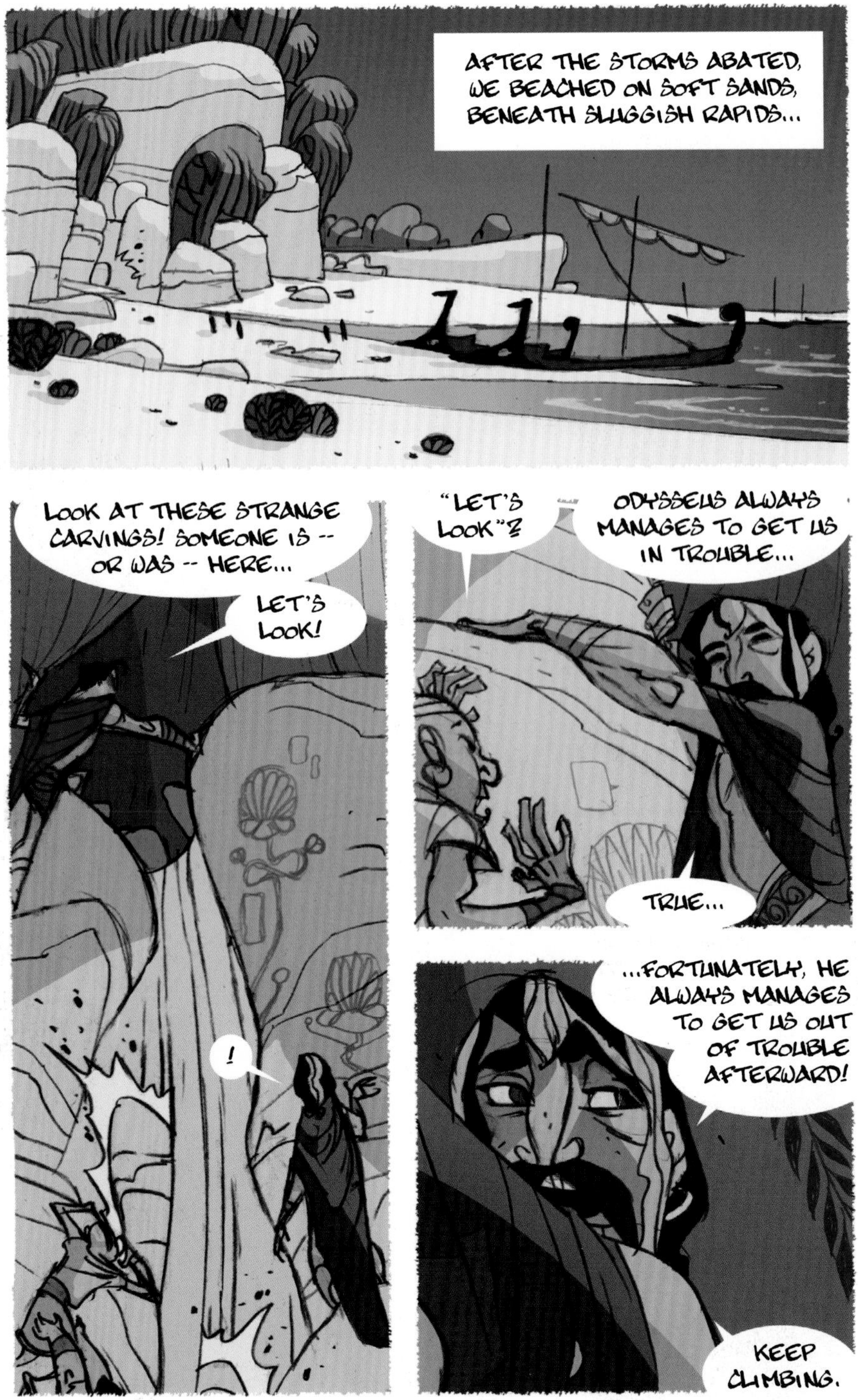
AFTER THE STORMS ABATED, WE BEACHED ON SOFT SANDS, BENEATH SLUGGISH RAPIDS...
LOOK AT THESE STRANGE CARVINGS! SOMEONE IS -- OR WAS -- HERE...
LET'S LOOK!
!
"LET'S LOOK"?
ODYSSEUS ALWAYS MANAGES TO GET US IN TROUBLE...
TRUE...
...FORTUNATELY, HE ALWAYS MANAGES TO GET US OUT OF TROUBLE AFTERWARD!
KEEP CLIMBING.

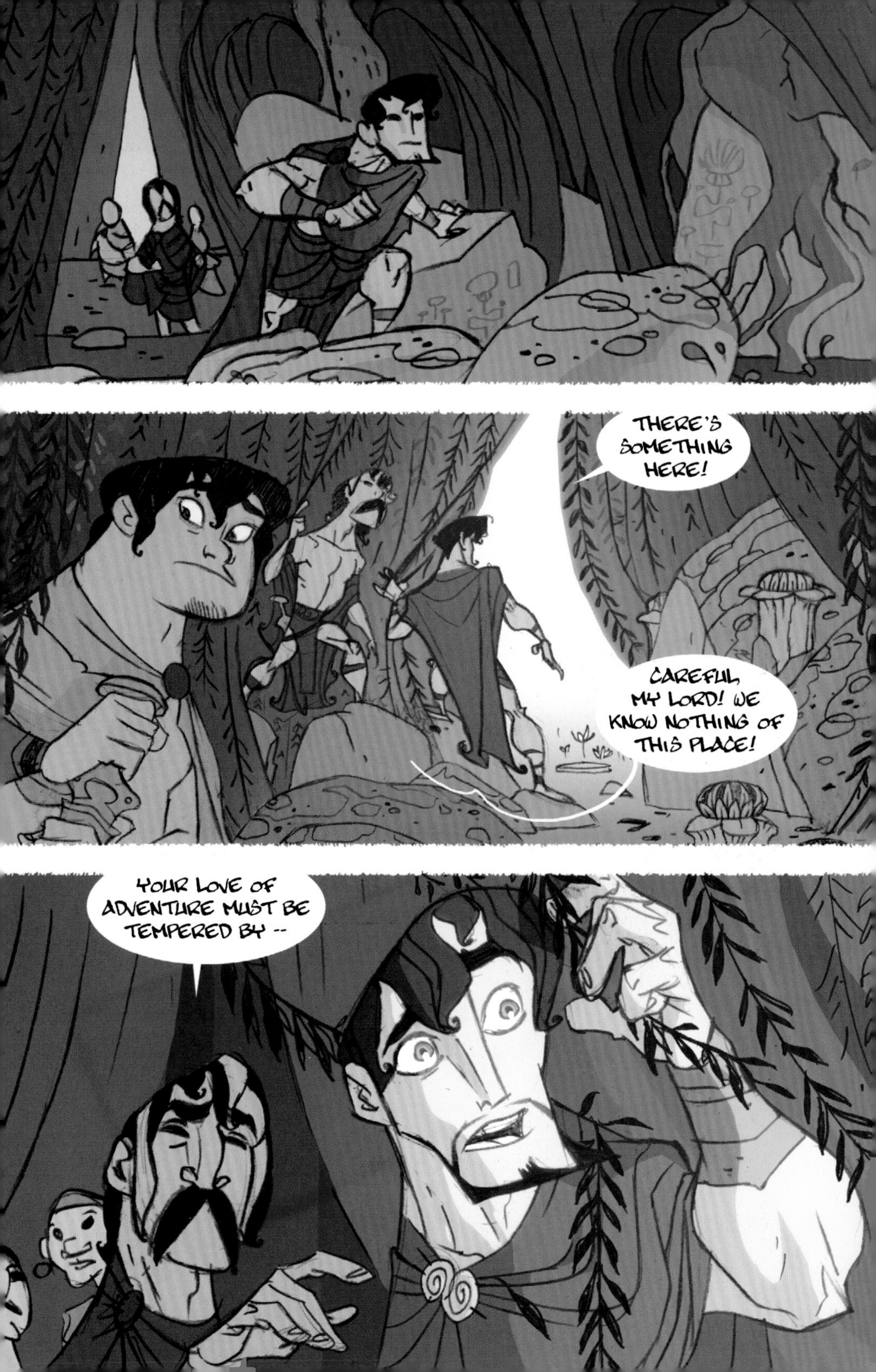
THERE'S SOMETHING HERE!
CAREFUL MY LORD! WE KNOW NOTHING OF THIS PLACE!
YOUR LOVE OF ADVENTURE MUST BE TEMPERED BY --

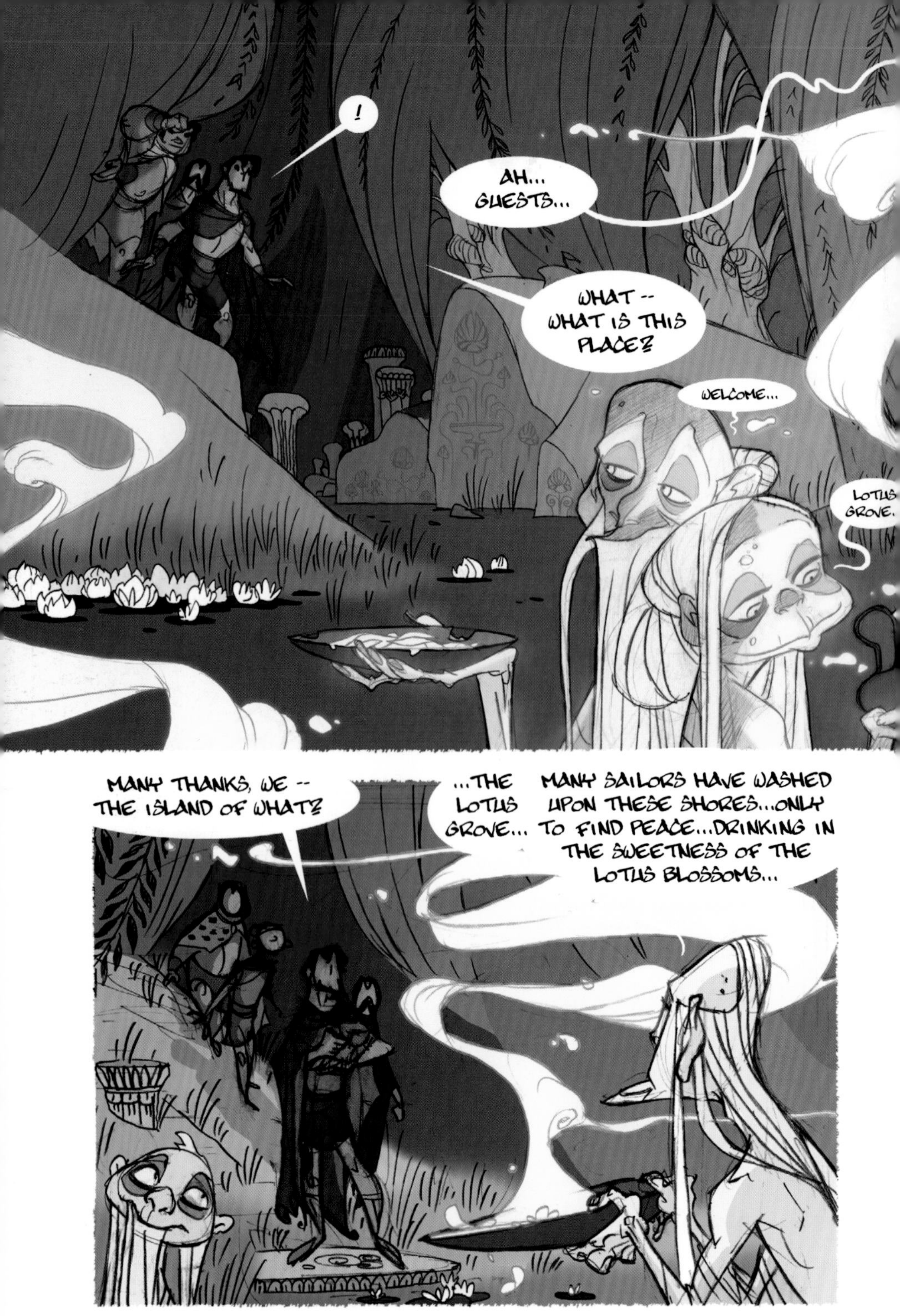
!
AH... GUESTS...
WHAT -- WHAT IS THIS PLACE?
WELCOME...
LOTUS GROVE.
MANY THANKS, WE -- THE ISLAND OF WHAT?
...THE LOTUS GROVE...
MANY SAILORS HAVE WASHED UPON THESE SHORES...ONLY TO FIND PEACE...DRINKING IN THE SWEETNESS OF THE LOTUS BLOSSOMS...

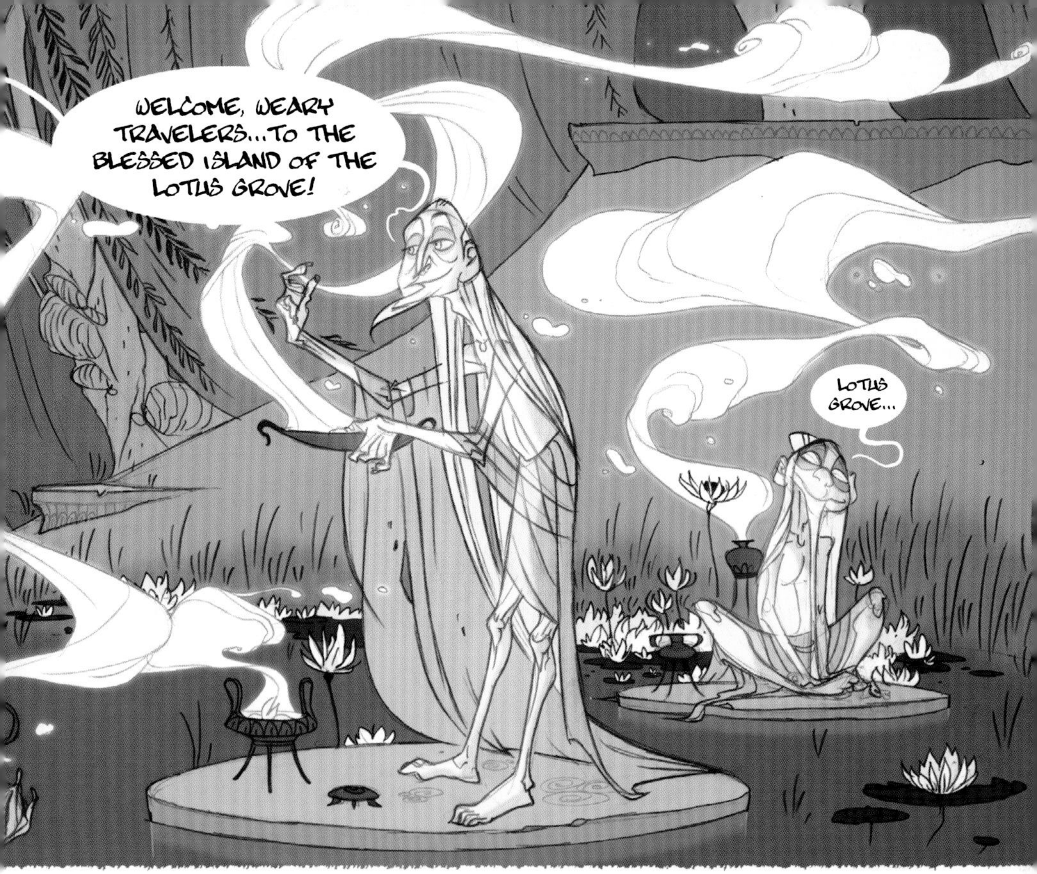
WELCOME, WEARY TRAVELERS...TO THE BLESSED ISLAND OF THE LOTUS GROVE!
LOTUS GROVE...

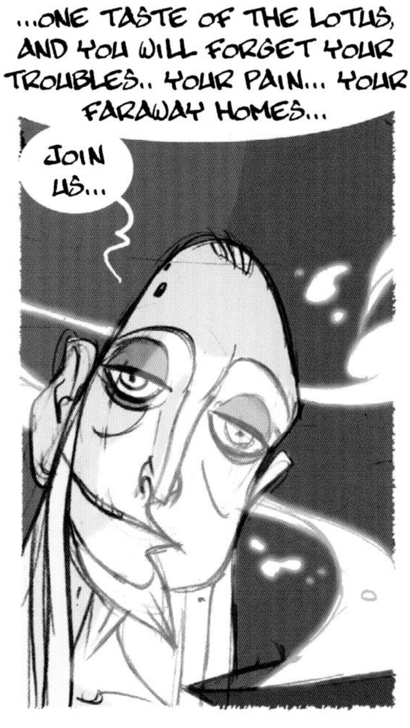
...ONE TASTE OF THE LOTUS, AND YOU WILL FORGET YOUR TROUBLES.. YOUR PAIN... YOUR FARAWAY HOMES...
JOIN US...

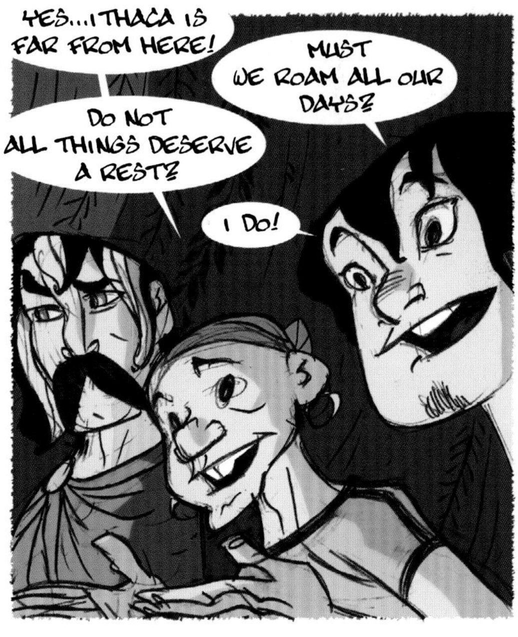
YES...ITHACA IS FAR FROM HERE!
MUST WE ROAM ALL OUR DAYS?
DO NOT ALL THINGS DESERVE A REST?
I DO!

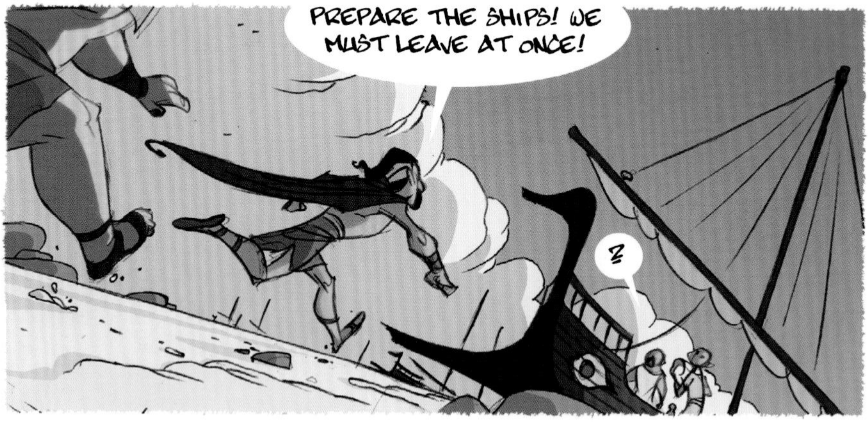
PREPARE THE SHIPS! WE MUST LEAVE AT ONCE!
Z

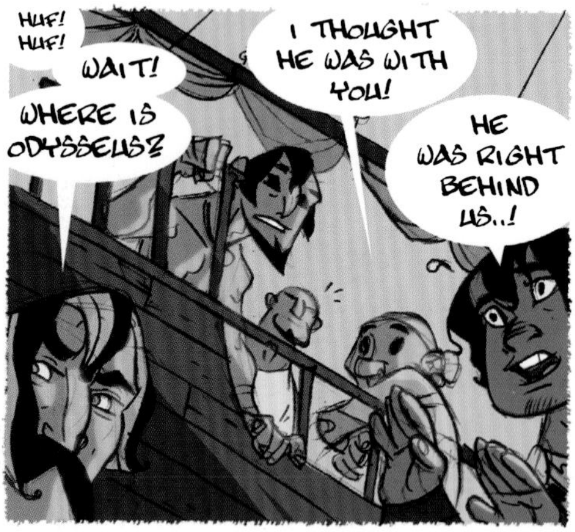
HUF! HUF!
WAIT!
WHERE IS ODYSSEUS?
I THOUGHT HE WAS WITH YOU!
HE WAS RIGHT BEHIND US..!

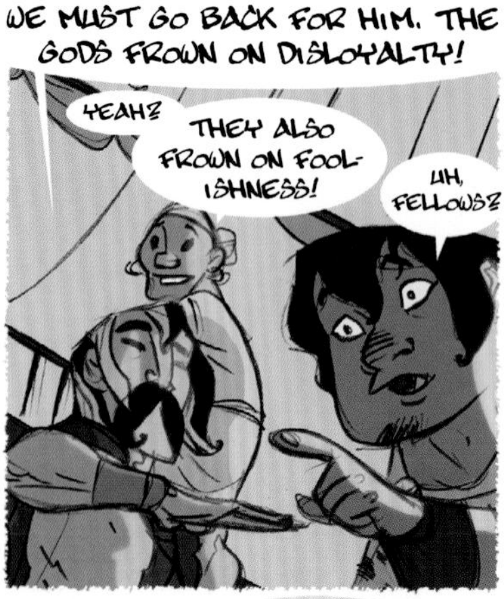
WE MUST GO BACK FOR HIM. THE GODS FROWN ON DISLOYALTY!
YEAH?
THEY ALSO FROWN ON FOOL-ISHNESS!
UH, FELLOWS?

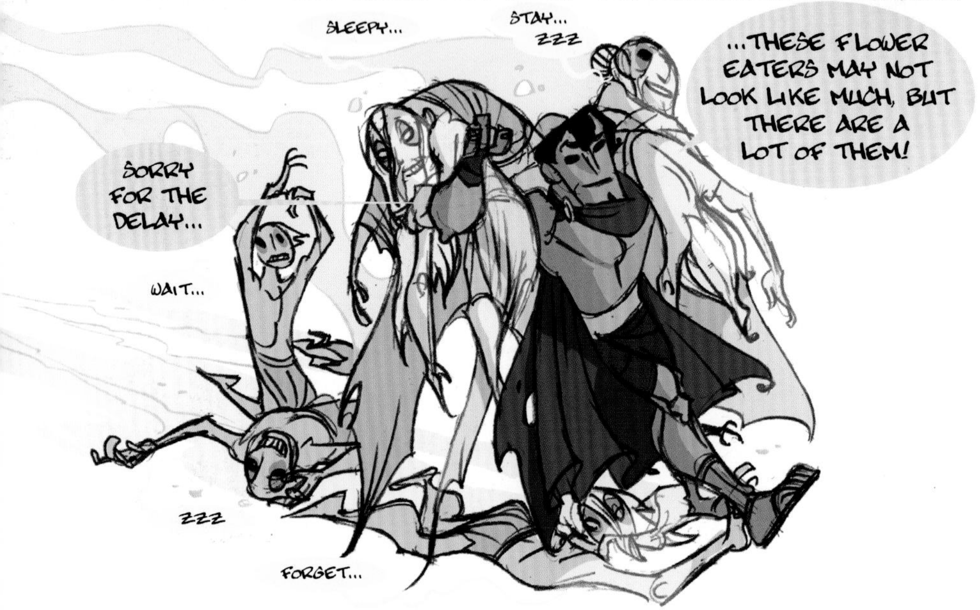
SLEEPY...
STAY... ZZZ
...THESE FLOWER EATERS MAY NOT LOOK LIKE MUCH, BUT THERE ARE A LOT OF THEM!
SORRY FOR THE DELAY...
WAIT...
ZZZ
FORGET...

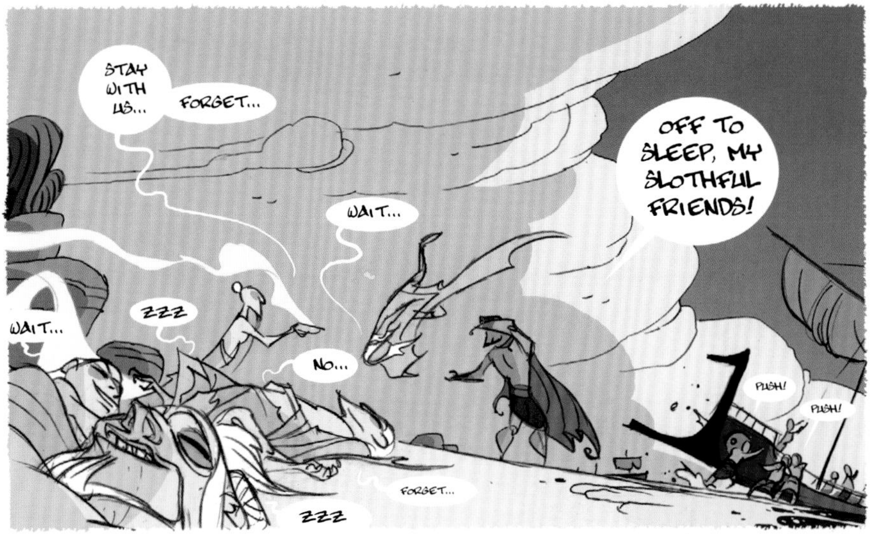
STAY WITH US...
FORGET...
OFF TO SLEEP, MY SLOTHFUL FRIENDS!
WAIT...
WAIT...
ZZZ
NO...
PUSH!
PUSH!
FORGET...
ZZZ

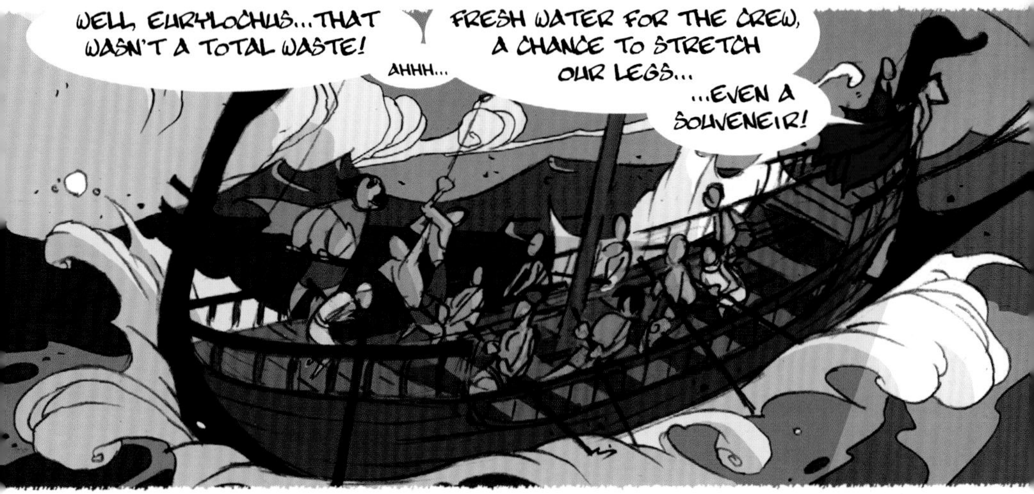
WELL, EURYLOCHUS...THAT WASN'T A TOTAL WASTE!
AHHH...
FRESH WATER FOR THE CREW, A CHANCE TO STRETCH OUR LEGS...
...EVEN A SOUVENEIR!

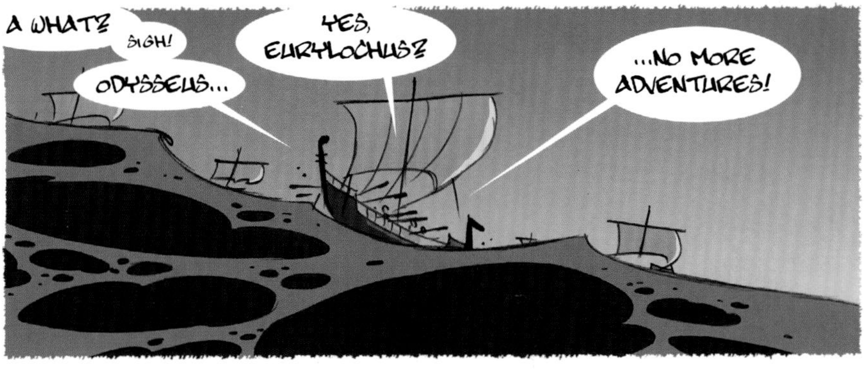
A WHAT?
SIGH!
ODYSSEUS...
YES, EURYLOCHUS?
...NO MORE ADVENTURES!

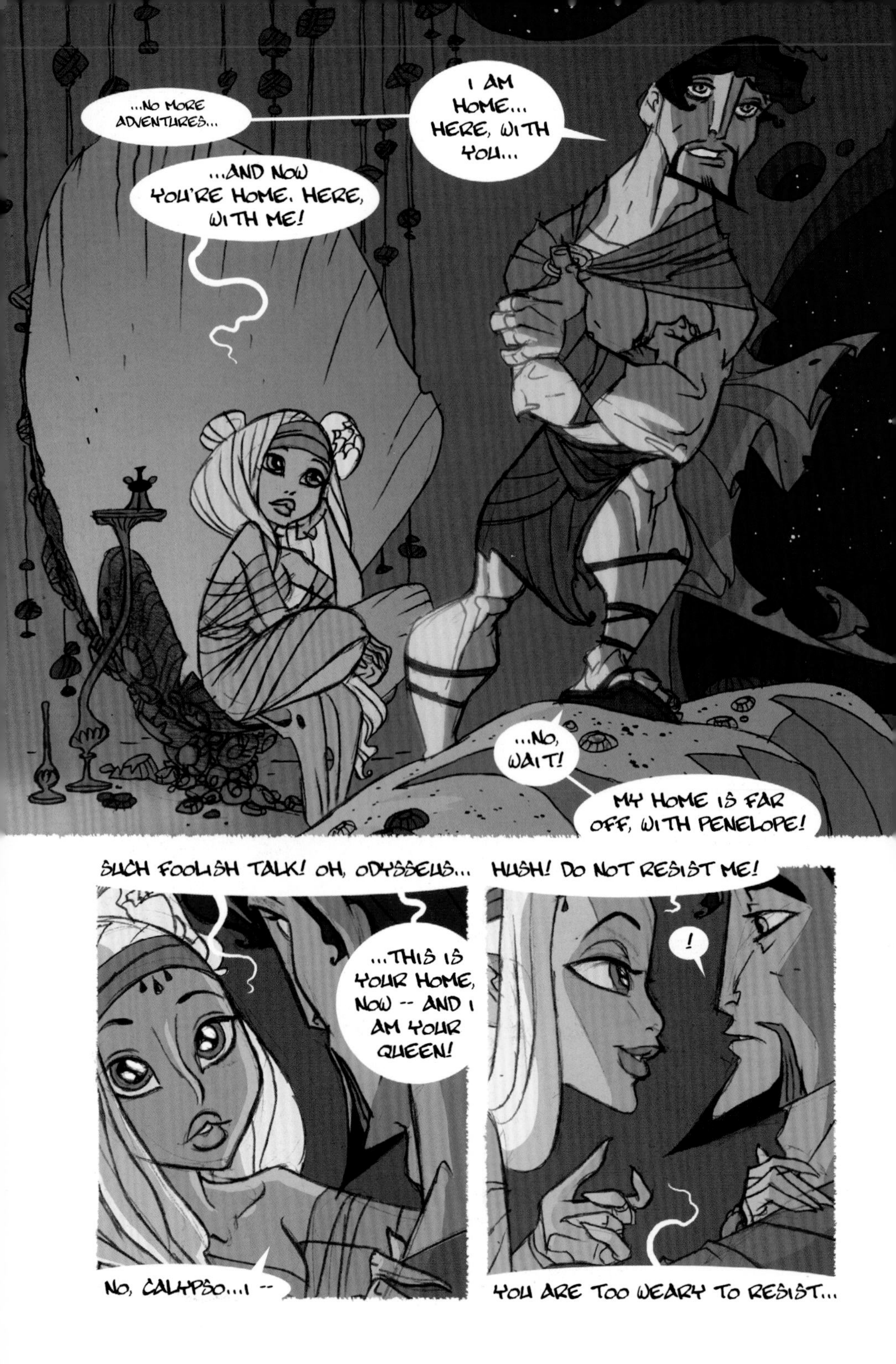
...NO MORE ADVENTURES...
I AM HOME... HERE, WITH YOU...
...AND NOW YOU'RE HOME. HERE, WITH ME!
...NO, WAIT!
MY HOME IS FAR OFF, WITH PENELOPE!
SUCH FOOLISH TALK! OH, ODYSSEUS...
...THIS IS YOUR HOME, NOW -- AND I AM YOUR QUEEN!
NO, CALYPSO...I --
HUSH! DO NOT RESIST ME!
!
YOU ARE TOO WEARY TO RESIST...

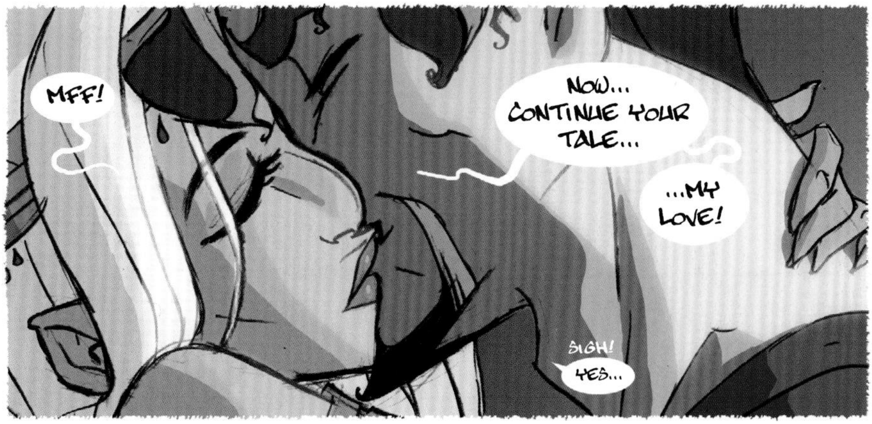
MFF!
NOW... CONTINUE YOUR TALE...
...MY LOVE!
SIGH!
YES...

WE ESCAPED THE LOTUS-EATERS, AND SAILED ON FOR DAYS. OUR SPIRITS BEGAN TO EBB...UNTIL FINALLY WE CAME TO A WILD, JAGGED LAND.

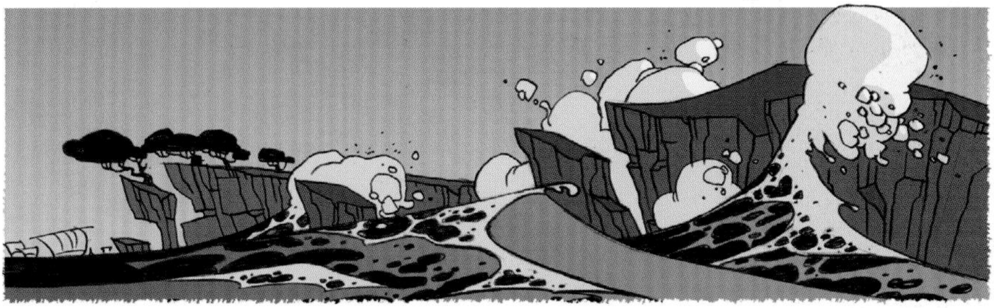

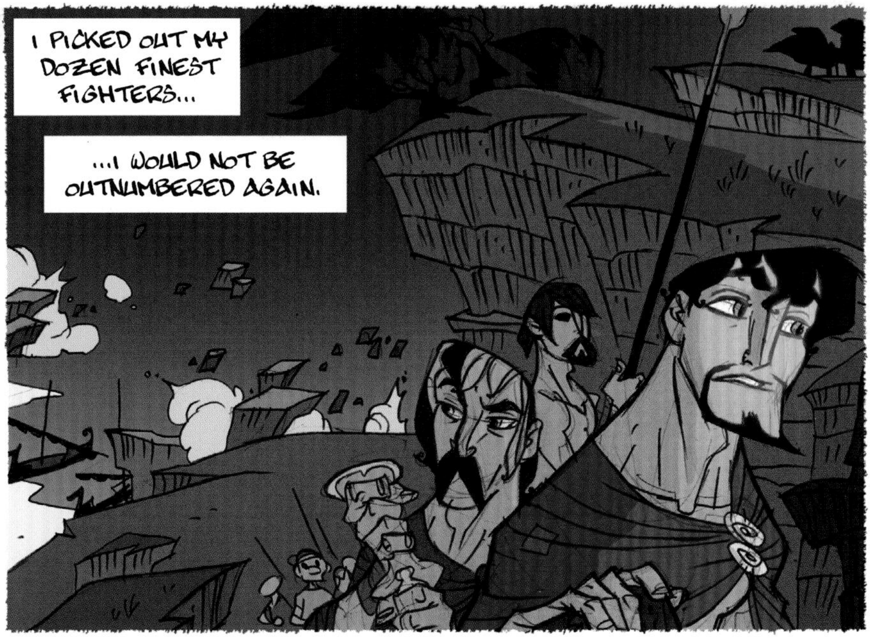
I PICKED OUT MY DOZEN FINEST FIGHTERS...
...I WOULD NOT BE OUTNUMBERED AGAIN.

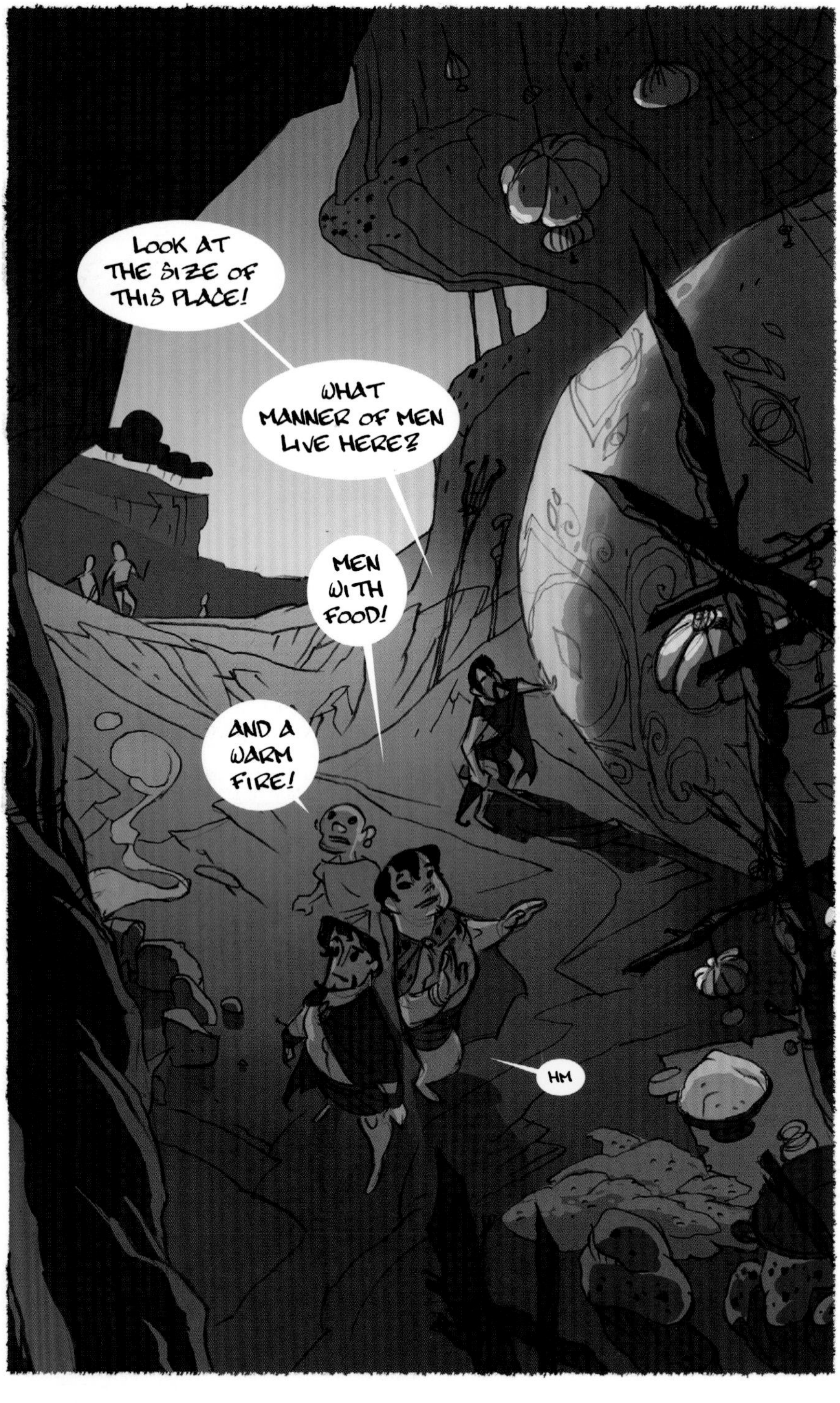
LOOK AT THE SIZE OF THIS PLACE!
WHAT MANNER OF MEN LIVE HERE?
MEN WITH FOOD!
AND A WARM FIRE!
HM

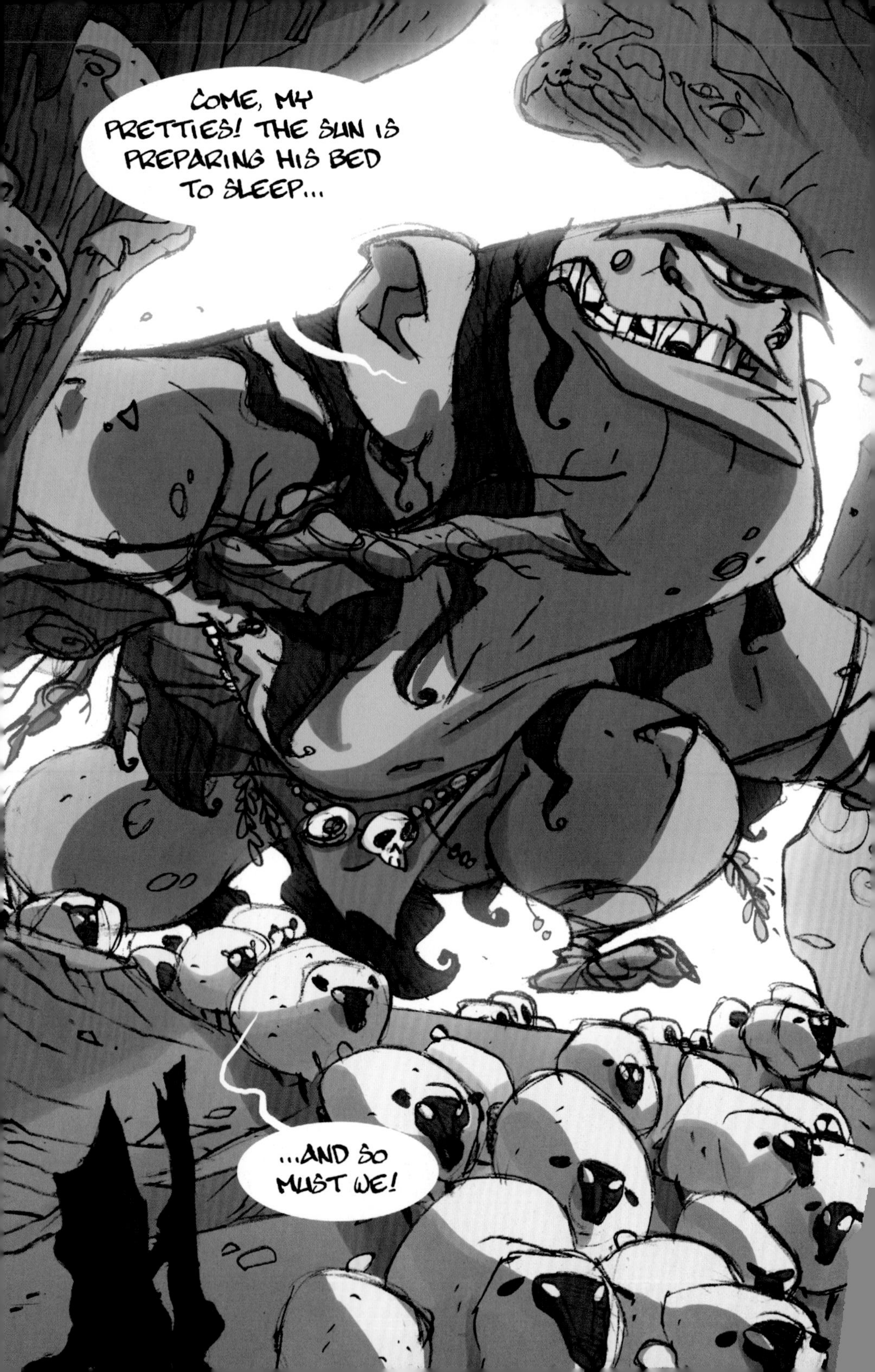
COME, MY PRETTIES! THE SUN IS PREPARING HIS BED TO SLEEP...
...AND SO MUST WE!

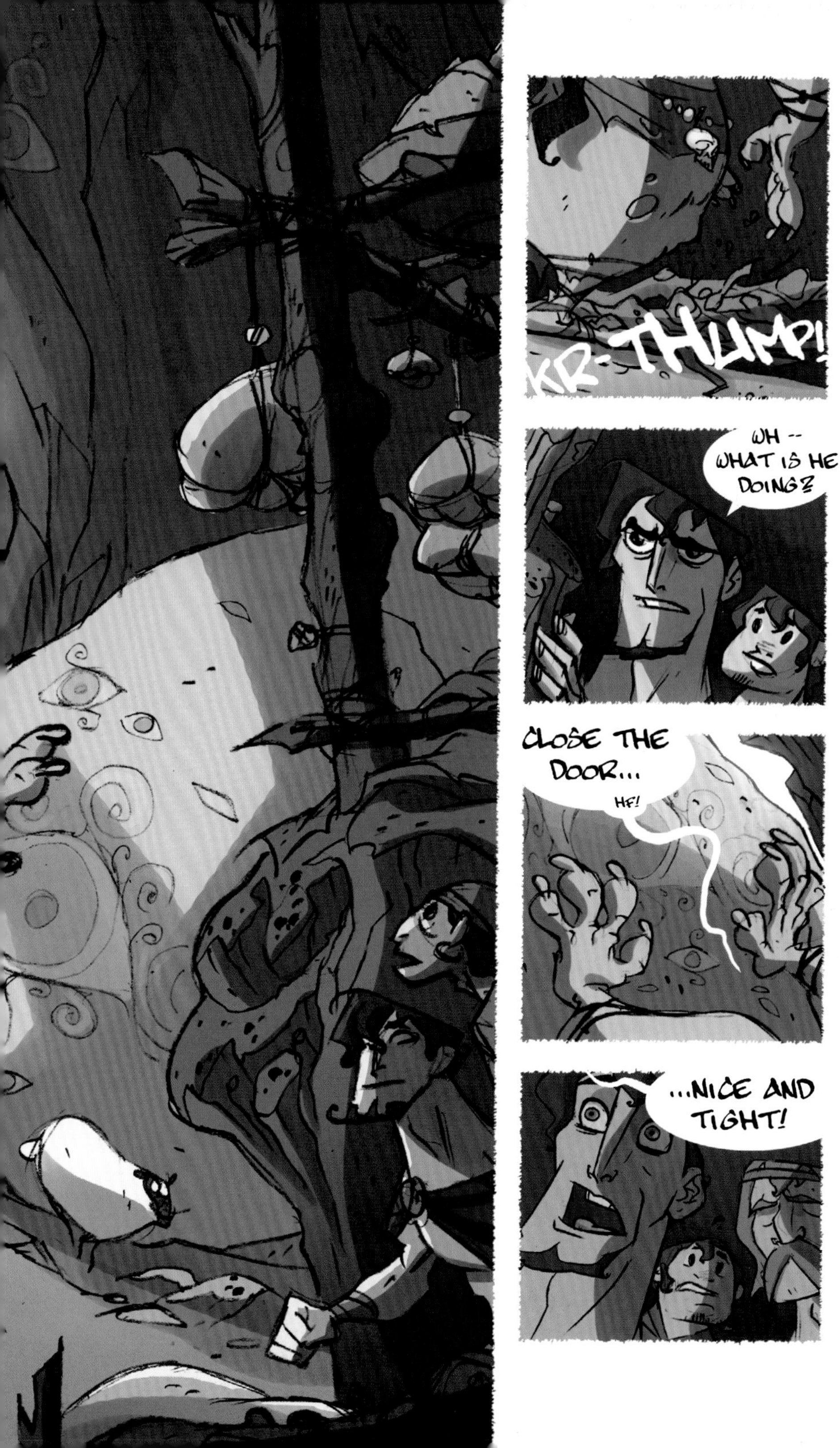
KR-THUMP!
WH -- WHAT IS HE DOING?
CLOSE THE DOOR...
HF!
...NICE AND TIGHT!

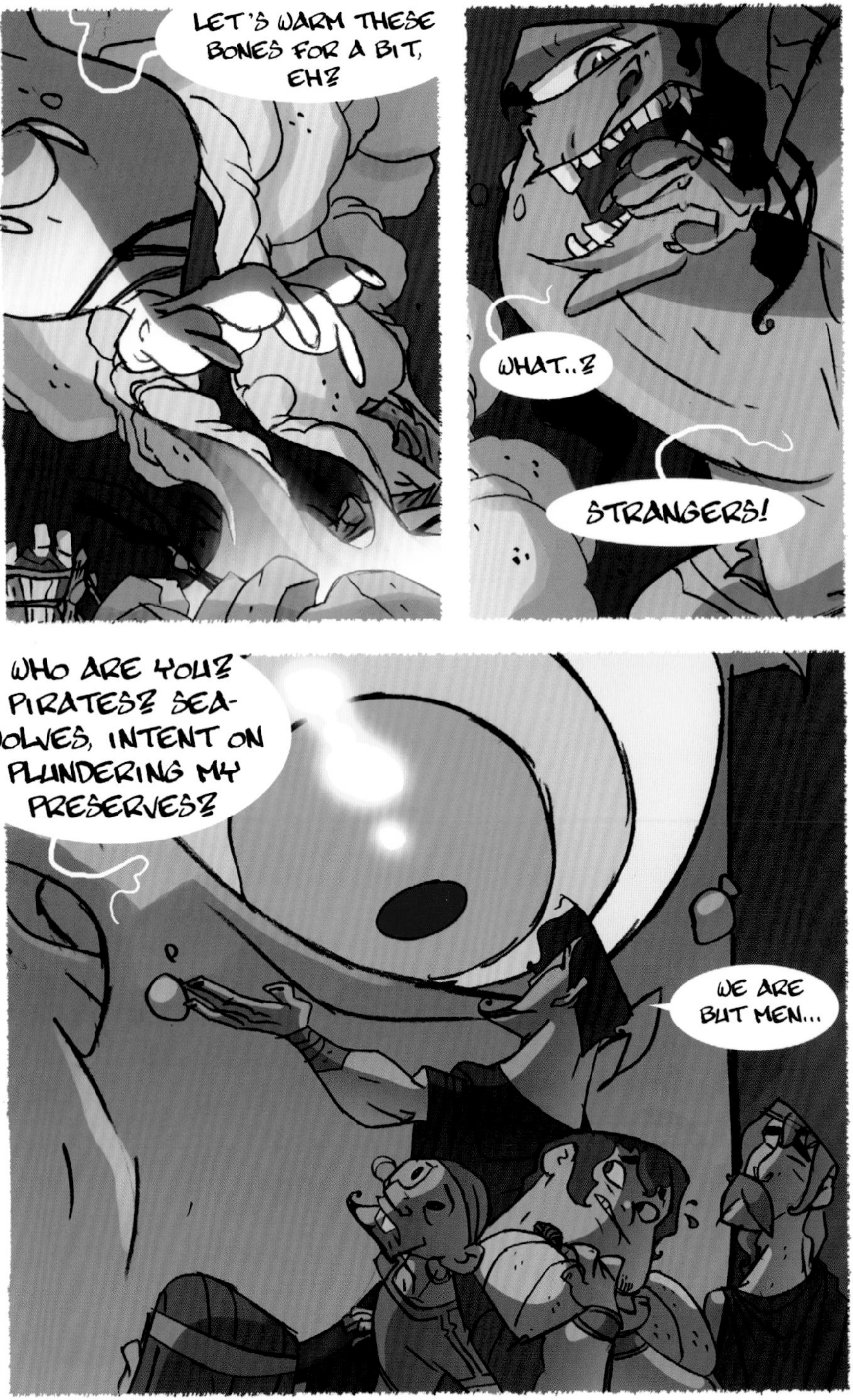
LET'S WARM THESE BONES FOR A BIT, EH?
WHAT..?
STRANGERS!
WHO ARE YOU? PIRATES? SEA-WOLVES, INTENT ON PLUNDERING MY PRESERVES?
WE ARE BUT MEN...

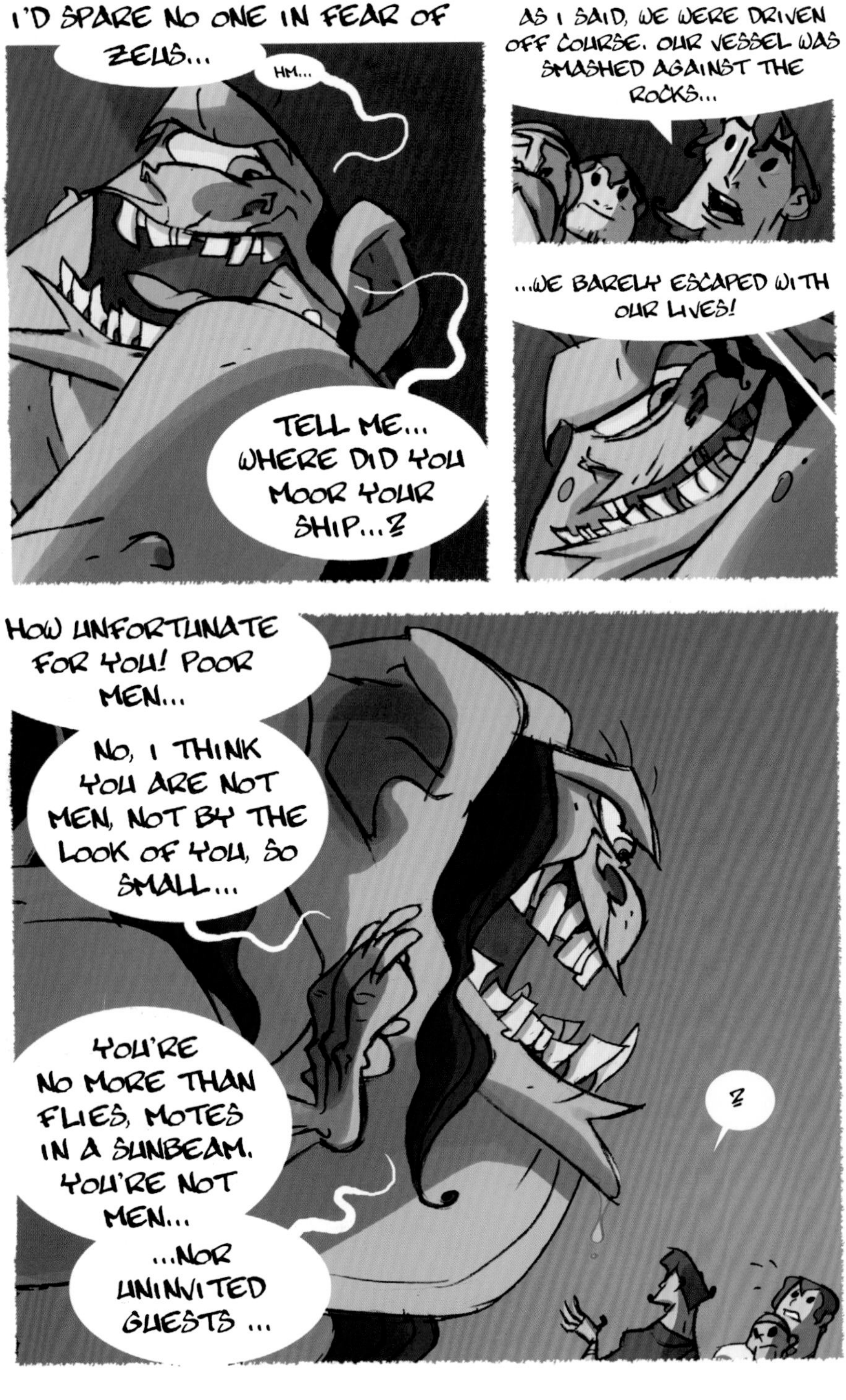
I'D SPARE NO ONE IN FEAR OF ZEUS...
HM...
TELL ME... WHERE DID YOU MOOR YOUR SHIP...?
AS I SAID, WE WERE DRIVEN OFF COURSE. OUR VESSEL WAS SMASHED AGAINST THE ROCKS...
...WE BARELY ESCAPED WITH OUR LIVES!
HOW UNFORTUNATE FOR YOU! POOR MEN...
NO, I THINK YOU ARE NOT MEN, NOT BY THE LOOK OF YOU, SO SMALL...
YOU'RE NO MORE THAN FLIES, MOTES IN A SUNBEAM. YOU'RE NOT MEN...
...NOR UNINVITED GUESTS ...
?

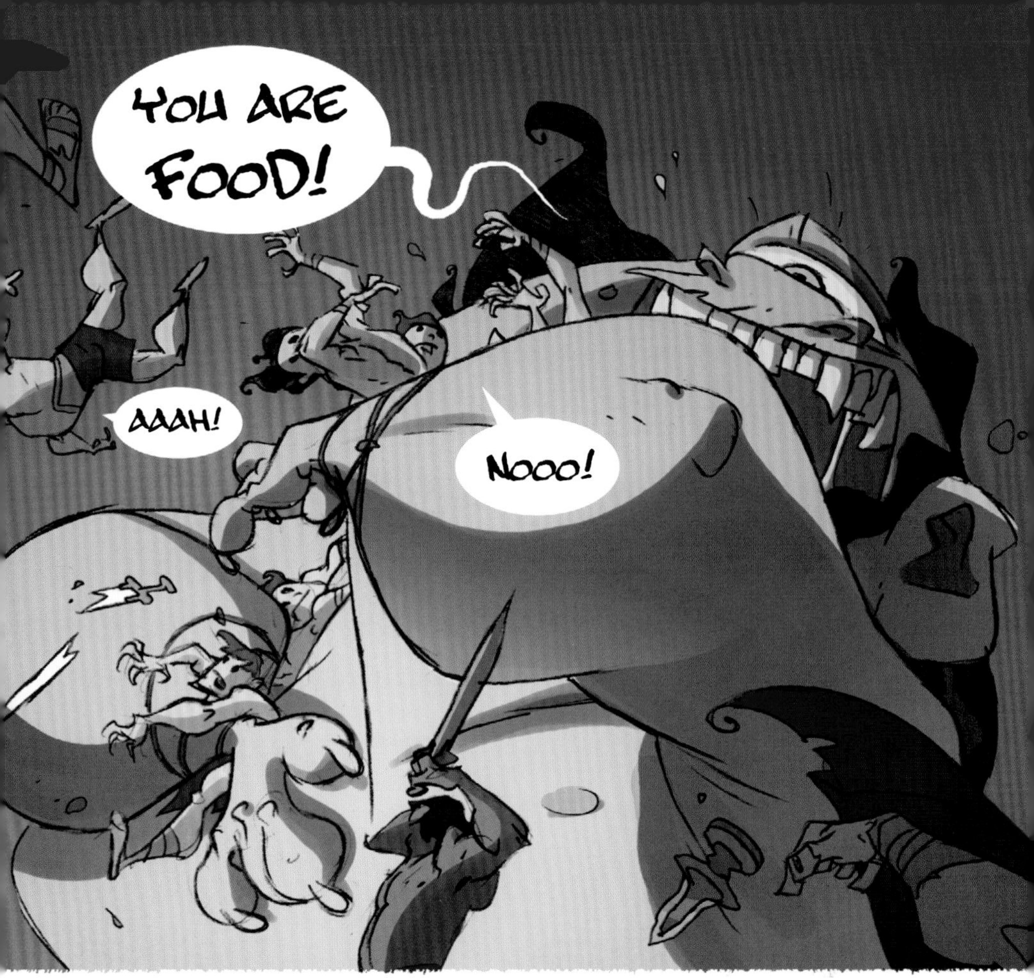
YOU ARE FOOD!
AAAH!
NOOO!

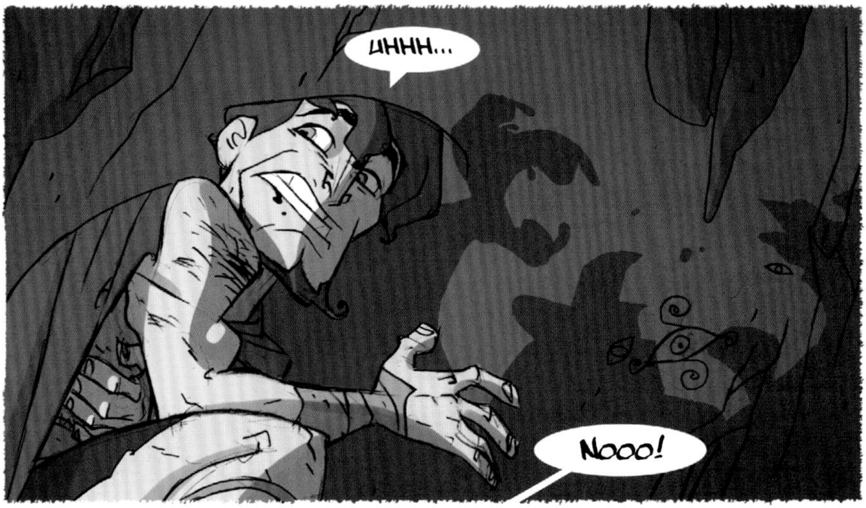
UHHH...
NOOO!

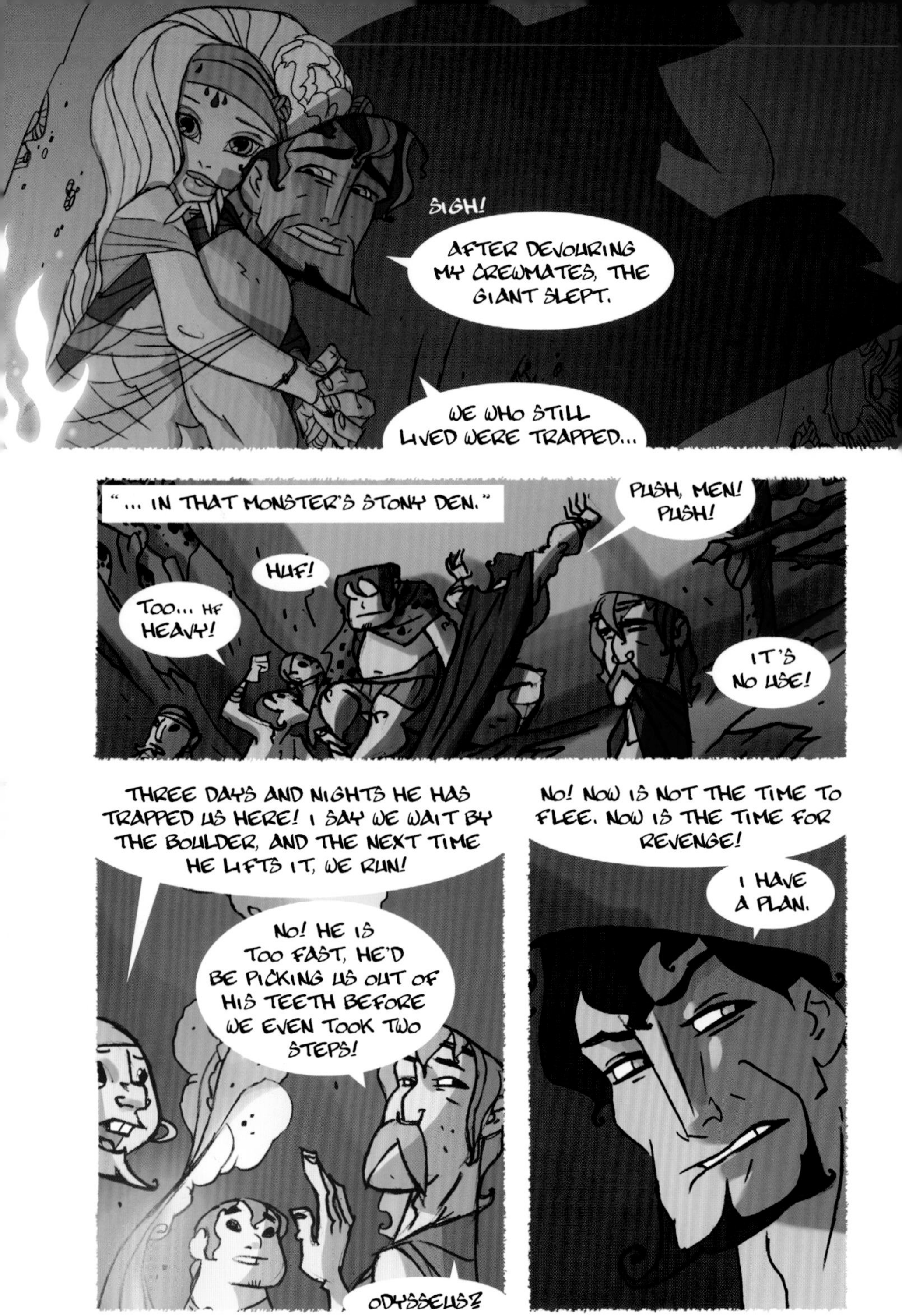
SIGH!
AFTER DEVOURING MY CREWMATES, THE GIANT SLEPT.
WE WHO STILL LIVED WERE TRAPPED...
"... IN THAT MONSTER'S STONY DEN."
PUSH, MEN! PUSH!
HUF!
TOO... HF HEAVY!
IT'S NO USE!
THREE DAYS AND NIGHTS HE HAS TRAPPED US HERE! I SAY WE WAIT BY THE BOULDER, AND THE NEXT TIME HE LIFTS IT, WE RUN!
NO! HE IS TOO FAST, HE'D BE PICKING US OUT OF HIS TEETH BEFORE WE EVEN TOOK TWO STEPS!
ODYSSEUS?
NO! NOW IS NOT THE TIME TO FLEE. NOW IS THE TIME FOR REVENGE!
I HAVE A PLAN.

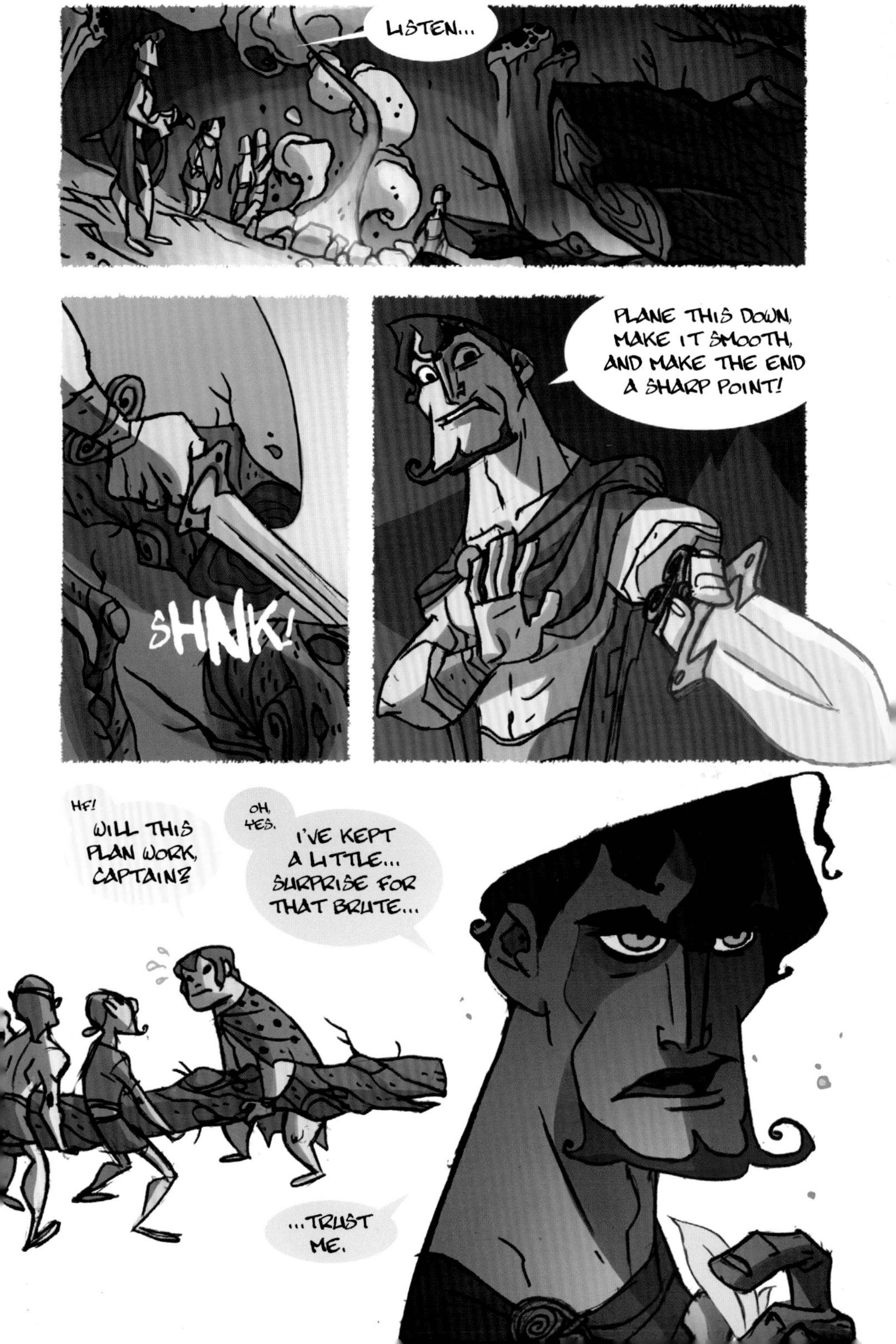
LISTEN...
SHNK!
PLANE THIS DOWN, MAKE IT SMOOTH, AND MAKE THE END A SHARP POINT!
HF!
WILL THIS PLAN WORK, CAPTAIN?
OH, YES.
I'VE KEPT A LITTLE... SURPRISE FOR THAT BRUTE...
...TRUST ME.

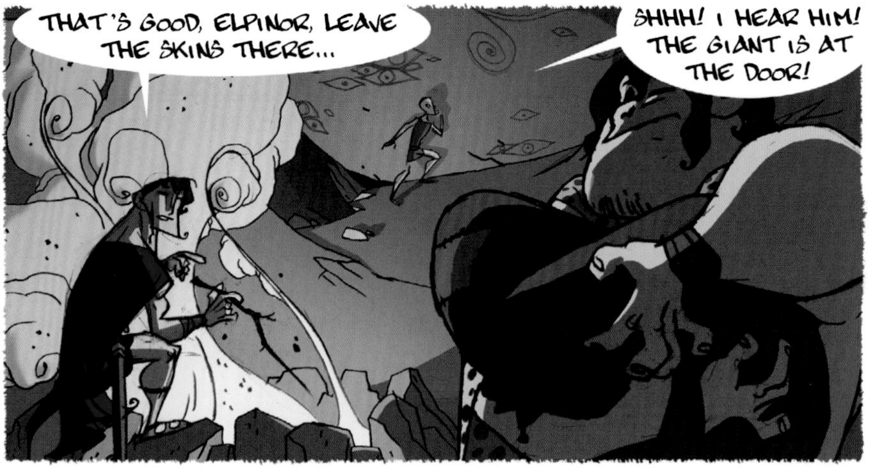
THAT'S GOOD, ELPINOR, LEAVE THE SKINS THERE...
SHHH! I HEAR HIM! THE GIANT IS AT THE DOOR!

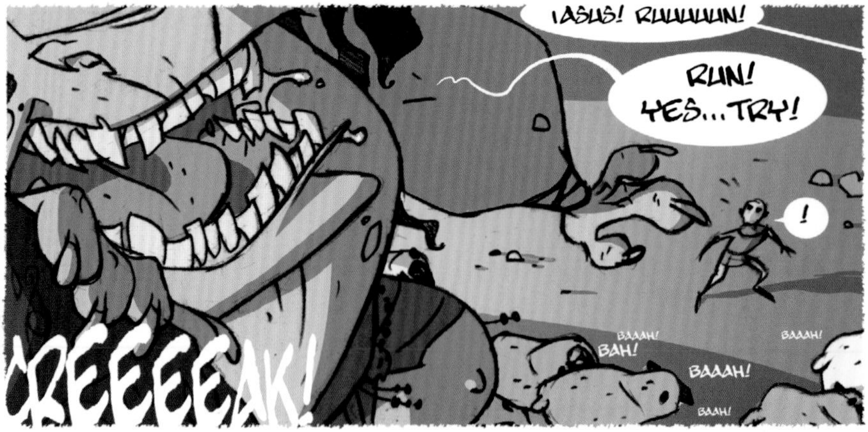
IASUS! RUUUUUN!
RUN! YES...TRY!
!
CREEEEAK!
BAAAH!
BAH!
BAAAH!
BAAAH!
BAAH!

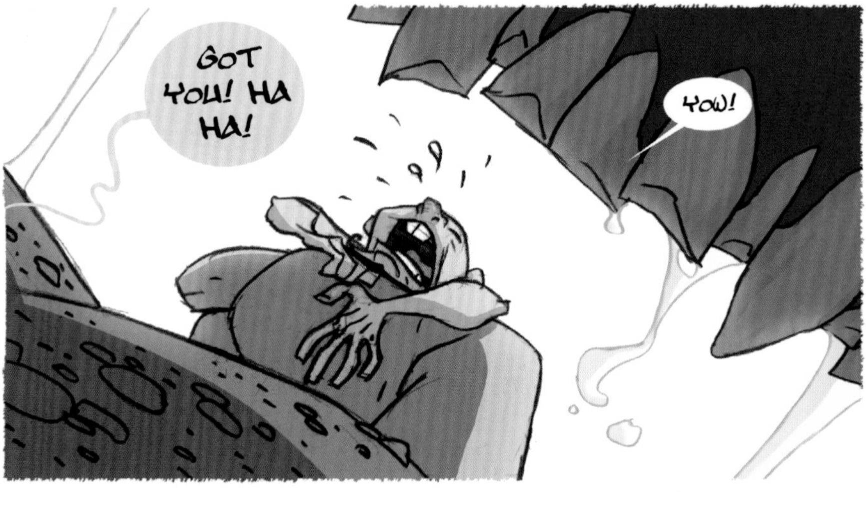
GOT YOU! HA HA!
YOW!

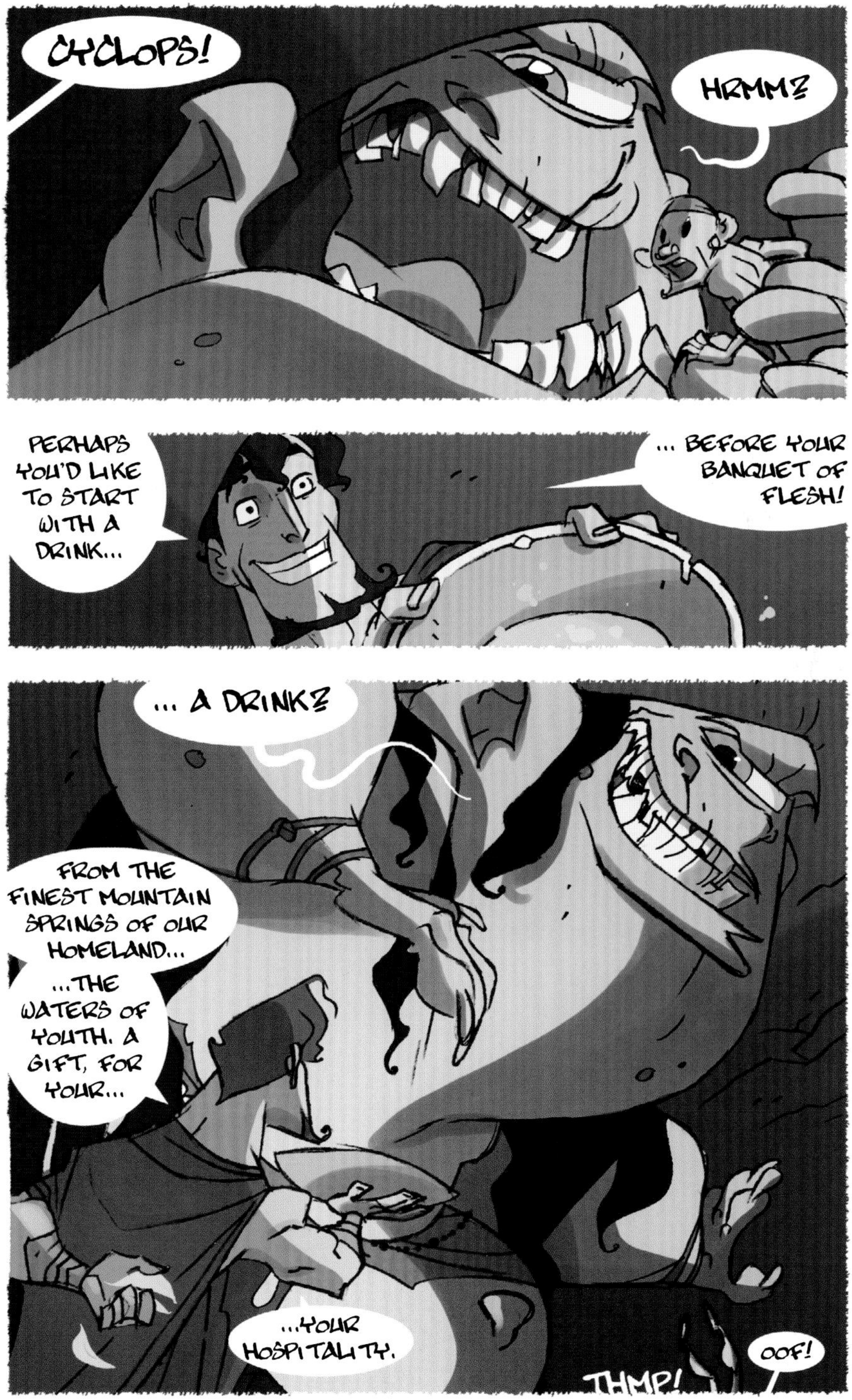
CYCLOPS!
HRMM?
PERHAPS YOU'D LIKE TO START WITH A DRINK...
... BEFORE YOUR BANQUET OF FLESH!
... A DRINK?
FROM THE FINEST MOUNTAIN SPRINGS OF OUR HOMELAND...
...THE WATERS OF YOUTH. A GIFT, FOR YOUR...
...YOUR HOSPITALITY.
THMP!
OOF!

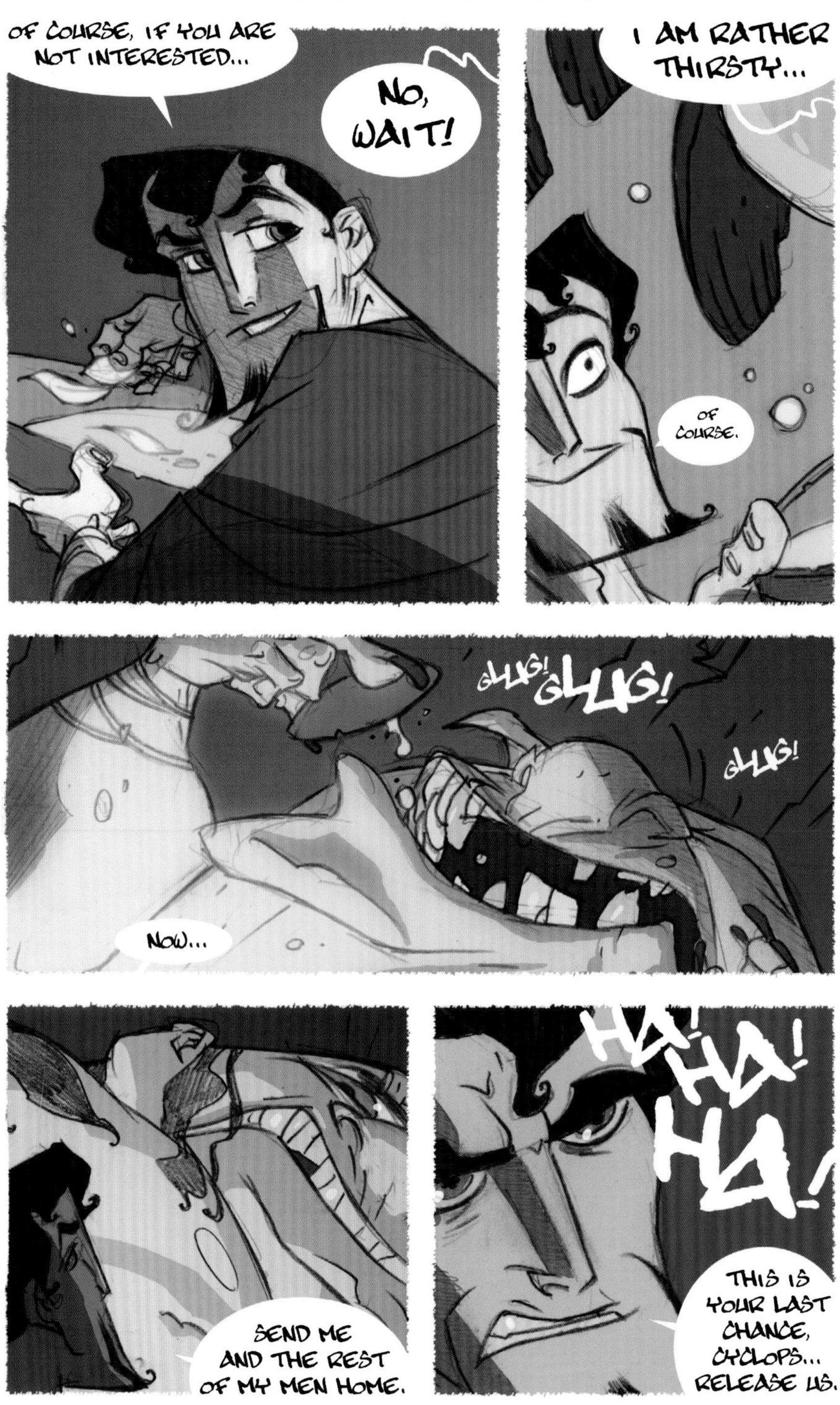

OF COURSE, IF YOU ARE NOT INTERESTED...
NO, WAIT!
I AM RATHER THIRSTY...
OF COURSE.
GLUG! GLUG!
GLUG!
NOW...
SEND ME AND THE REST OF MY MEN HOME.
HA! HA! HA!
THIS IS YOUR LAST CHANCE, CYCLOPS... RELEASE US.

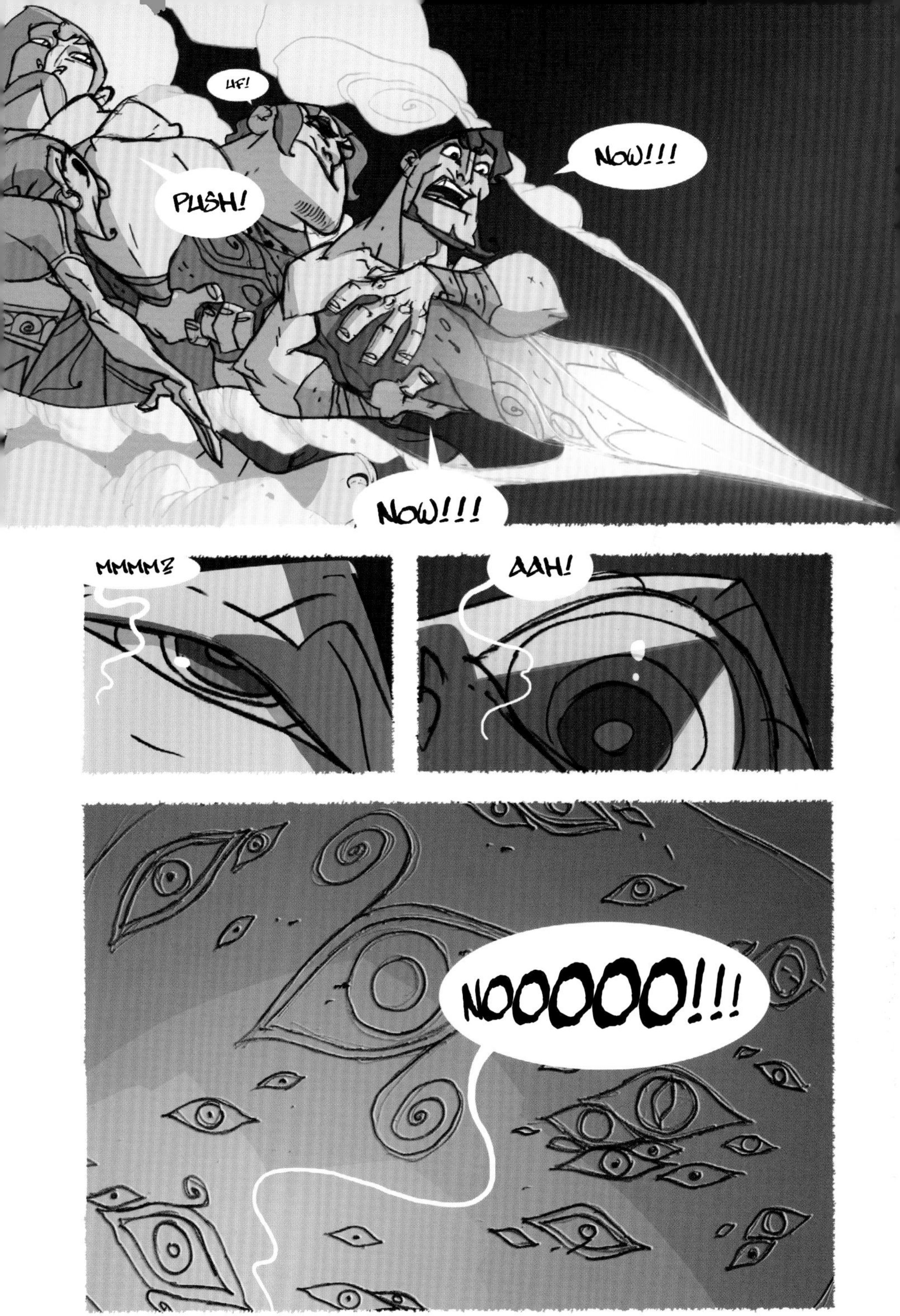
UF!
PUSH!
NOW!!!
NOW!!!
MMMM?
AAH!
NOOOOO!!!

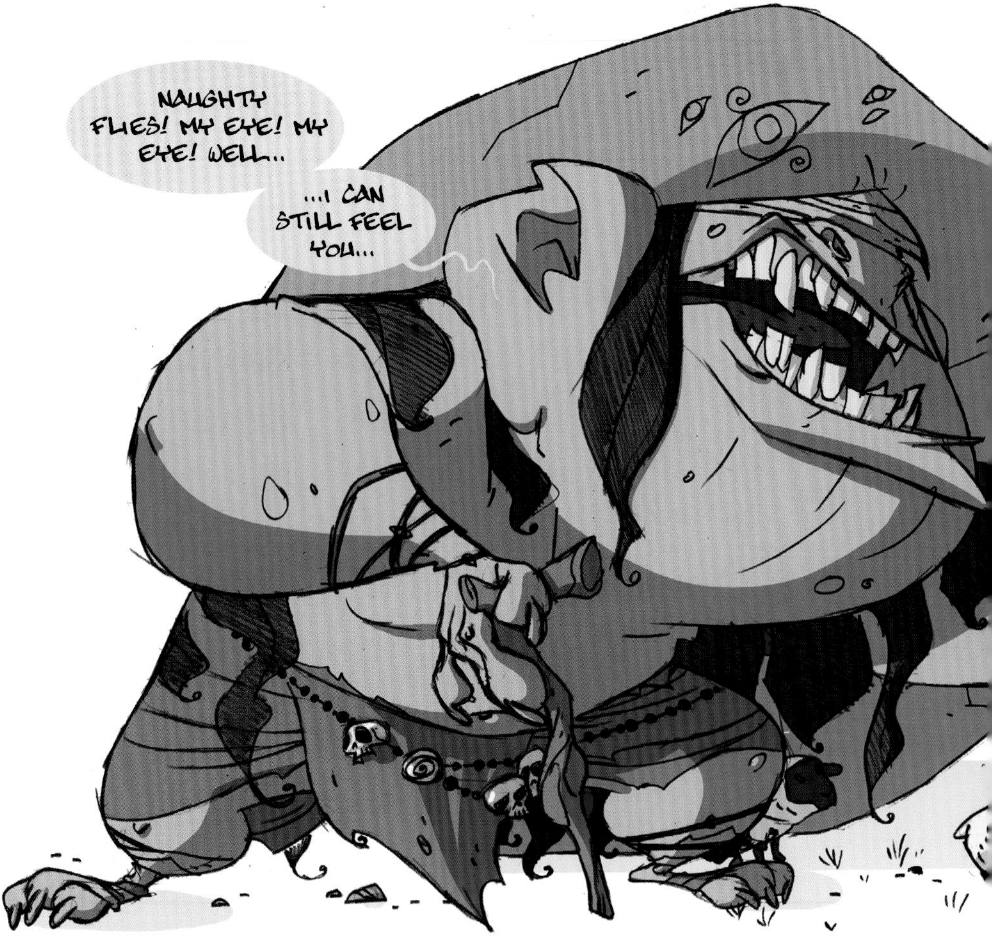
NAUGHTY FLIES! MY EYE! MY EYE! WELL...
...I CAN STILL FEEL YOU...

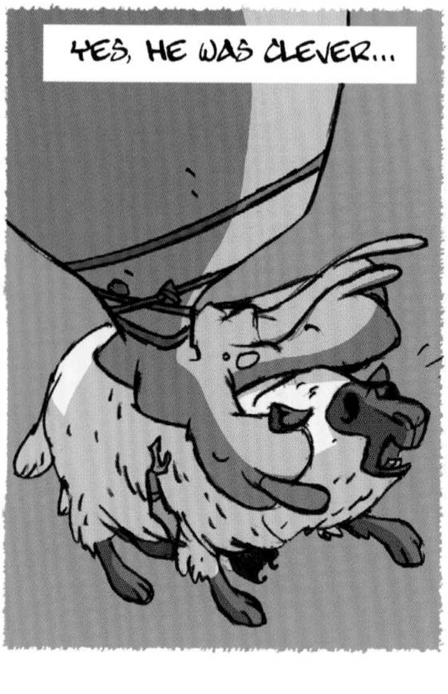
YES, HE WAS CLEVER...

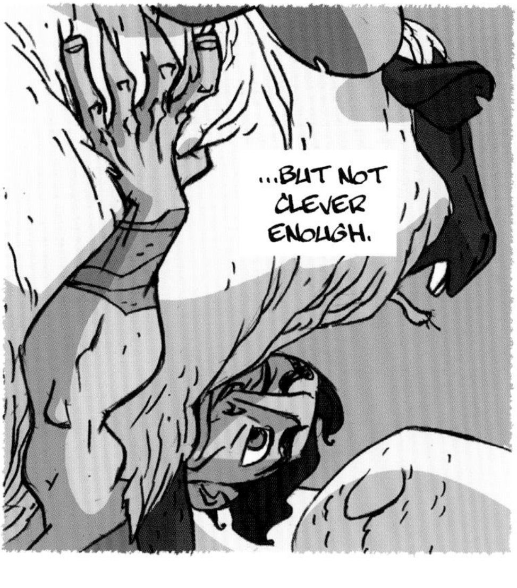
...BUT NOT CLEVER ENOUGH.

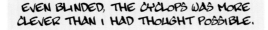

EVEN BLINDED, THE CYCLOPS WAS MORE CLEVER THAN I HAD THOUGHT POSSIBLE.

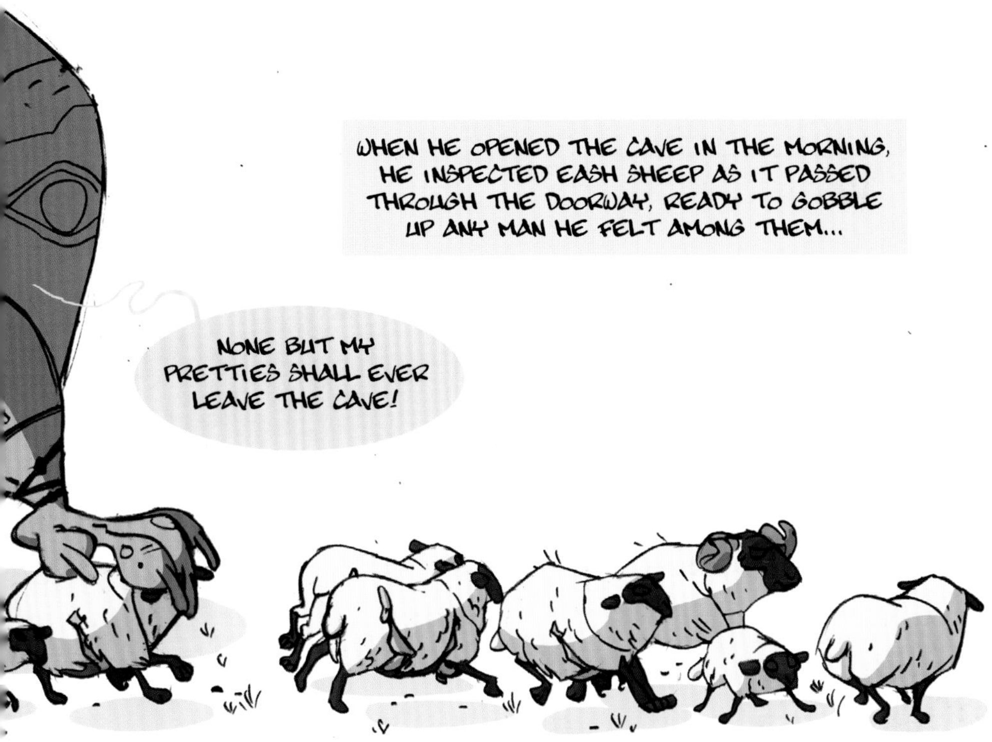
WHEN HE OPENED THE CAVE IN THE MORNING, HE INSPECTED EASH SHEEP AS IT PASSED THROUGH THE DOORWAY, READY TO GOBBLE UP ANY MAN HE FELT AMONG THEM...
NONE BUT MY PRETTIES SHALL EVER LEAVE THE CAVE!

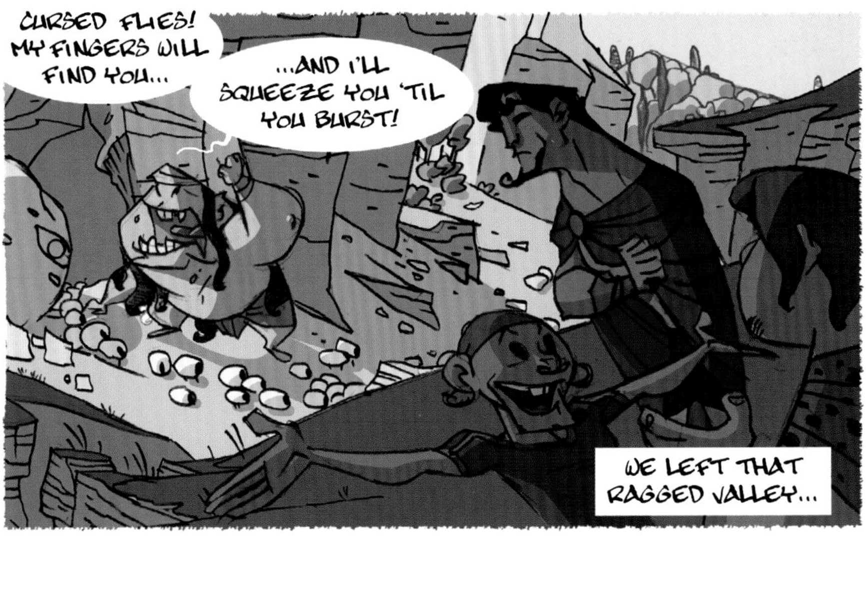
CURSED FLIES! MY FINGERS WILL FIND YOU...
...AND I'LL SQUEEZE YOU 'TIL YOU BURST!
WE LEFT THAT RAGGED VALLEY...

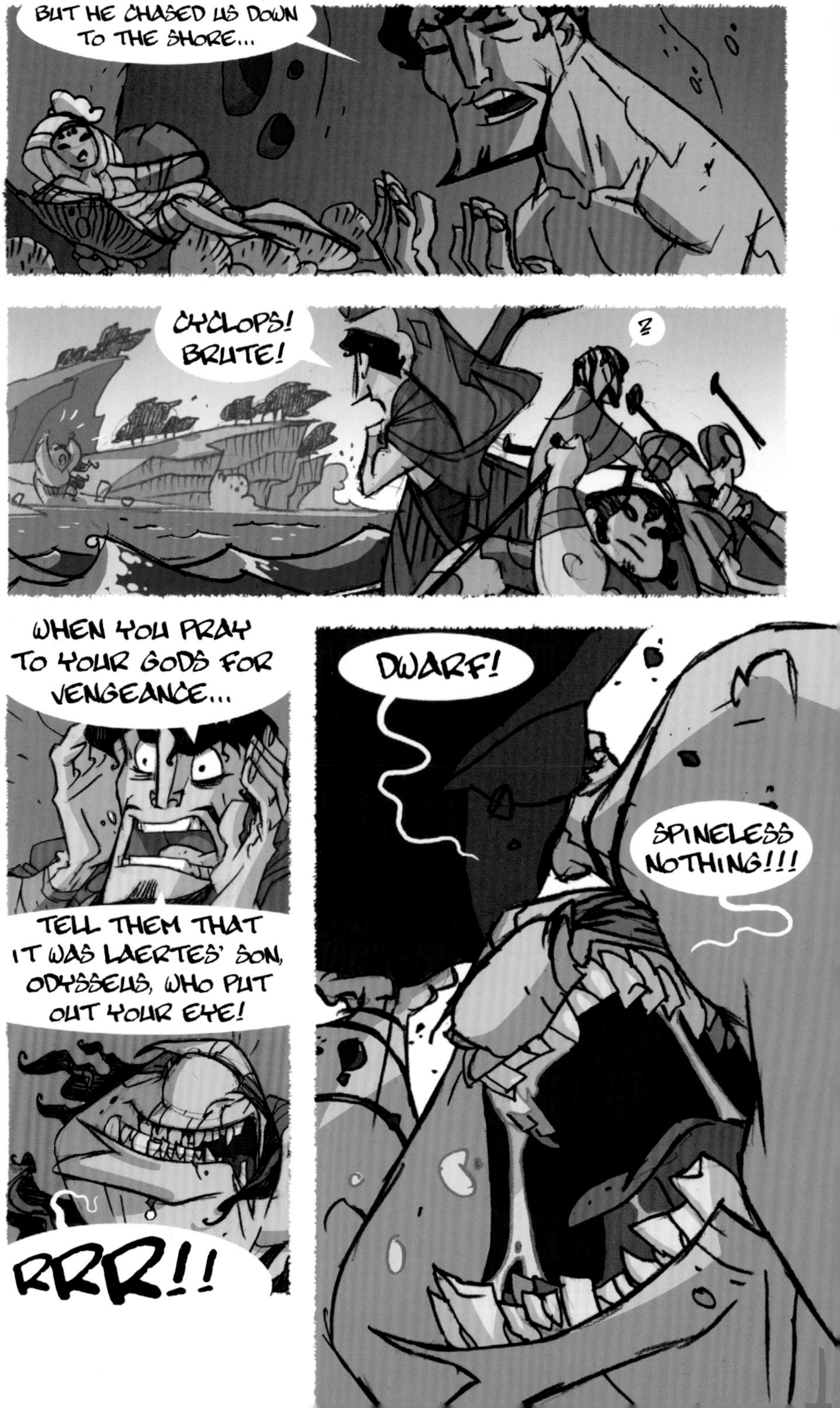
BUT HE CHASED US DOWN TO THE SHORE...
CYCLOPS! BRUTE!
Z
WHEN YOU PRAY TO YOUR GODS FOR VENGEANCE...
TELL THEM THAT IT WAS LAERTES' SON, ODYSSEUS, WHO PUT OUT YOUR EYE!
RRR!!
DWARF!
SPINELESS NOTHING!!!

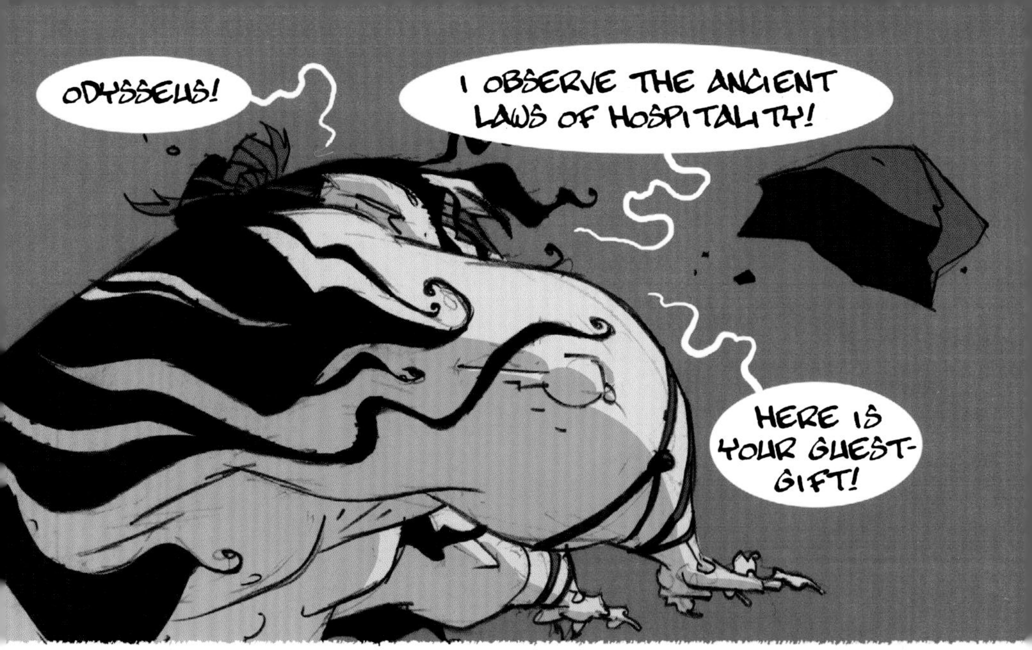
ODYSSEUS!
I OBSERVE THE ANCIENT LAWS OF HOSPITALITY!
HERE IS YOUR GUEST-GIFT!

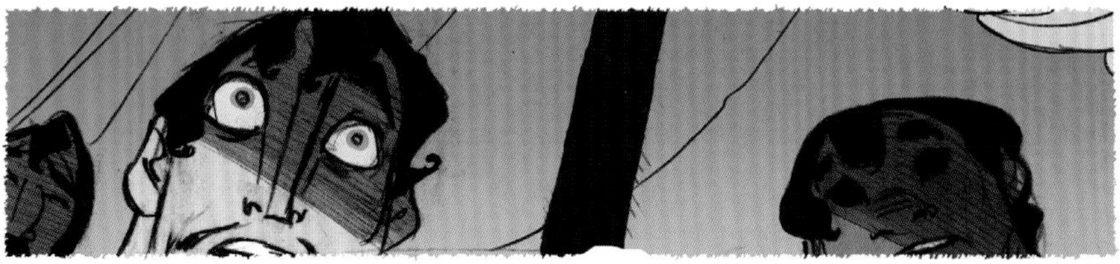

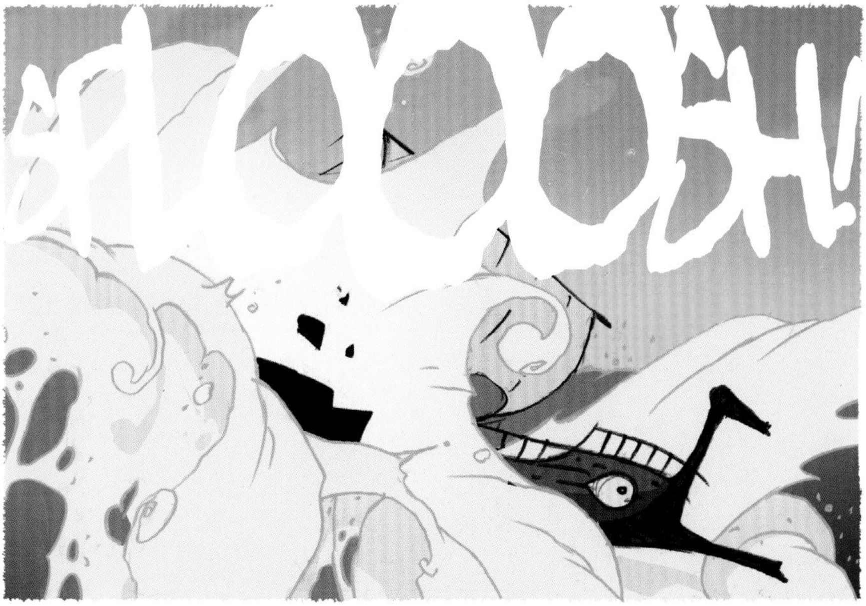

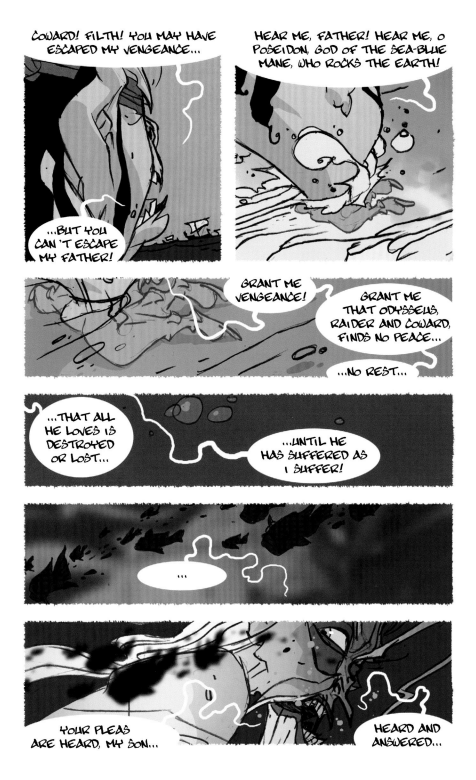

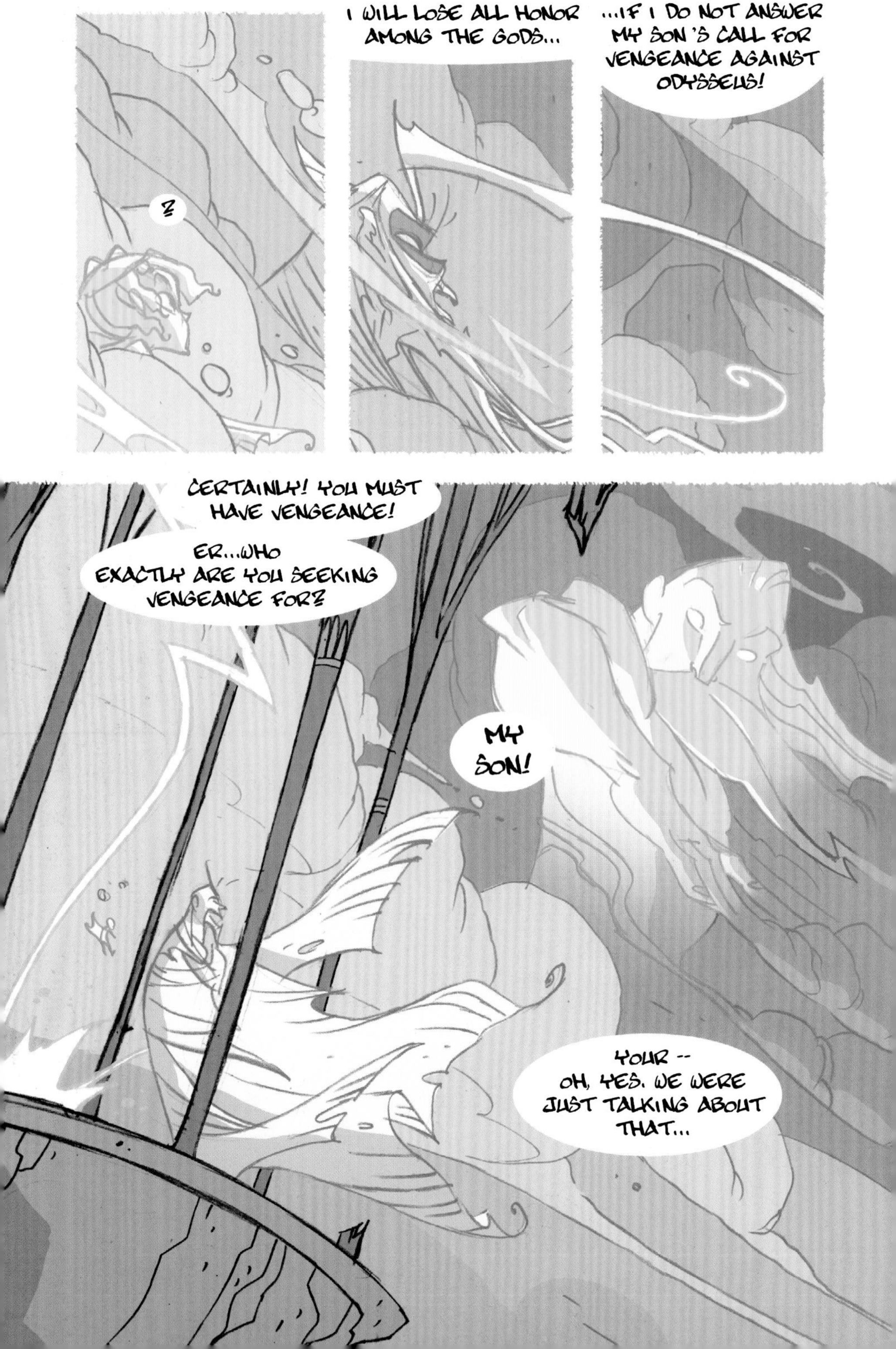
Z
I WILL LOSE ALL HONOR AMONG THE GODS...
...IF I DO NOT ANSWER MY SON'S CALL FOR VENGEANCE AGAINST ODYSSEUS!
CERTAINLY! YOU MUST HAVE VENGEANCE!
ER...WHO EXACTLY ARE YOU SEEKING VENGEANCE FOR?
MY SON!
YOUR -- OH, YES. WE WERE JUST TALKING ABOUT THAT...

WELL...IF THIS ODYSSEUS HAS SO GREATLY WRONGED YOU, MIGHTY EARTH-SHAKER, YOU HAVE MY BLESSING TO PAY HIM BACK...

YOUR POWER IS YOURS TO DO WHAT YOU LIKE. WARM YOUR HEART IN... ER... WHAT'S-HIS-NAME'S MISERY.

FINALLY!

NOW... IF YOU'LL EXCUSE ME...

I'VE GOT A TRICKY BIT OF PRECIPITATION I'M WORKING ON...

THANK YOU, MY BROTHER...

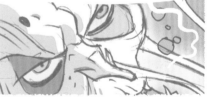

...AS WE SPEAK THE OCEAN CURRENTS WILL DELIVER HIM INTO EVEN MORE PAIN AND SUFFERING!

Z

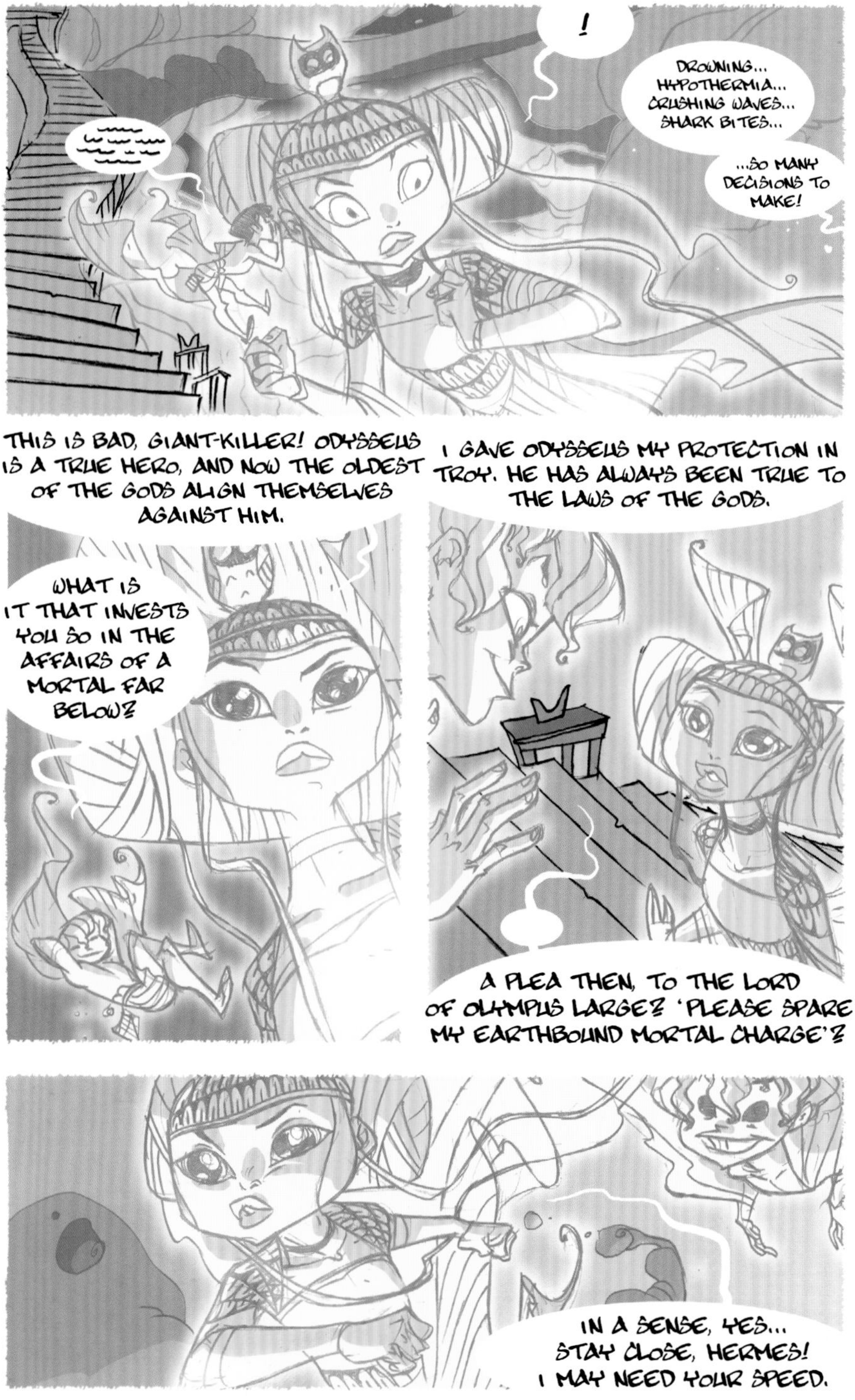

!
DROWNING... HYPOTHERMIA... CRUSHING WAVES... SHARK BITES...
...SO MANY DECISIONS TO MAKE!
THIS IS BAD, GIANT-KILLER! ODYSSEUS IS A TRUE HERO, AND NOW THE OLDEST OF THE GODS ALIGN THEMSELVES AGAINST HIM.
I GAVE ODYSSEUS MY PROTECTION IN TROY. HE HAS ALWAYS BEEN TRUE TO THE LAWS OF THE GODS.
WHAT IS IT THAT INVESTS YOU SO IN THE AFFAIRS OF A MORTAL FAR BELOW?
A PLEA THEN, TO THE LORD OF OLYMPUS LARGE? 'PLEASE SPARE MY EARTHBOUND MORTAL CHARGE'?
IN A SENSE, YES... STAY CLOSE, HERMES! I MAY NEED YOUR SPEED.

FATHER! I SEEK AN AUDIENCE! FATHER!

EH?

OH...ATHENA!

FATHER! I --

SHH!!! NOT SO LOUD, MY DEAR...YOUR UNCLE IS STORMING AROUND IN A FOUL MOOD, WON'T LET ME WORK ON MY NEW CLOUDS...

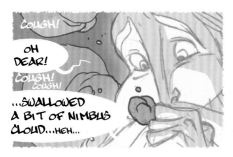

COUGH!

OH DEAR!

COUGH! COUGH!

...SWALLOWED A BIT OF NIMBUS CLOUD...HEH...

WHY HAVE YOU AGREED TO LAY THESE LOW PLOTS AGAINST ODYSSEUS? HE HAS NEVER NEGLECTED HIS SACRIFICES FOR YOU! WHY SET YOUR POWERS AGAINST HIM?

MY POWERS? CERTAINLY NOT!

ER...

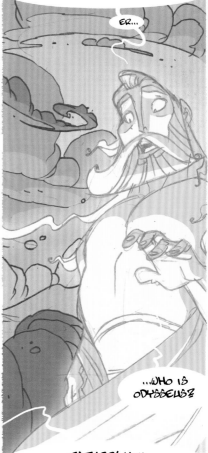

...WHO IS ODYSSEUS?

FATHER! YOU WERE JUST...TALKING...ABOUT...HIM!

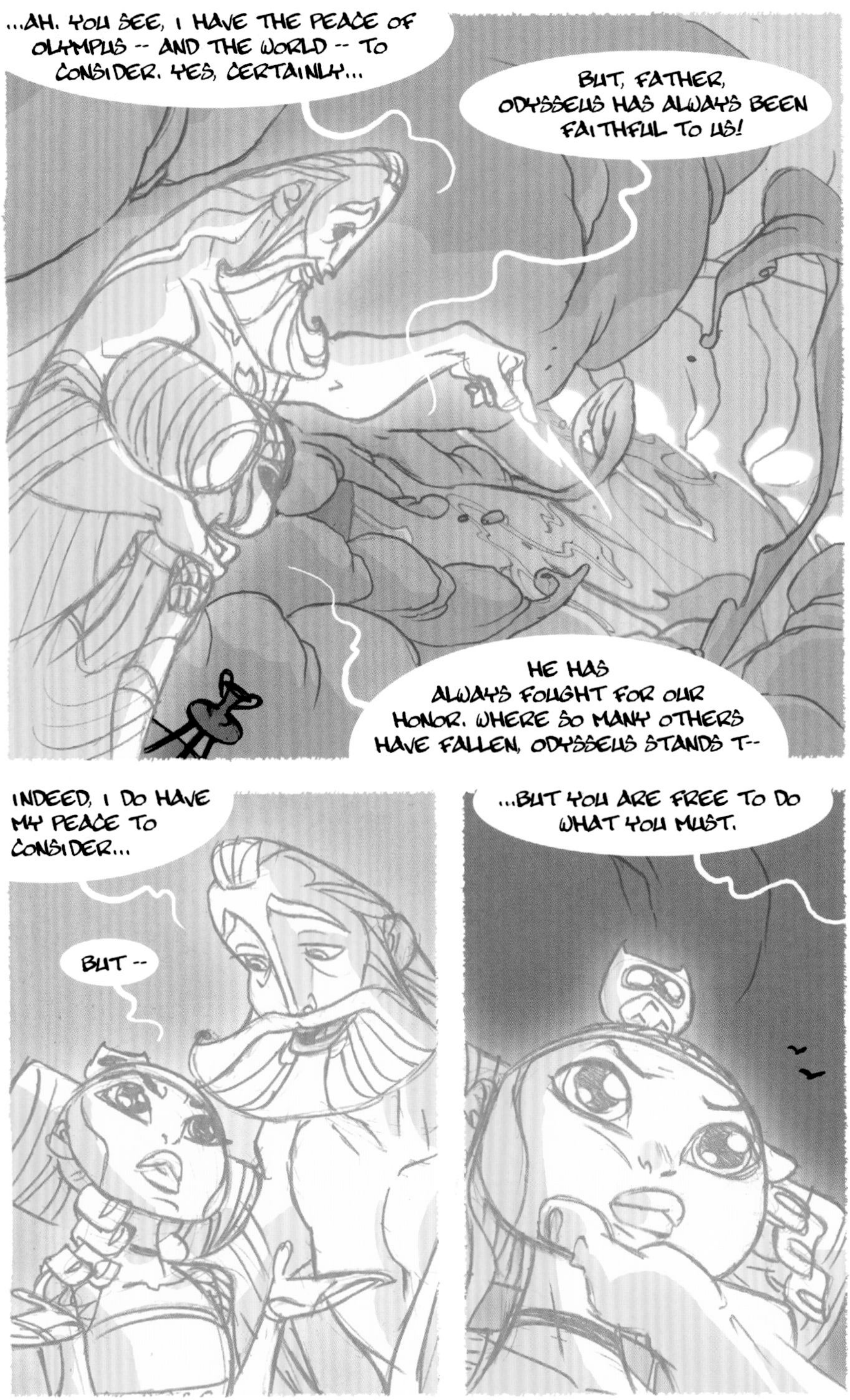
...AH. YOU SEE, I HAVE THE PEACE OF OLYMPUS -- AND THE WORLD -- TO CONSIDER. YES, CERTAINLY...
BUT, FATHER, ODYSSEUS HAS ALWAYS BEEN FAITHFUL TO US!
HE HAS ALWAYS FOUGHT FOR OUR HONOR. WHERE SO MANY OTHERS HAVE FALLEN, ODYSSEUS STANDS T--
INDEED, I DO HAVE MY PEACE TO CONSIDER...
BUT --
...BUT YOU ARE FREE TO DO WHAT YOU MUST.

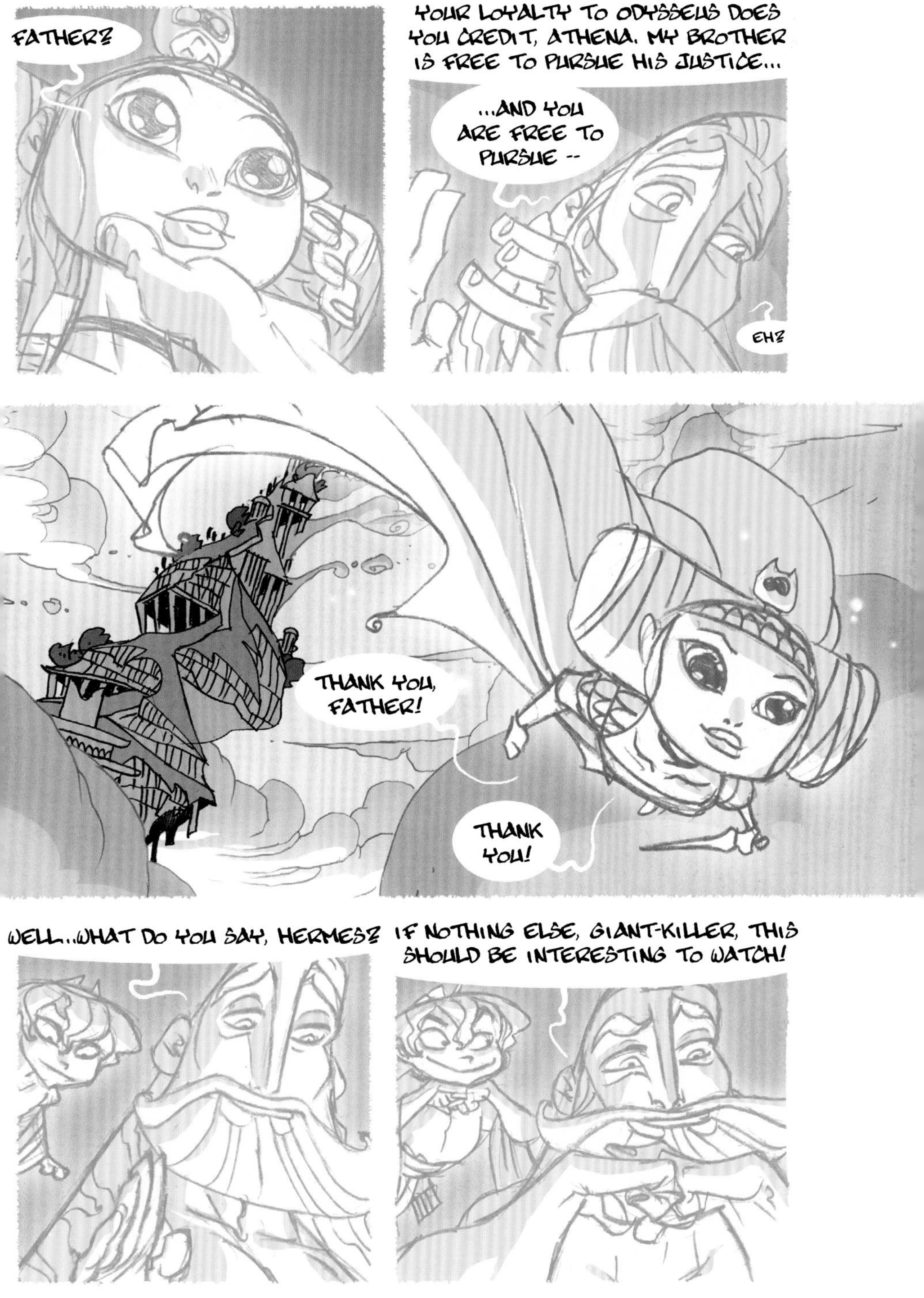
FATHER?
YOUR LOYALTY TO ODYSSEUS DOES YOU CREDIT, ATHENA. MY BROTHER IS FREE TO PURSUE HIS JUSTICE...
...AND YOU ARE FREE TO PURSUE --
EH?
THANK YOU, FATHER!
THANK YOU!
WELL...WHAT DO YOU SAY, HERMES?
IF NOTHING ELSE, GIANT-KILLER, THIS SHOULD BE INTERESTING TO WATCH!

MORE STORMS! THE MEN ARE BEGINNING TO DOUBT YOU, MY PRINCE!

THE MEN...OR YOU?

HAVE FAITH, EURYLOCHUS ...I DIDN'T SUCCESSFULLY LEAD YOU OUT OF TROY, JUST TO HAVE YOU PERISH FROM A LITTLE WATER!

CAPTAIN!

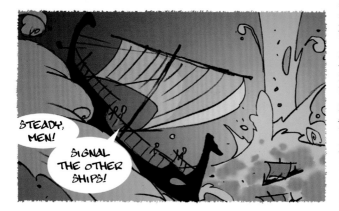

STEADY, MEN!

SIGNAL THE OTHER SHIPS!

ODYSSEUS...

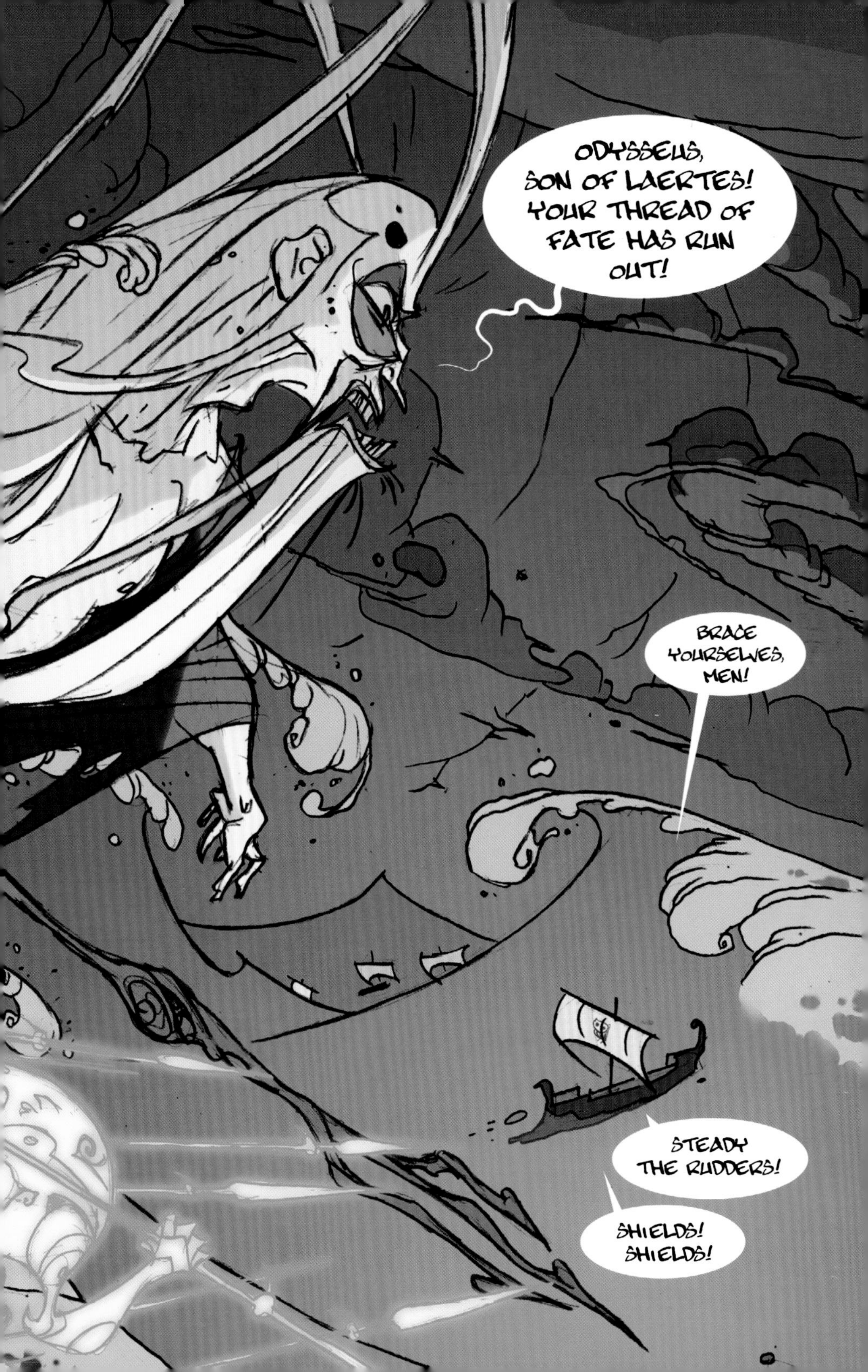
ODYSSEUS, SON OF LAERTES! YOUR THREAD OF FATE HAS RUN OUT!
BRACE YOURSELVES, MEN!
STEADY THE RUDDERS!
SHIELDS! SHIELDS!

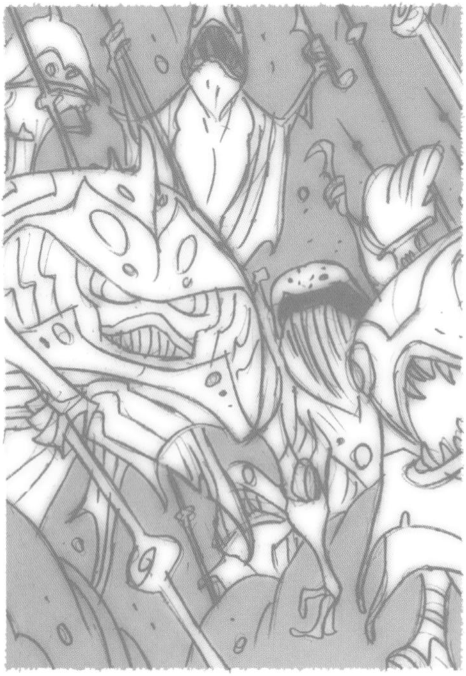

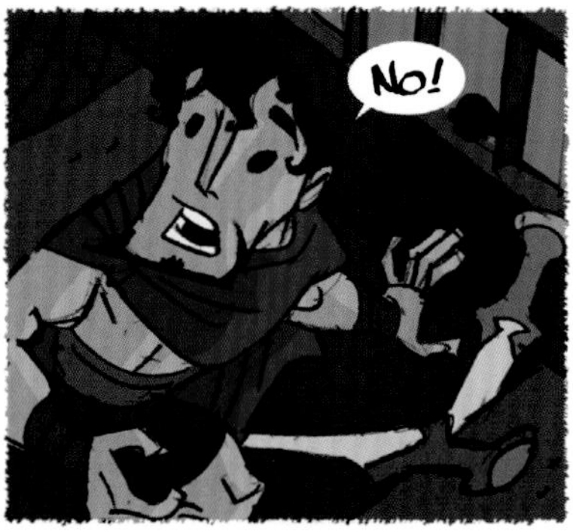
NO!

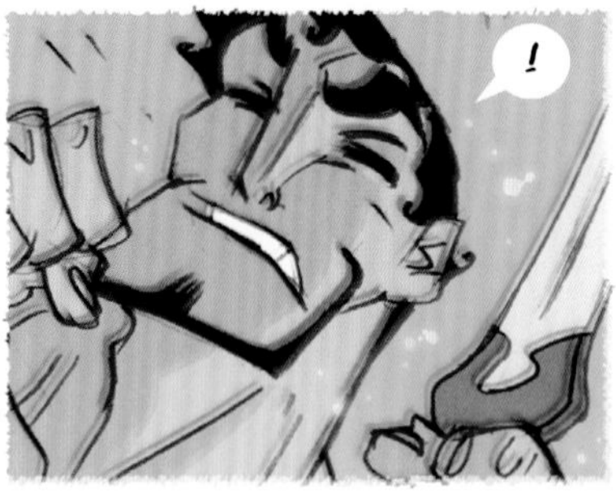
!

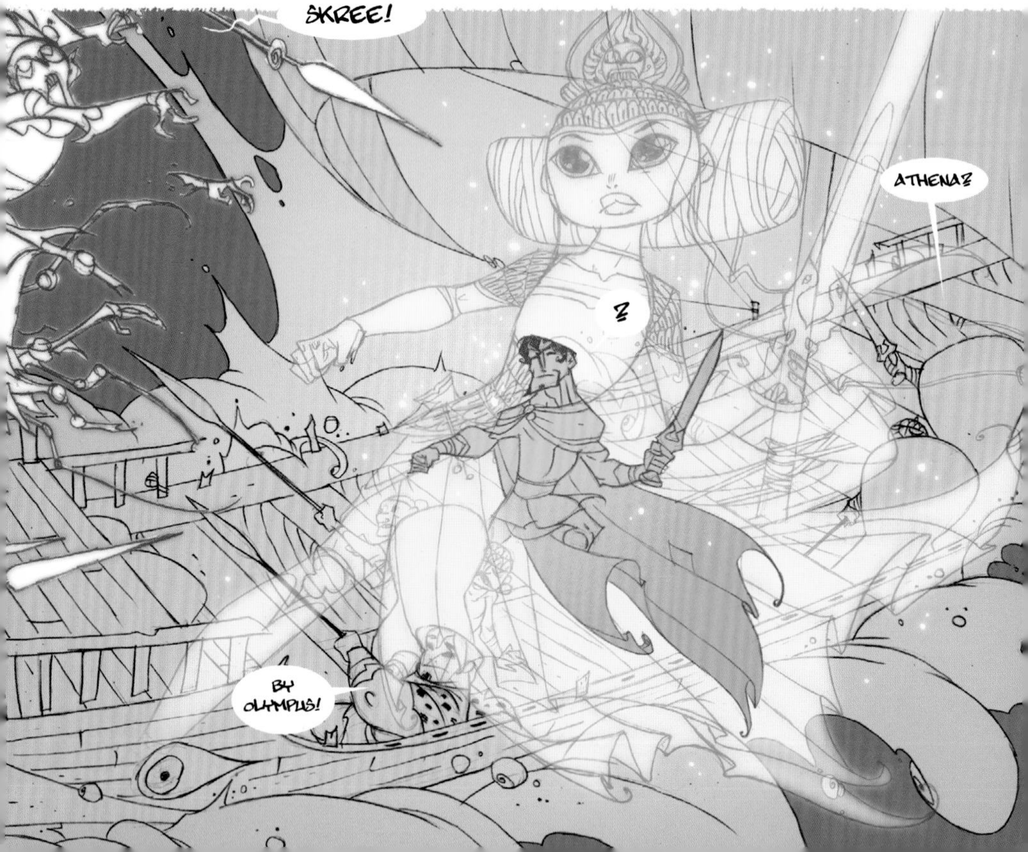
SKREE!
ATHENA?
?
BY OLYMPUS!

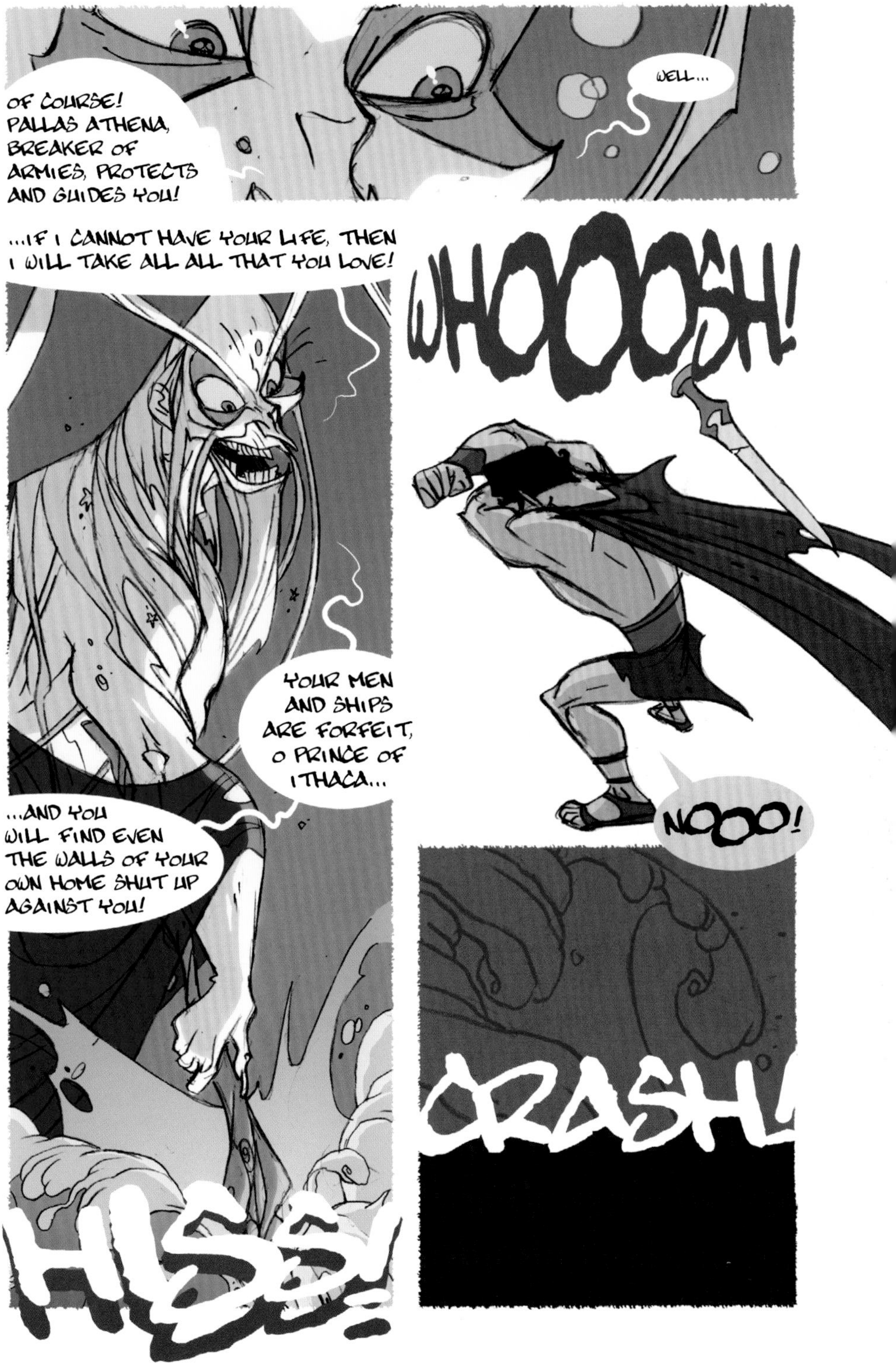
OF COURSE! PALLAS ATHENA, BREAKER OF ARMIES, PROTECTS AND GUIDES YOU!
WELL...
...IF I CANNOT HAVE YOUR LIFE, THEN I WILL TAKE ALL ALL THAT YOU LOVE!
YOUR MEN AND SHIPS ARE FORFEIT, O PRINCE OF ITHACA...
...AND YOU WILL FIND EVEN THE WALLS OF YOUR OWN HOME SHUT UP AGAINST YOU!
HISS!
WHOOOOSH!
NOOO!
CRASH!

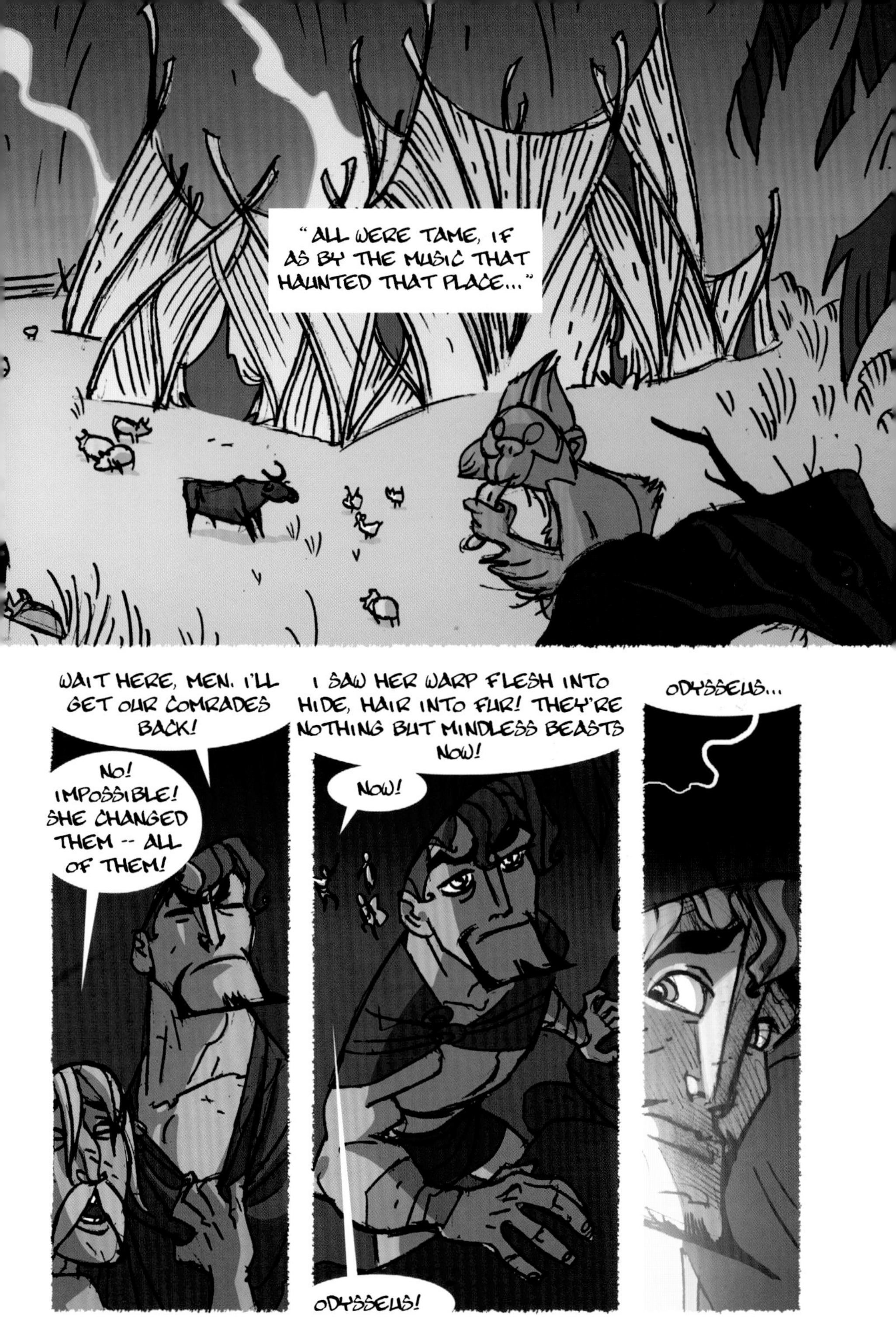
"ALL WERE TAME, IF AS BY THE MUSIC THAT HAUNTED THAT PLACE..."
WAIT HERE, MEN. I'LL GET OUR COMRADES BACK!
NO! IMPOSSIBLE! SHE CHANGED THEM -- ALL OF THEM!
I SAW HER WARP FLESH INTO HIDE, HAIR INTO FUR! THEY'RE NOTHING BUT MINDLESS BEASTS NOW!
NOW!
ODYSSEUS!
ODYSSEUS...

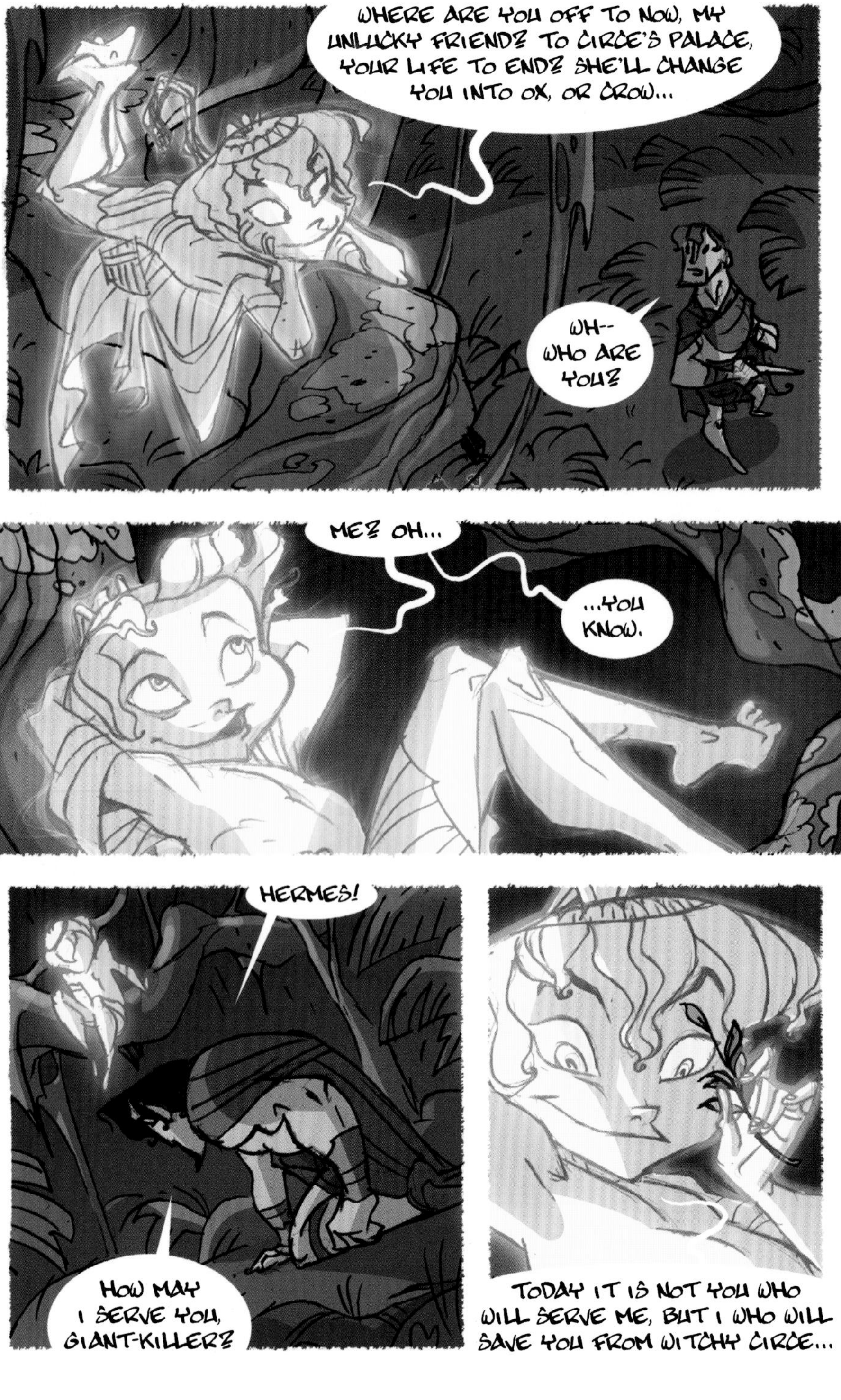
WHERE ARE YOU OFF TO NOW, MY UNLUCKY FRIEND? TO CIRCE'S PALACE, YOUR LIFE TO END? SHE'LL CHANGE YOU INTO OX, OR CROW...
WH-- WHO ARE YOU?
ME? OH...
...YOU KNOW.
HERMES!
HOW MAY I SERVE YOU, GIANT-KILLER?
TODAY IT IS NOT YOU WHO WILL SERVE ME, BUT I WHO WILL SAVE YOU FROM WITCHY CIRCE...

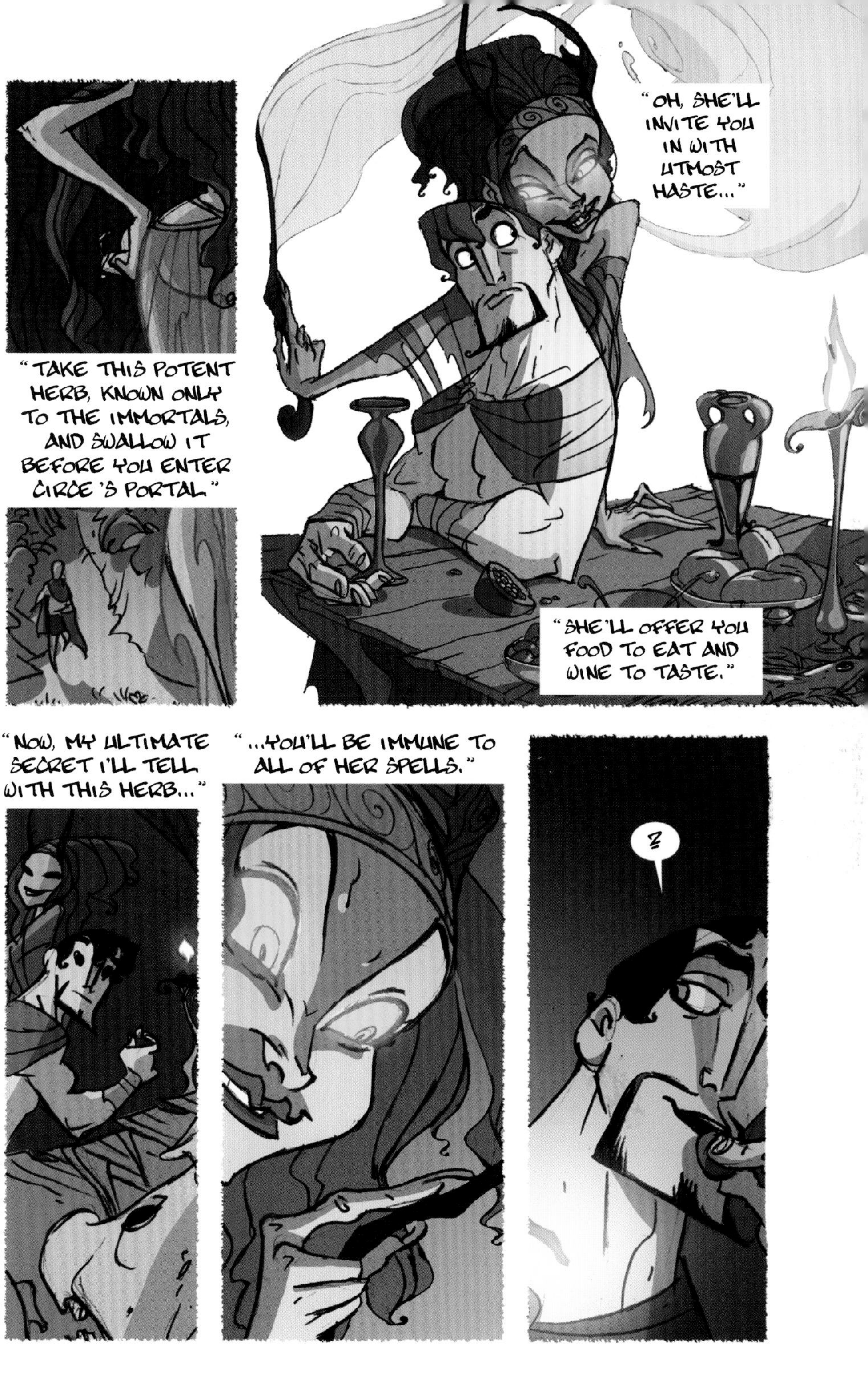
"TAKE THIS POTENT HERB, KNOWN ONLY TO THE IMMORTALS, AND SWALLOW IT BEFORE YOU ENTER CIRCE'S PORTAL."
"OH, SHE'LL INVITE YOU IN WITH UTMOST HASTE..."
"SHE'LL OFFER YOU FOOD TO EAT AND WINE TO TASTE."
"NOW, MY ULTIMATE SECRET I'LL TELL WITH THIS HERB..."
"...YOU'LL BE IMMUNE TO ALL OF HER SPELLS."
?

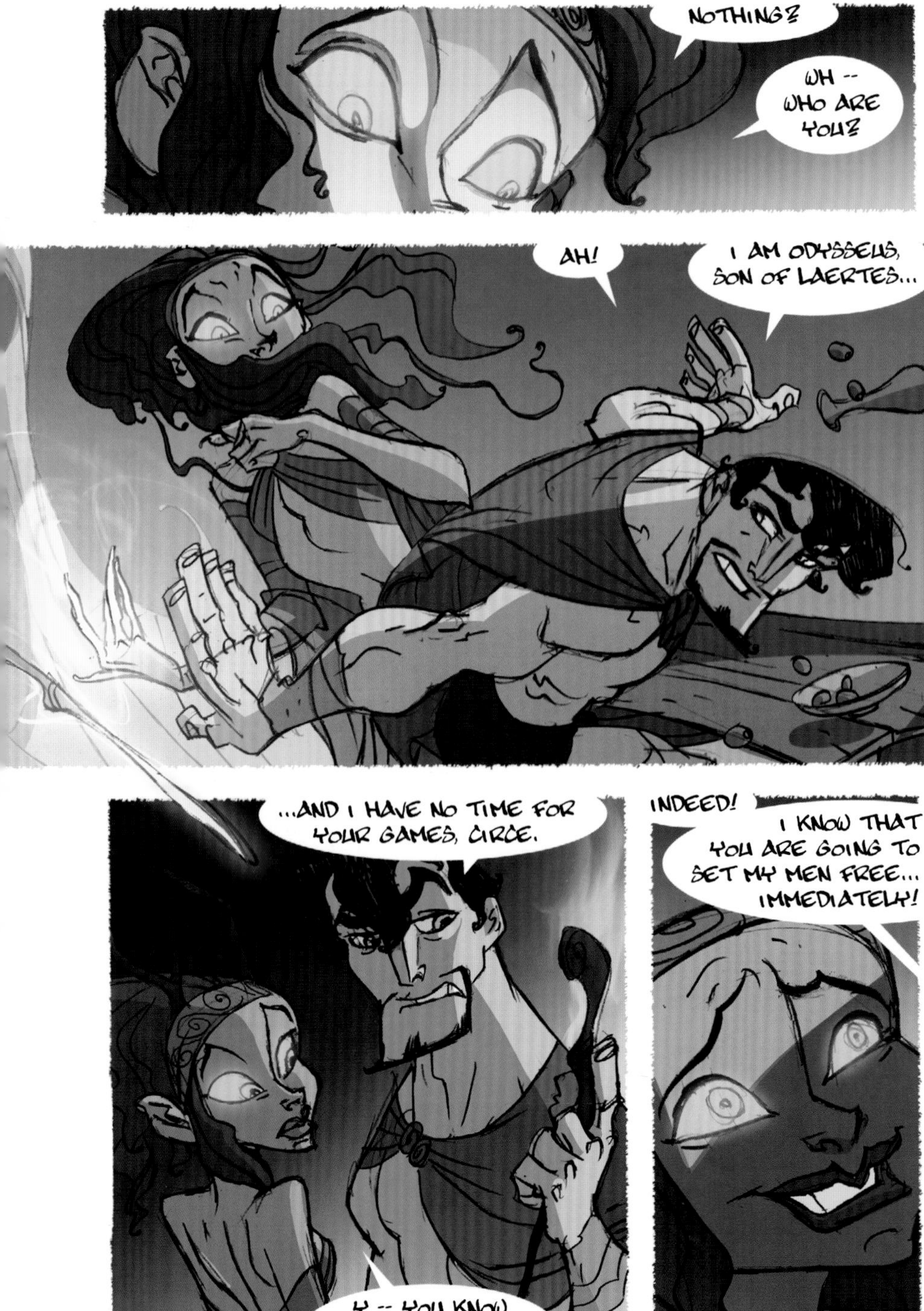
NOTHING?
WH -- WHO ARE YOU?
AH!
I AM ODYSSEUS, SON OF LAERTES...
...AND I HAVE NO TIME FOR YOUR GAMES, CIRCE.
Y -- YOU KNOW MUCH, WANDERER...
INDEED!
I KNOW THAT YOU ARE GOING TO SET MY MEN FREE... IMMEDIATELY!

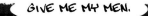

OH, VERY WELL!

BUT SURELY YOU CANNOT BEGRUDGE A WOMAN...

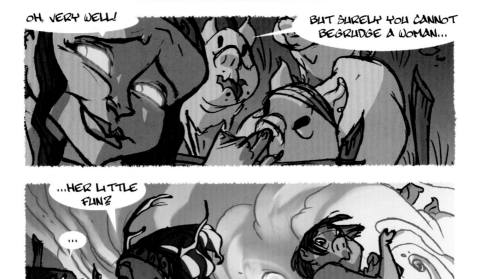

...HER LITTLE FUN?

...

ODYSSEUS, YOU HAVE BESTED MY MAGIC, A FEAT NO OTHER MORTAL CAN CLAIM. I URGE YOU AND YOUR MEN TO JOIN ME HERE.

REST, RE-SUPPLY... NO TRICKS, NO MAGIC! YOU HAVE MY WORD.

SNORT?

?

!

SIGH!

HMM.

THE WORD OF A GODDESS IS NOT TO BE TAKEN LIGHTLY. I ACCEPT YOUR OFFER, AND I THANK YOU.

MEN! FETCH YOUR COMRADES FROM THE BEACH...

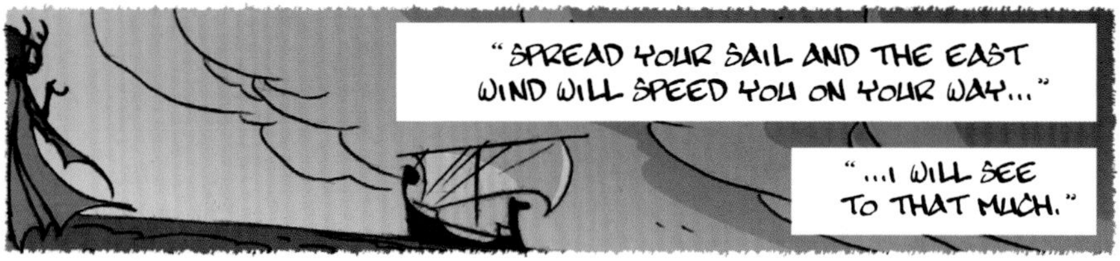
"SPREAD YOUR SAIL AND THE EAST WIND WILL SPEED YOU ON YOUR WAY..."
"...I WILL SEE TO THAT MUCH."

"ACROSS THE OCEAN RIVER, YOU WILL COME UPON THE CHURNING BLACK SHORES OF PERSEPHONE'S GROVE. BEWARE THE SHADES OF LETHE, WHICH ROB YOU OF YOUR EARTHLY MEMORIES..."

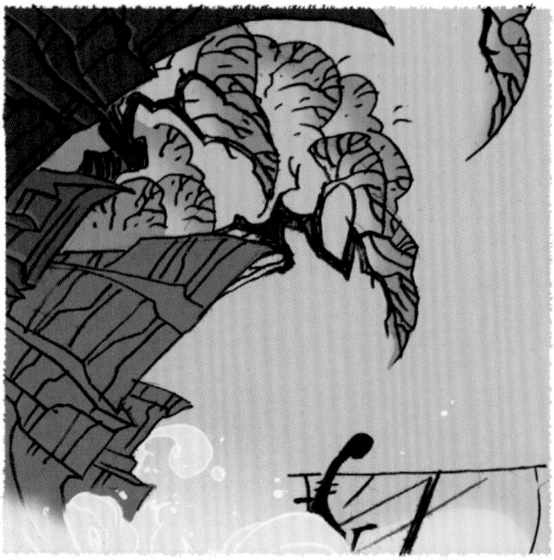

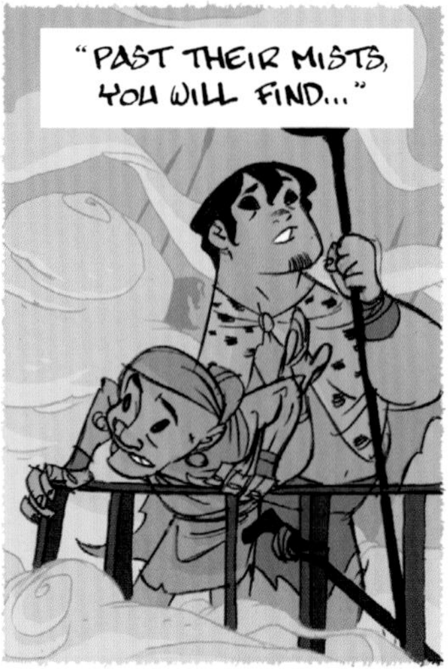
"PAST THEIR MISTS, YOU WILL FIND..."

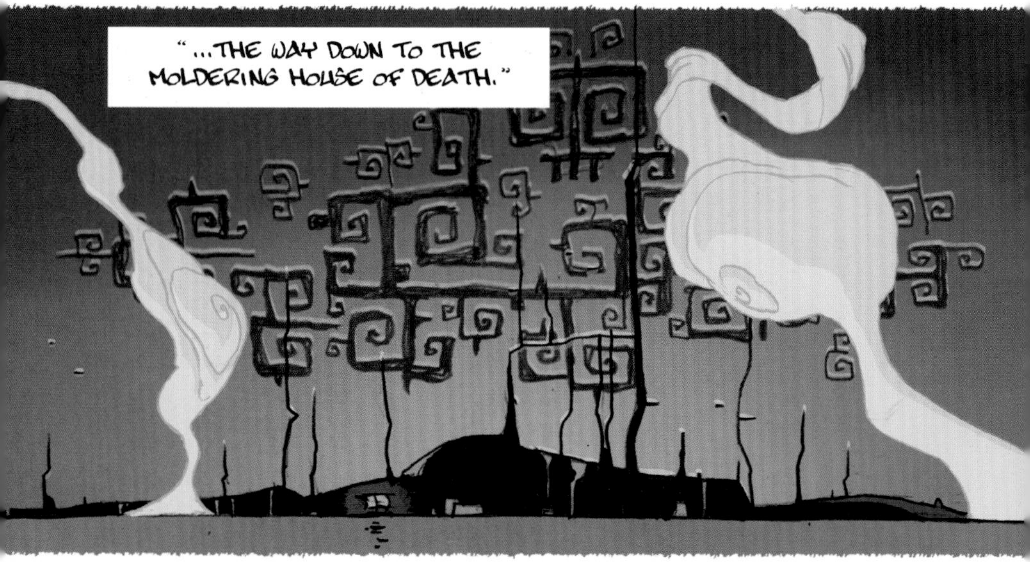
"...THE WAY DOWN TO THE MOLDERING HOUSE OF DEATH."

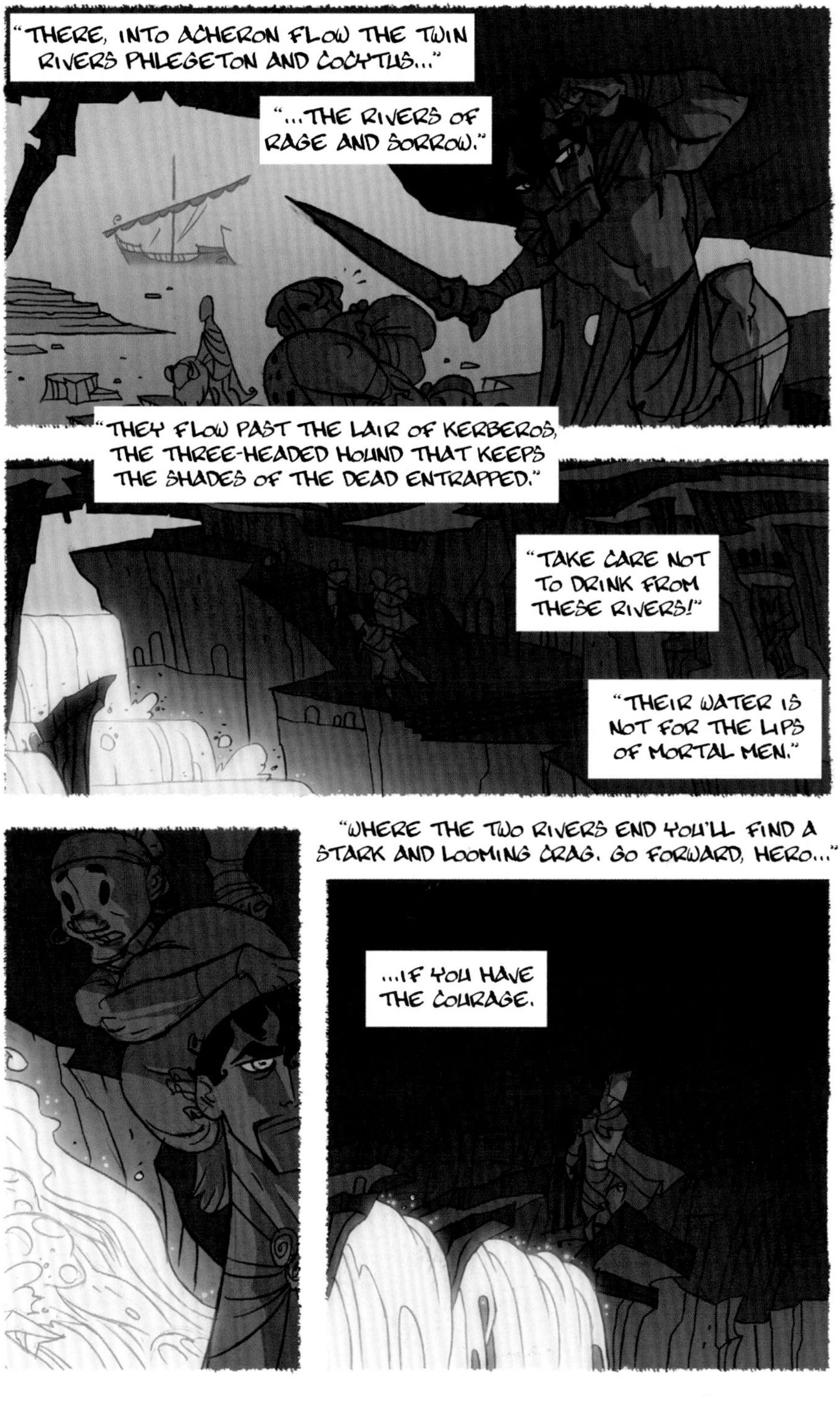
"THERE, INTO ACHERON FLOW THE TWIN RIVERS PHLEGETON AND COCYTUS..."
"...THE RIVERS OF RAGE AND SORROW."
"THEY FLOW PAST THE LAIR OF KERBEROS, THE THREE-HEADED HOUND THAT KEEPS THE SHADES OF THE DEAD ENTRAPPED."
"TAKE CARE NOT TO DRINK FROM THESE RIVERS!"
"THEIR WATER IS NOT FOR THE LIPS OF MORTAL MEN."
"WHERE THE TWO RIVERS END YOU'LL FIND A STARK AND LOOMING CRAG. GO FORWARD, HERO..."
...IF YOU HAVE THE COURAGE.

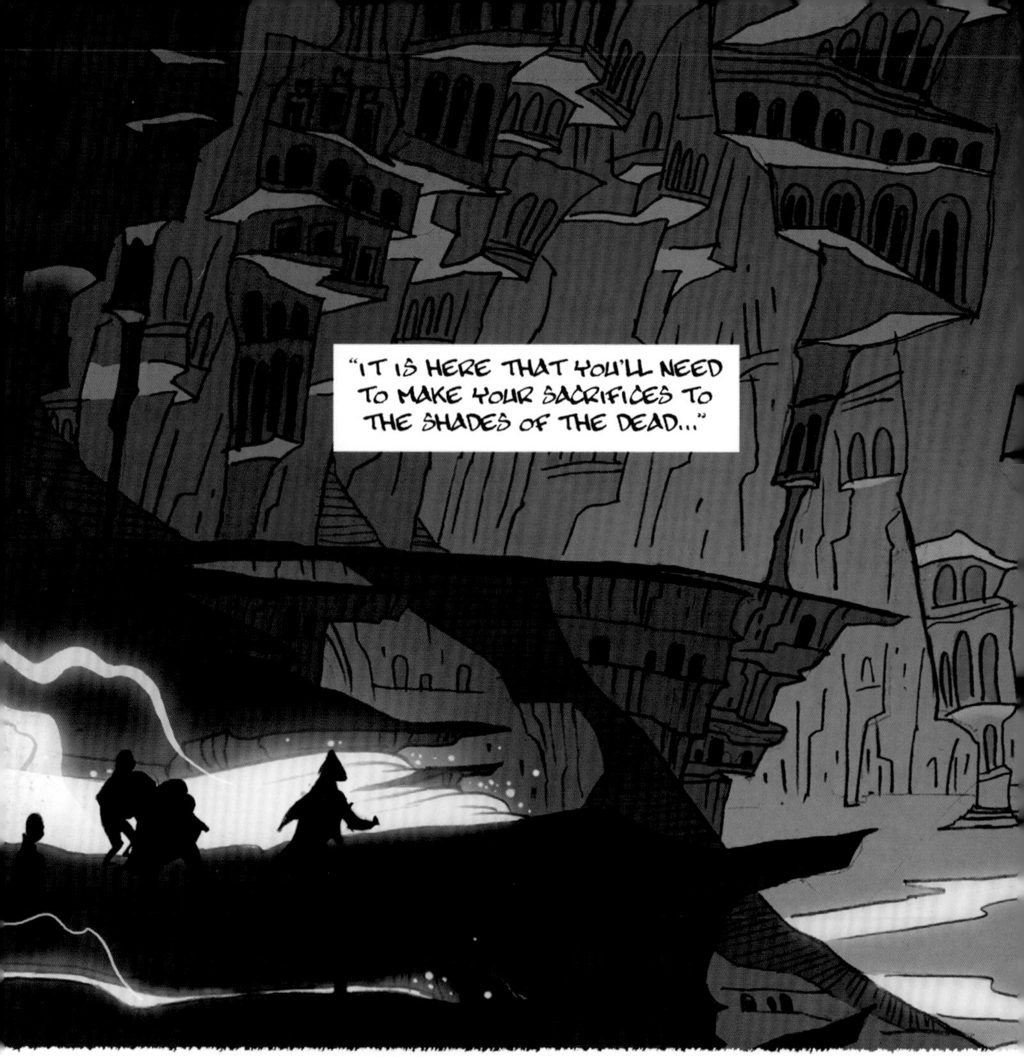
"IT IS HERE THAT YOU'LL NEED TO MAKE YOUR SACRIFICES TO THE SHADES OF THE DEAD..."

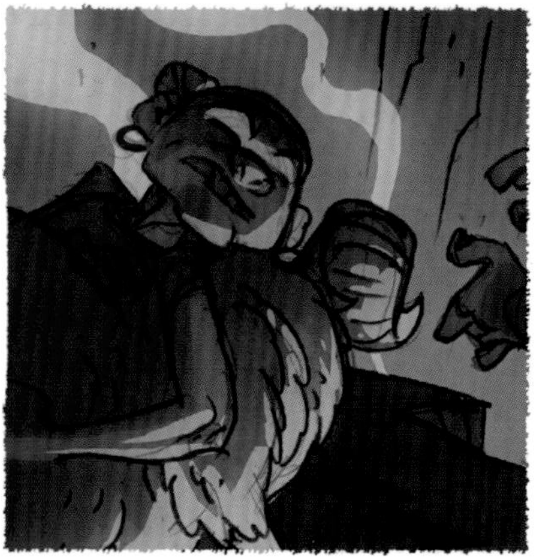

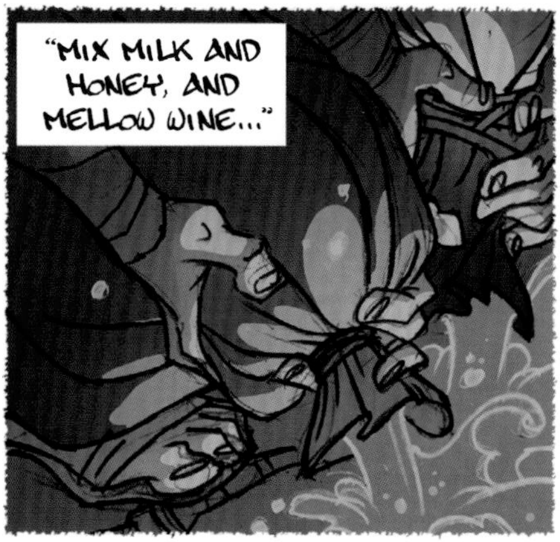
"MIX MILK AND HONEY, AND MELLOW WINE..."

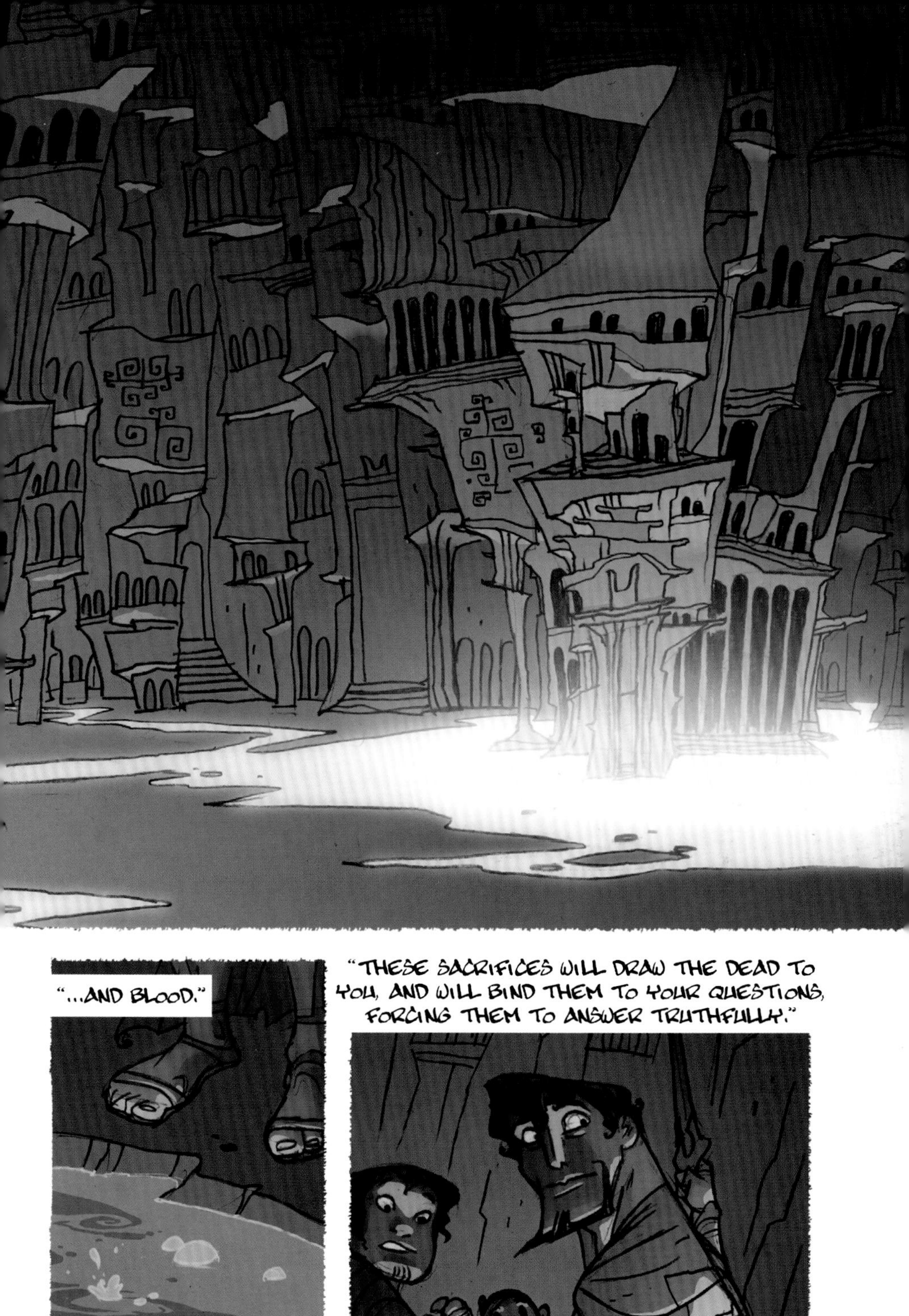
"...AND BLOOD."
"THESE SACRIFICES WILL DRAW THE DEAD TO YOU, AND WILL BIND THEM TO YOUR QUESTIONS, FORCING THEM TO ANSWER TRUTHFULLY."

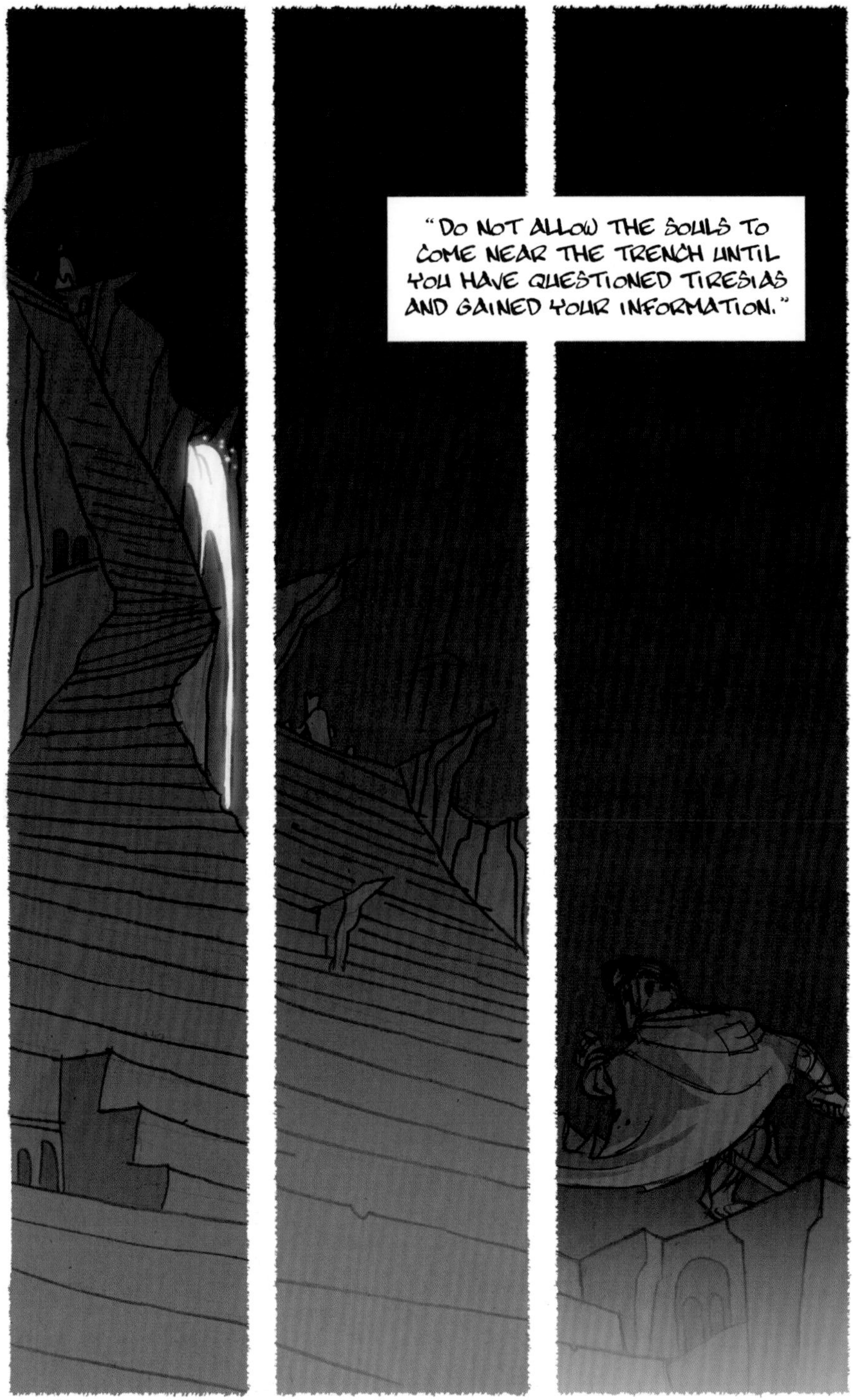
"DO NOT ALLOW THE SOULS TO COME NEAR THE TRENCH UNTIL YOU HAVE QUESTIONED TIRESIAS AND GAINED YOUR INFORMATION."

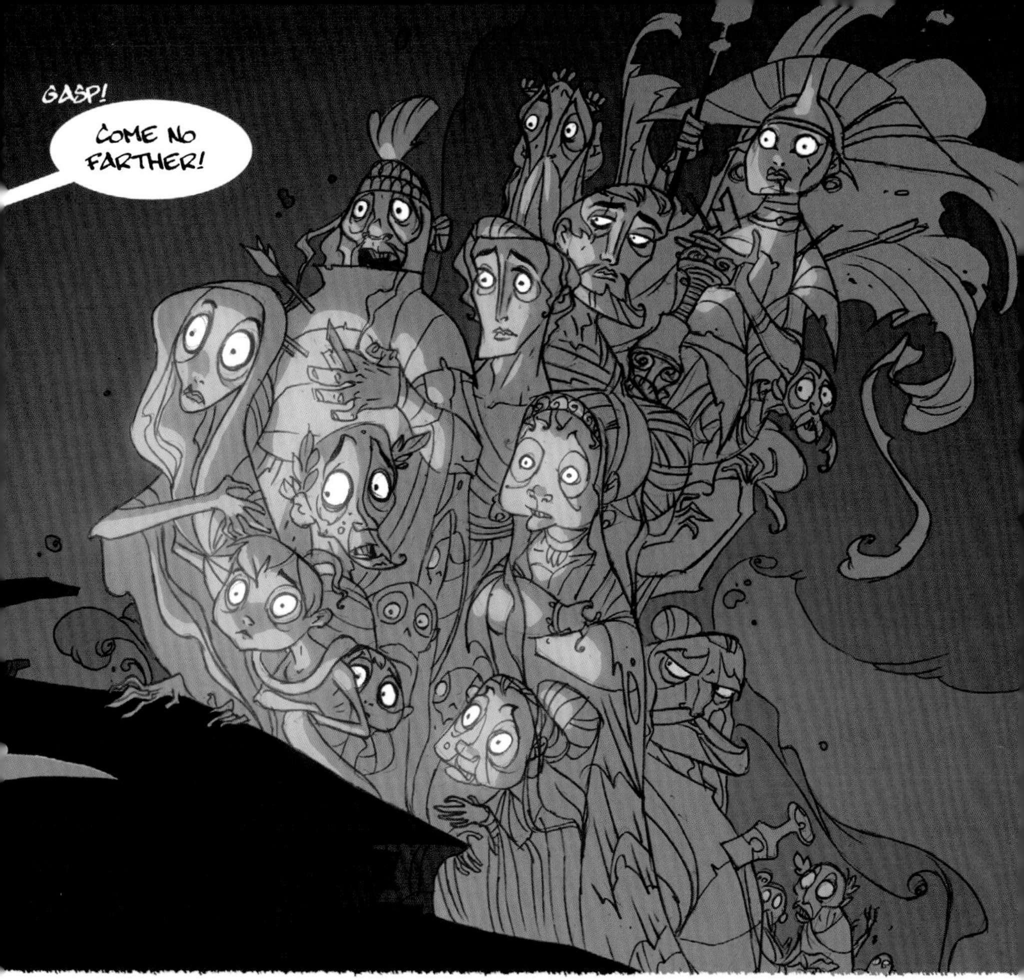
GASP!
COME NO FARTHER!

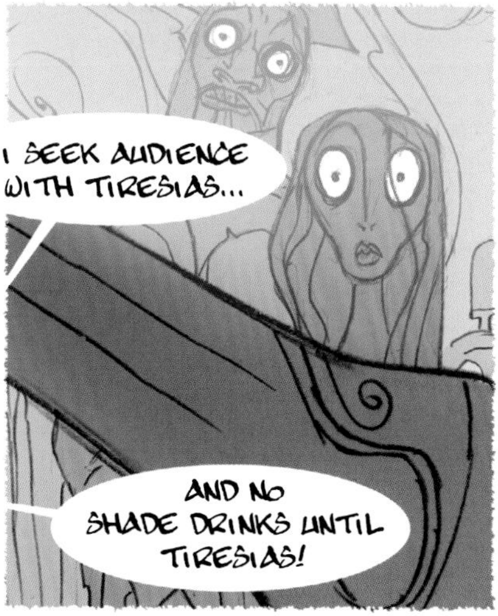
I SEEK AUDIENCE WITH TIRESIAS...
AND NO SHADE DRINKS UNTIL TIRESIAS!

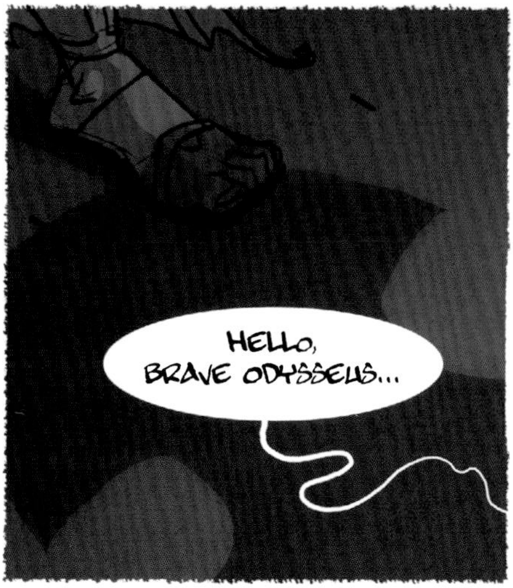
HELLO, BRAVE ODYSSEUS...

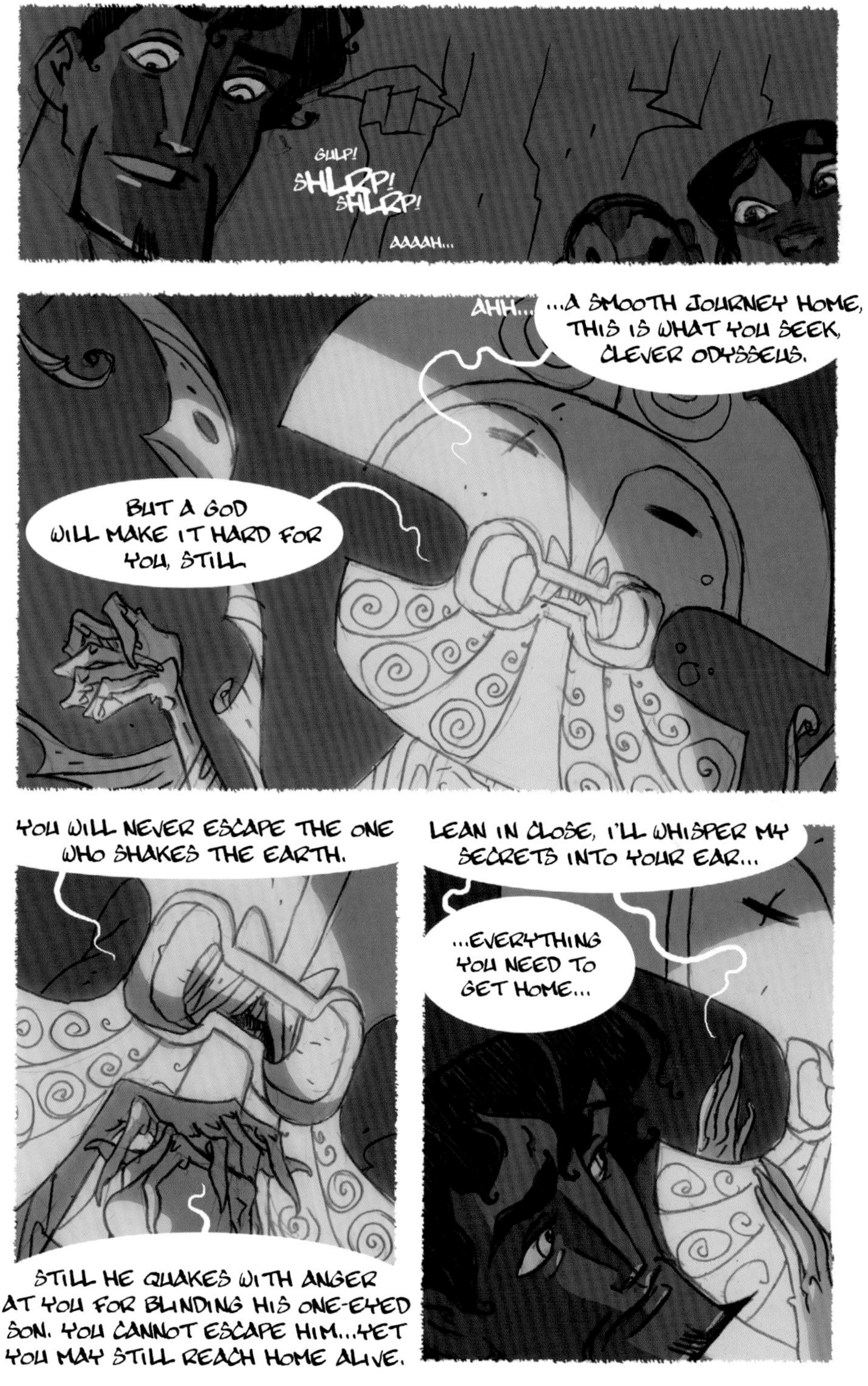
GULP!
SHLRP!
SHLRP!
AAAAH...
AHH...
...A SMOOTH JOURNEY HOME, THIS IS WHAT YOU SEEK, CLEVER ODYSSEUS.
BUT A GOD WILL MAKE IT HARD FOR YOU, STILL.
YOU WILL NEVER ESCAPE THE ONE WHO SHAKES THE EARTH.
STILL HE QUAKES WITH ANGER AT YOU FOR BLINDING HIS ONE-EYED SON. YOU CANNOT ESCAPE HIM...YET YOU MAY STILL REACH HOME ALIVE.
LEAN IN CLOSE, I'LL WHISPER MY SECRETS INTO YOUR EAR...
...EVERYTHING YOU NEED TO GET HOME...

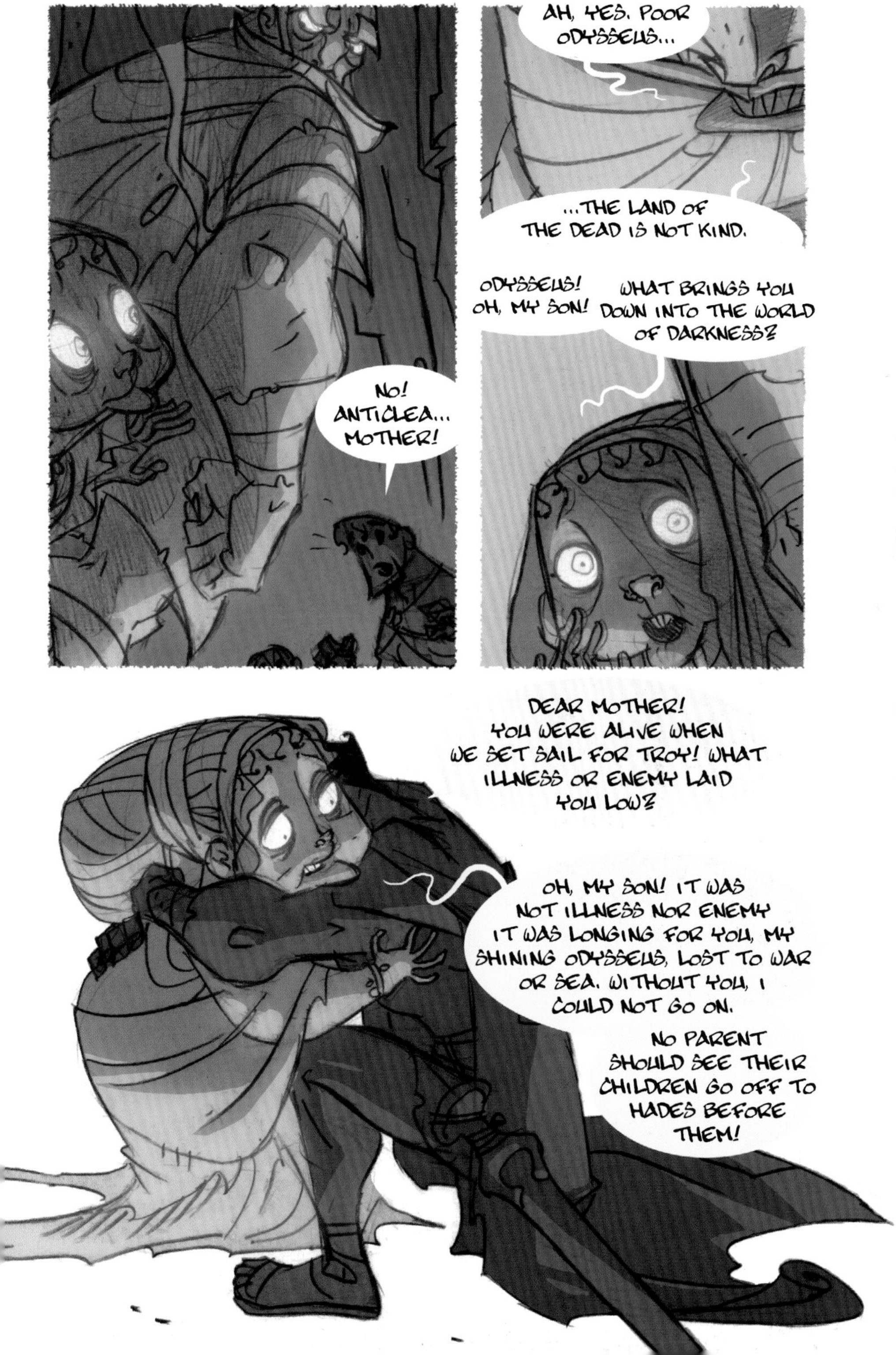
No! ANTICLEA... MOTHER!
AH, YES. POOR ODYSSEUS...
...THE LAND OF THE DEAD IS NOT KIND.
ODYSSEUS! OH, MY SON!
WHAT BRINGS YOU DOWN INTO THE WORLD OF DARKNESS?
DEAR MOTHER! YOU WERE ALIVE WHEN WE SET SAIL FOR TROY! WHAT ILLNESS OR ENEMY LAID YOU LOW?
OH, MY SON! IT WAS NOT ILLNESS NOR ENEMY IT WAS LONGING FOR YOU, MY SHINING ODYSSEUS, LOST TO WAR OR SEA. WITHOUT YOU, I COULD NOT GO ON.
NO PARENT SHOULD SEE THEIR CHILDREN GO OFF TO HADES BEFORE THEM!

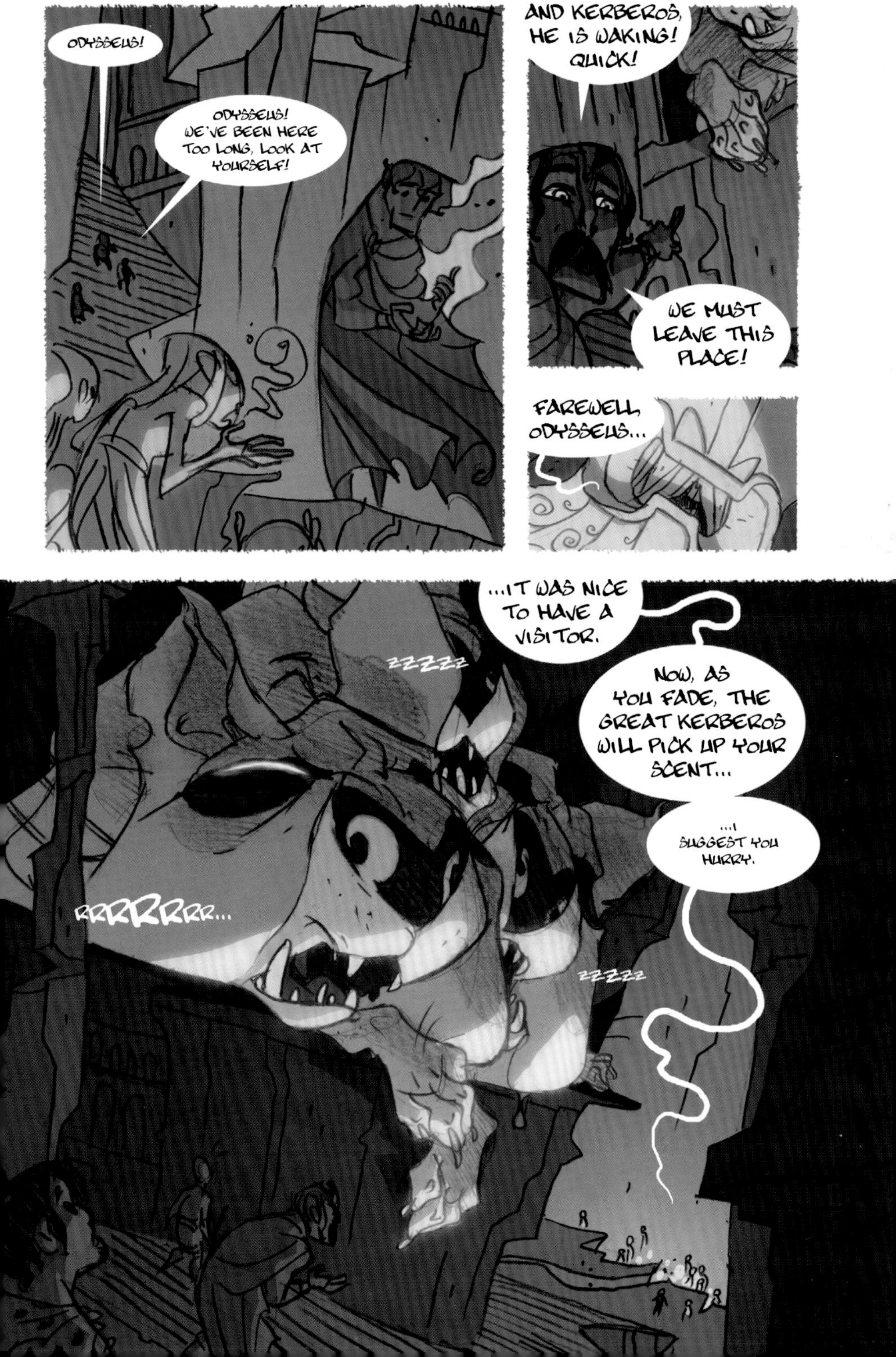
ODYSSEUS!
ODYSSEUS! WE'VE BEEN HERE TOO LONG, LOOK AT YOURSELF!
AND KERBEROS, HE IS WAKING! QUICK!
WE MUST LEAVE THIS PLACE!
FAREWELL ODYSSEUS...
...IT WAS NICE TO HAVE A VISITOR.
ZZZZZZ
NOW, AS YOU FADE, THE GREAT KERBEROS WILL PICK UP YOUR SCENT...
...I SUGGEST YOU HURRY.
RRRRRRRR...
ZZZZZ

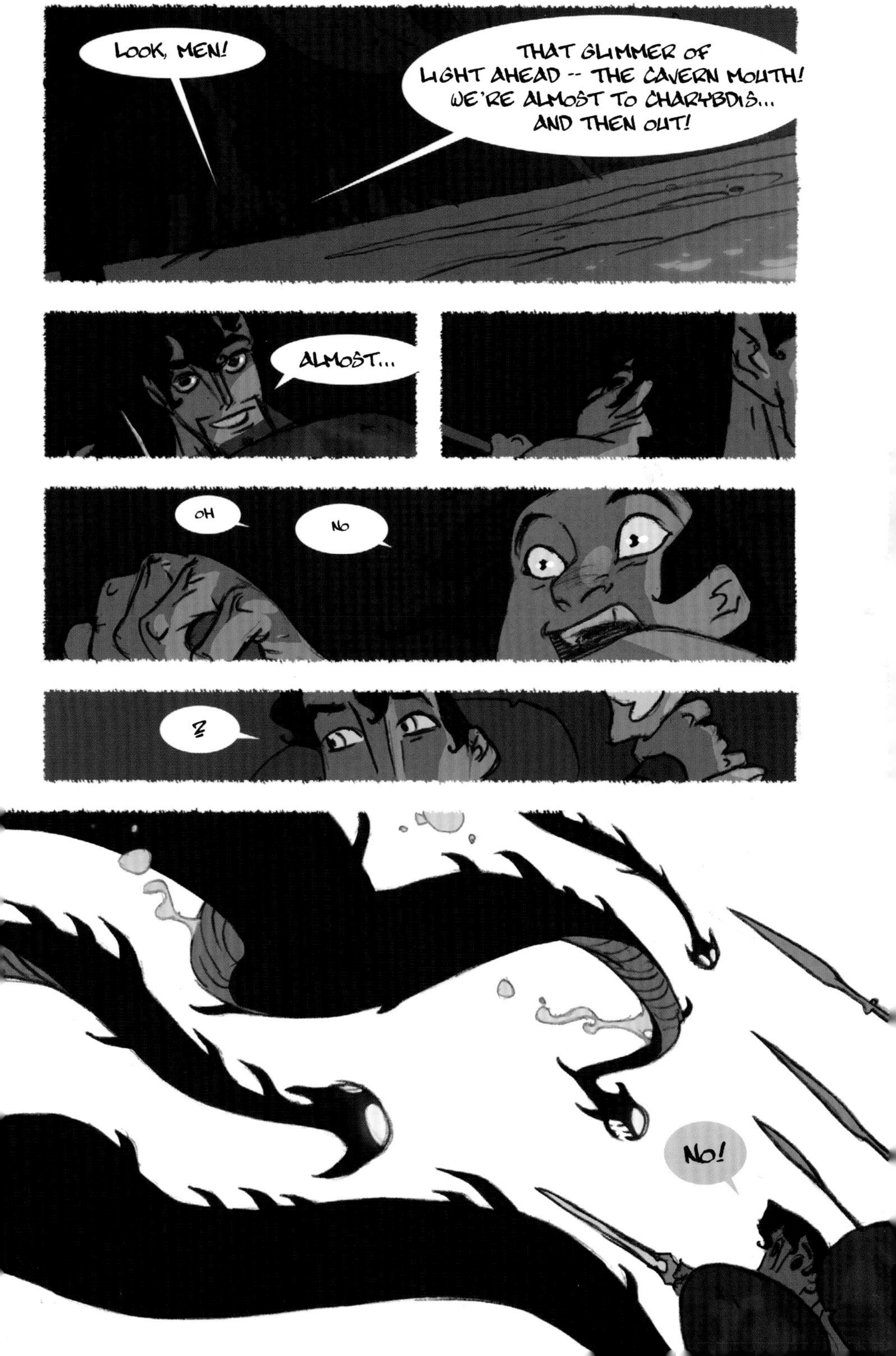
LOOK, MEN!
THAT GLIMMER OF LIGHT AHEAD -- THE CAVERN MOUTH! WE'RE ALMOST TO CHARYBDIS... AND THEN OUT!
ALMOST...
OH
NO
NO!

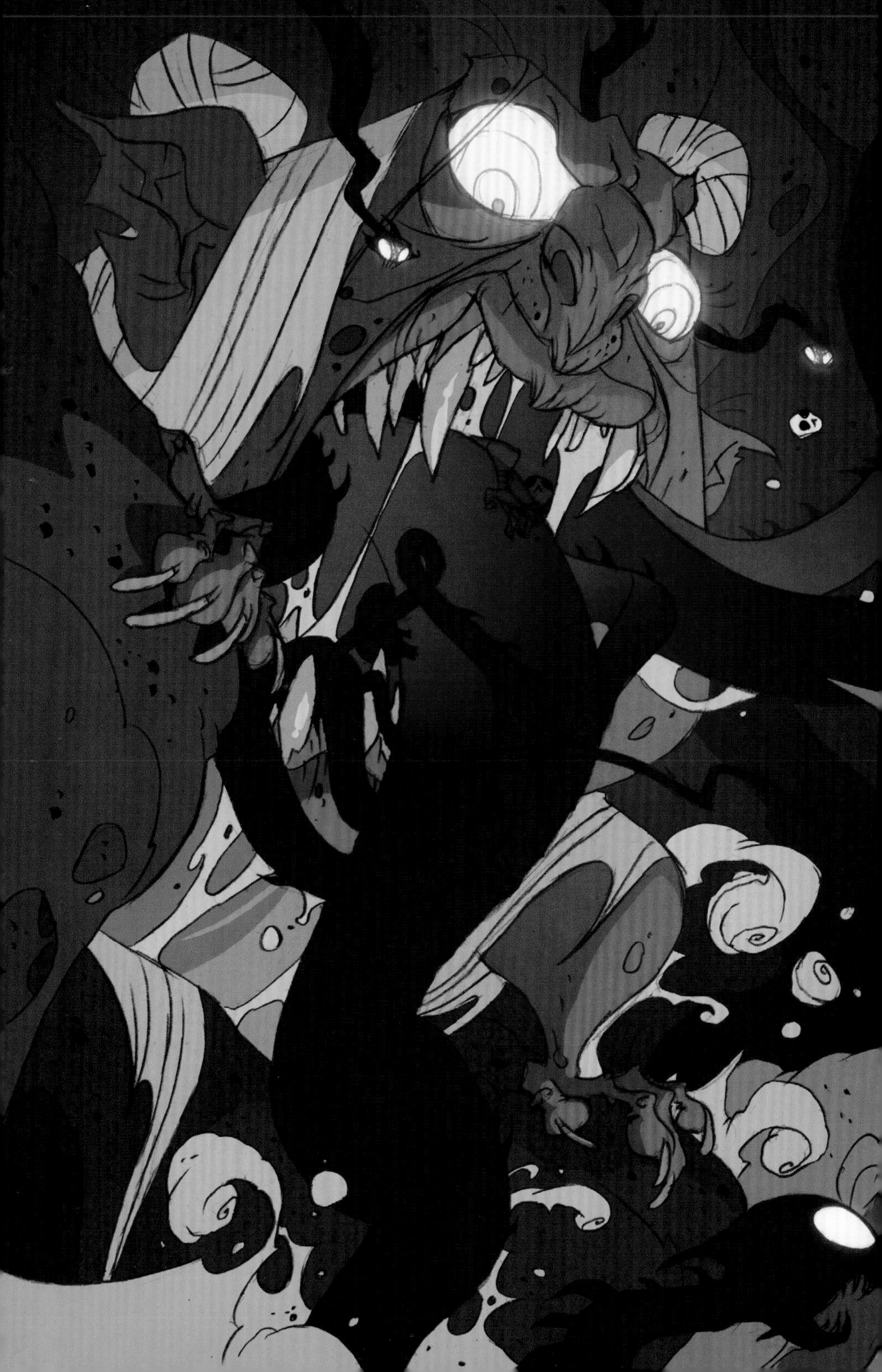

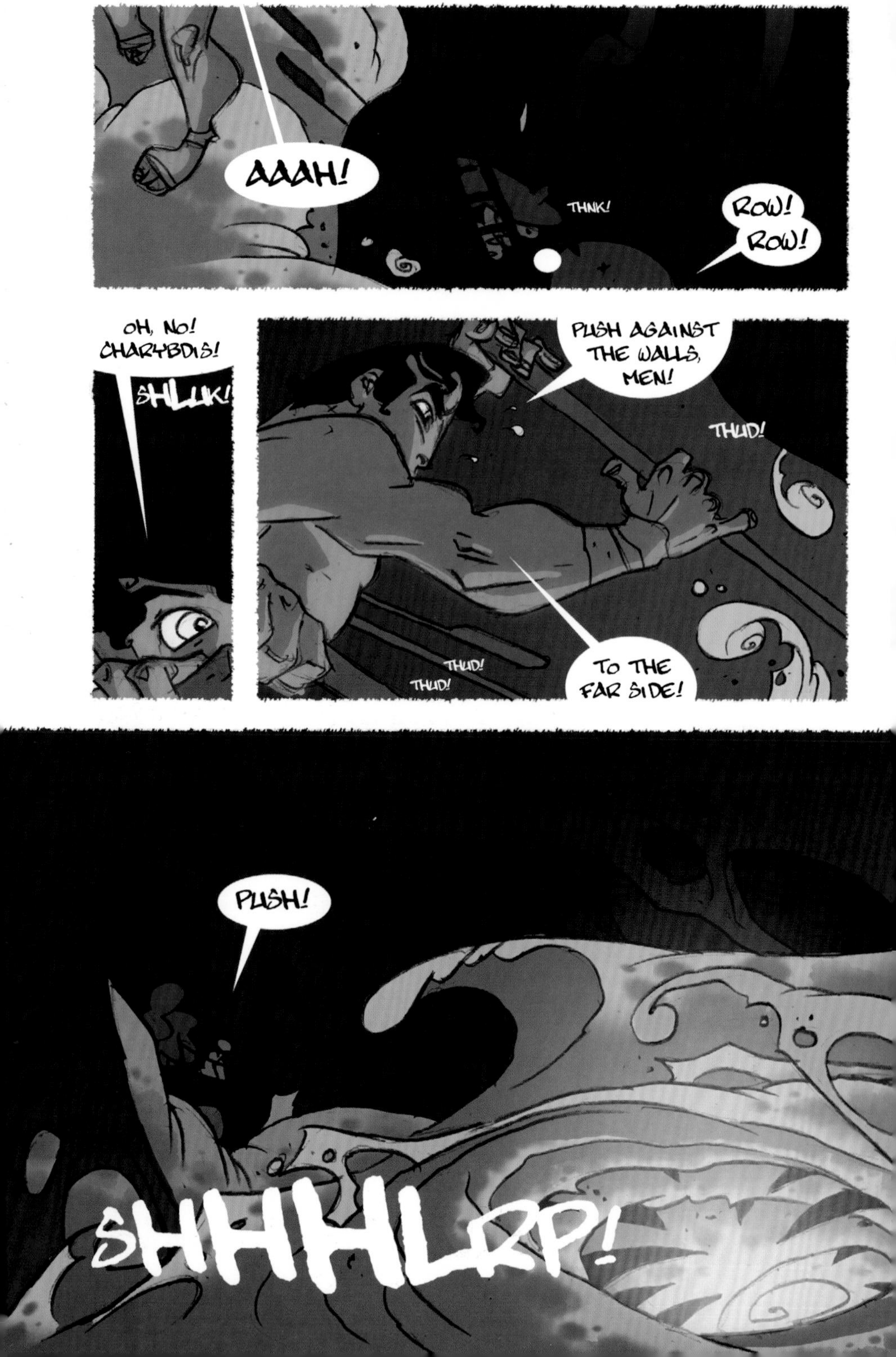
AAAH!
THNK!
ROW! ROW!
OH, NO! CHARYBDIS!
SHLLLK!
PUSH AGAINST THE WALLS, MEN!
THUD!
THUD!
THUD!
TO THE FAR SIDE!
PUSH!
SHHHLRP!

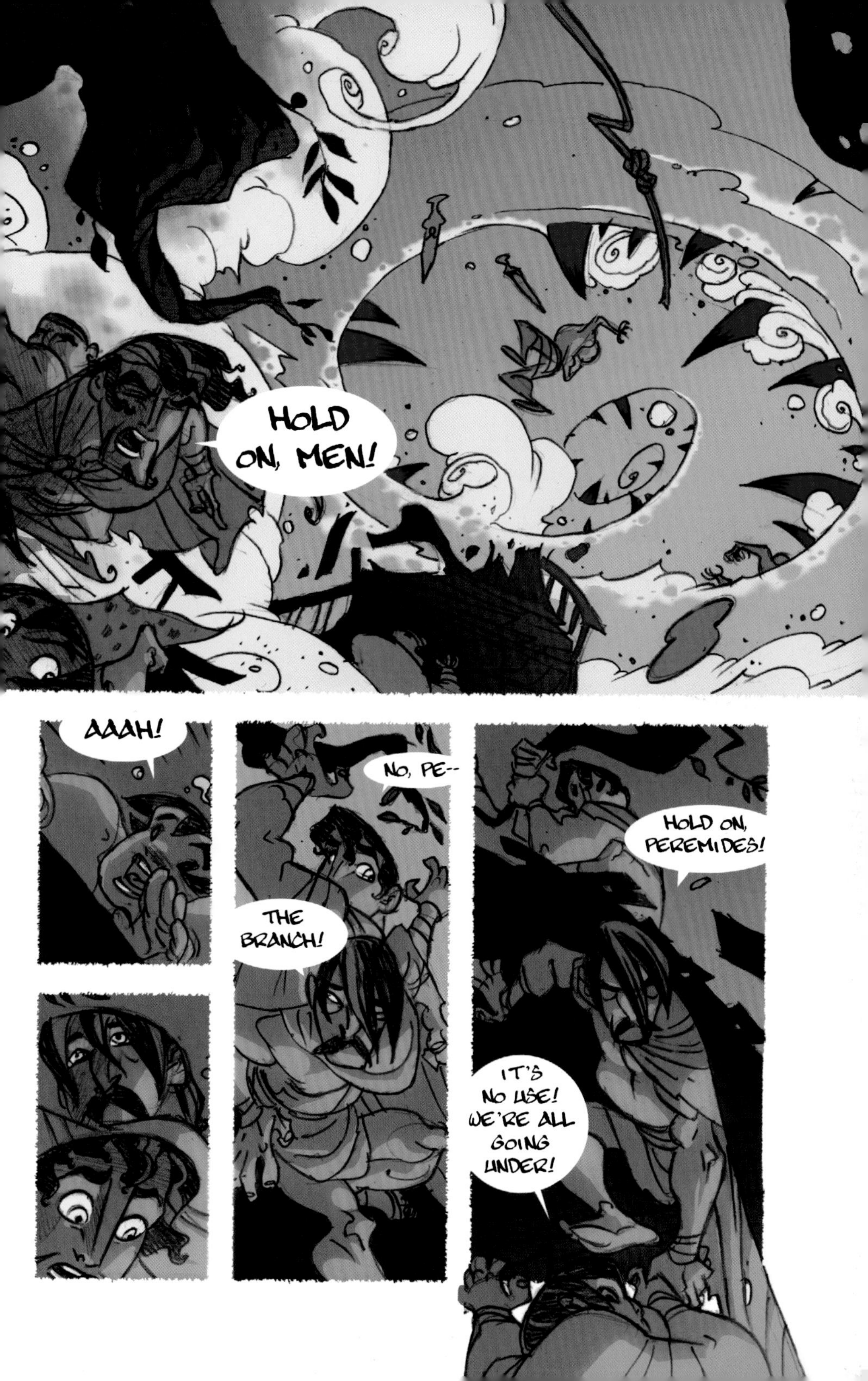
HOLD ON, MEN!
AAAH!
NO, PE--
THE BRANCH!
HOLD ON, PEREMIDES!
IT'S NO USE! WE'RE ALL GOING UNDER!

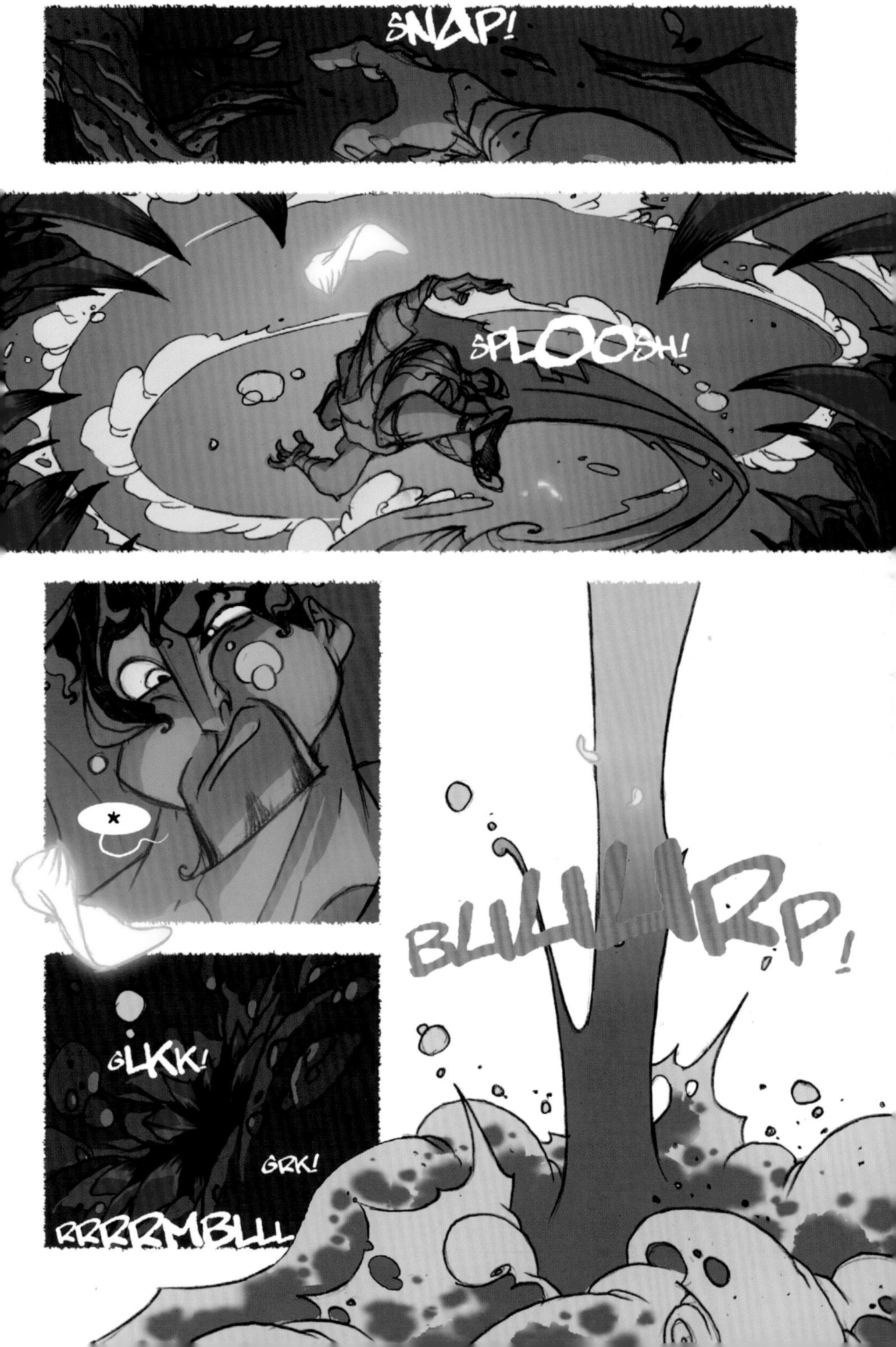
SNAP!
SPLOOOSH!
*
BLLLLLRP!
GLKK!
GRK!
RRRRRMBLLL

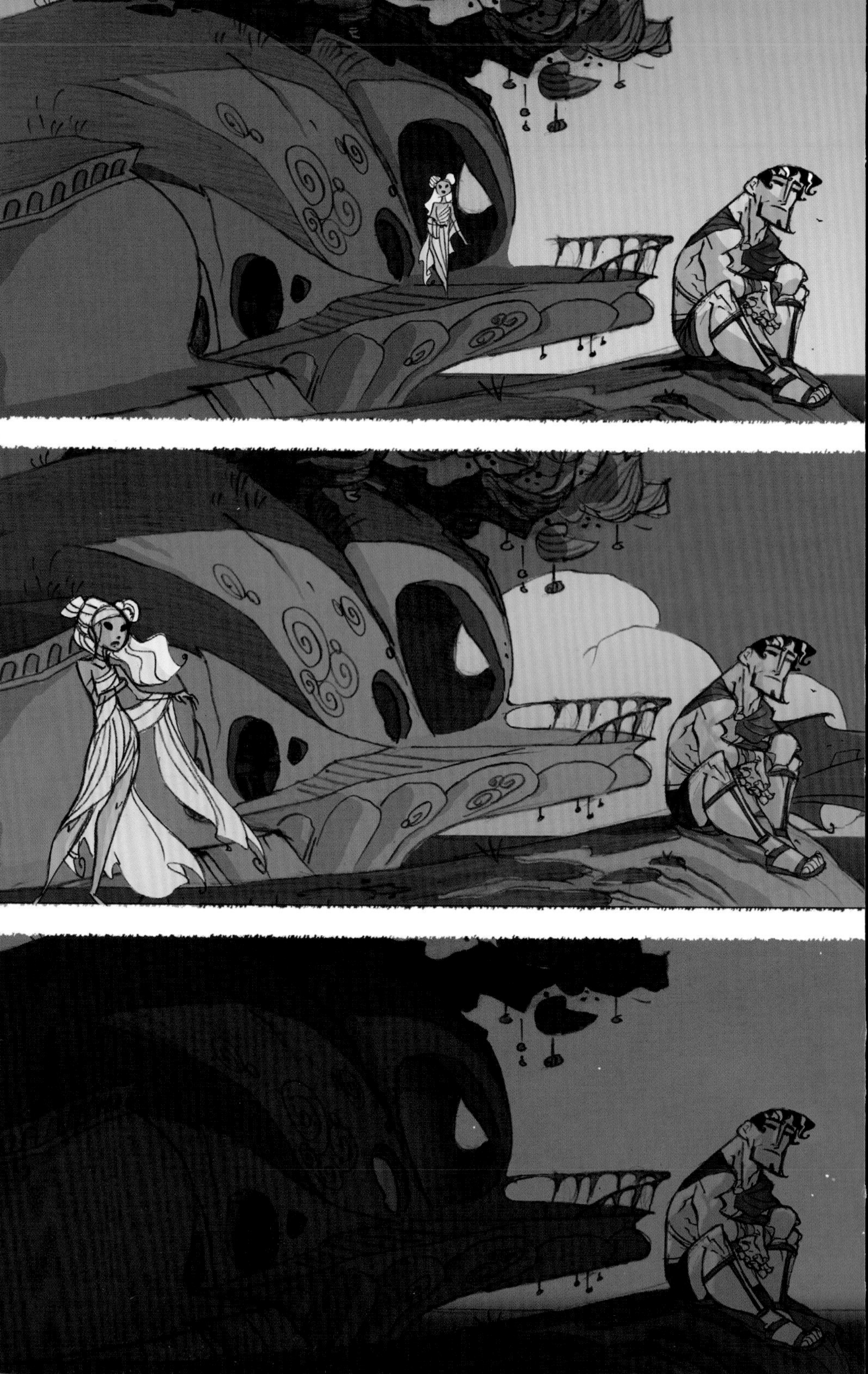

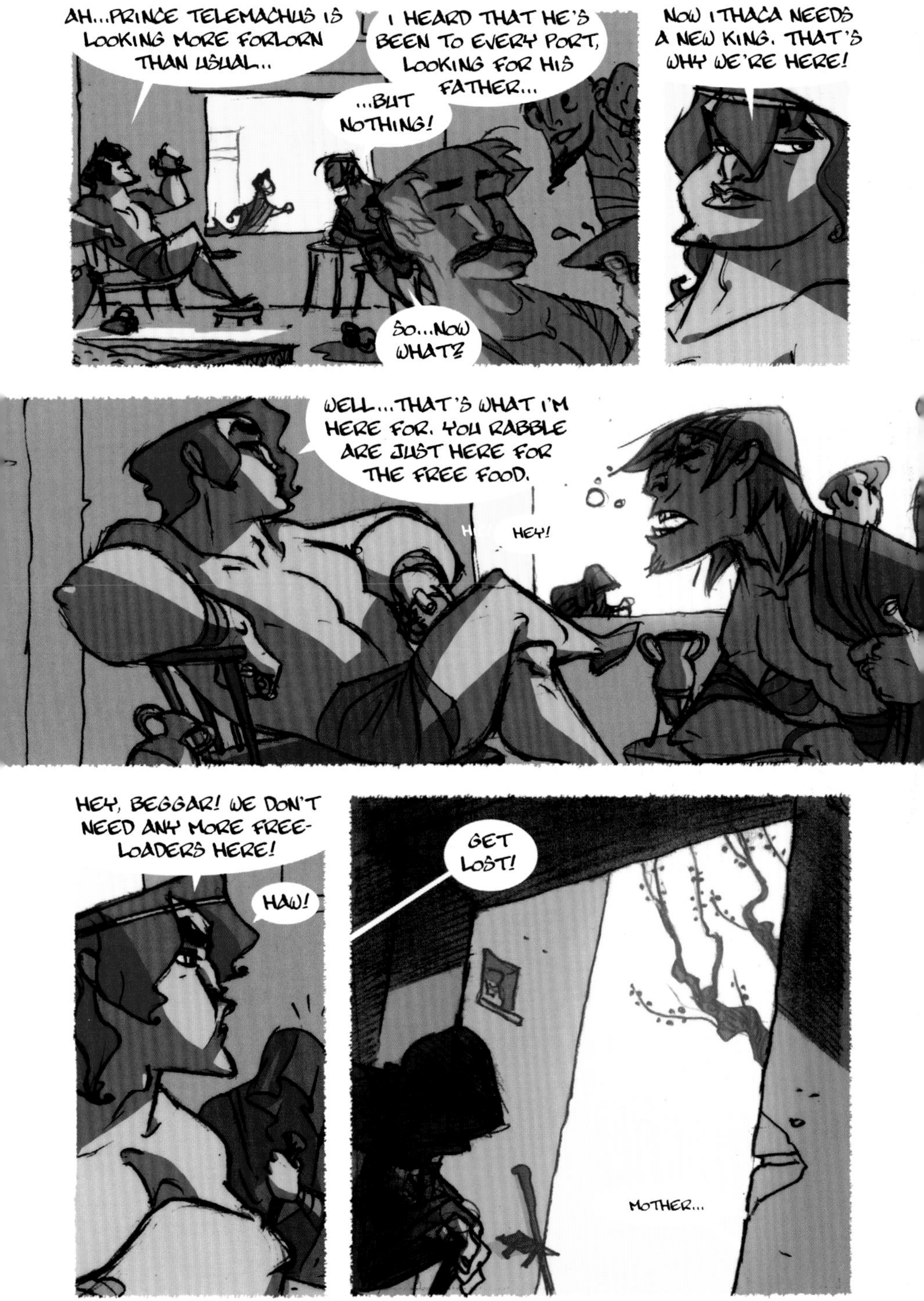

AH...PRINCE TELEMACHUS IS LOOKING MORE FORLORN THAN USUAL..
I HEARD THAT HE'S BEEN TO EVERY PORT, LOOKING FOR HIS FATHER...
...BUT NOTHING!
SO...NOW WHAT?
NOW ITHACA NEEDS A NEW KING. THAT'S WHY WE'RE HERE!
WELL...THAT'S WHAT I'M HERE FOR. YOU RABBLE ARE JUST HERE FOR THE FREE FOOD.
HEY!
HEY, BEGGAR! WE DON'T NEED ANY MORE FREE-LOADERS HERE!
HAW!
GET LOST!
MOTHER...

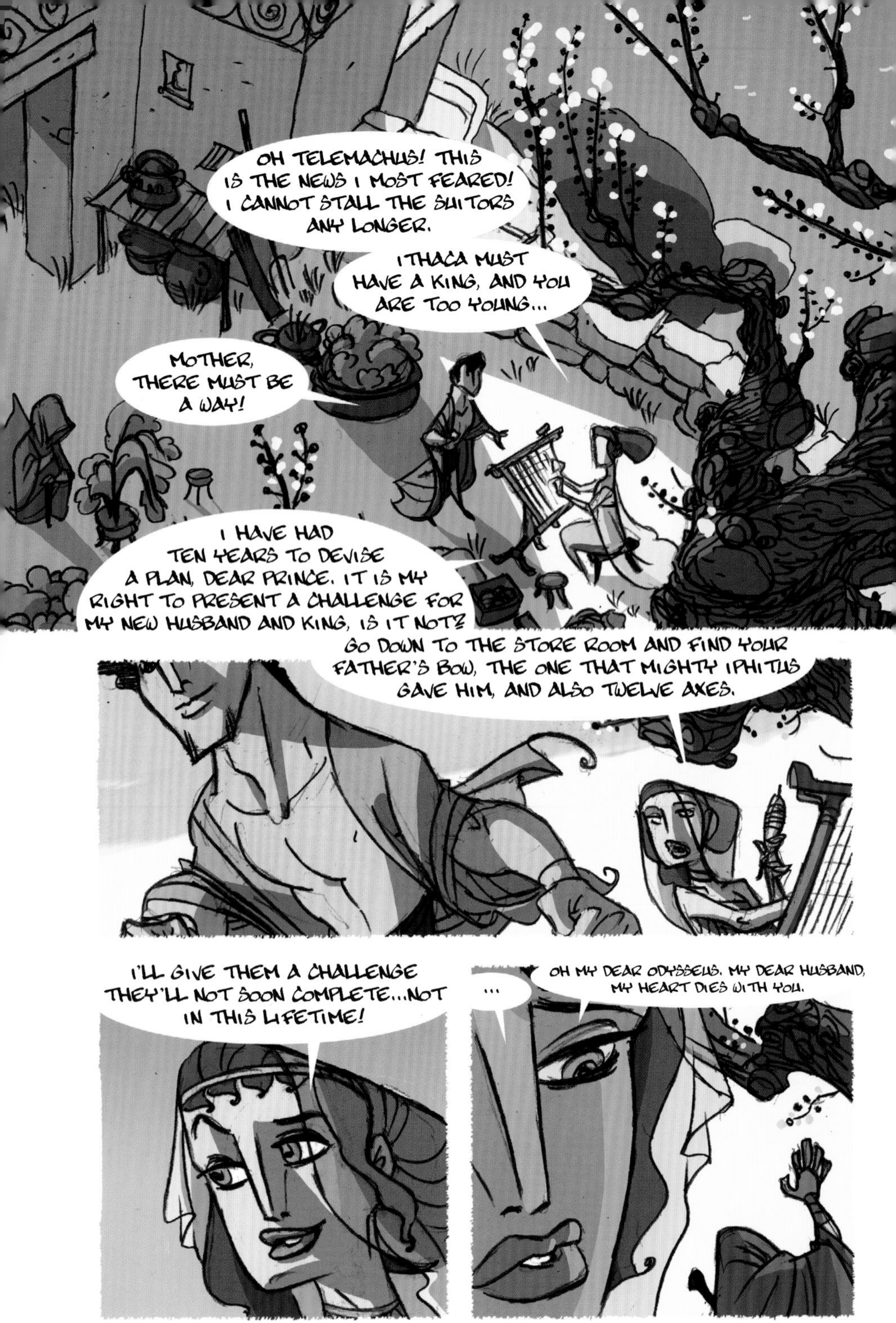
OH TELEMACHUS! THIS IS THE NEWS I MOST FEARED! I CANNOT STALL THE SUITORS ANY LONGER.
ITHACA MUST HAVE A KING, AND YOU ARE TOO YOUNG...
MOTHER, THERE MUST BE A WAY!
I HAVE HAD TEN YEARS TO DEVISE A PLAN, DEAR PRINCE. IT IS MY RIGHT TO PRESENT A CHALLENGE FOR MY NEW HUSBAND AND KING, IS IT NOT?
GO DOWN TO THE STORE ROOM AND FIND YOUR FATHER'S BOW, THE ONE THAT MIGHTY IPHITUS GAVE HIM, AND ALSO TWELVE AXES.
I'LL GIVE THEM A CHALLENGE THEY'LL NOT SOON COMPLETE...NOT IN THIS LIFETIME!
...
OH MY DEAR ODYSSEUS. MY DEAR HUSBAND, MY HEART DIES WITH YOU.

LISTEN TO ME, MY OVERBEARING FRIENDS!

YOU PLAGUE THIS PALACE DAY AND NIGHT, SEEKING MY HAND IN MARRIAGE.

HEE HEE!

THE HAND THAT CAN STRING HIS BOW...

...AND SHOOT AN ARROW CLEAN THROUGH ALL TWELVE AXES, WILL BE THE HAND TO TAKE MINE IN MARRIAGE.

AH...I'LL JUST WAIT HERE UNTIL IT IS MY TURN TO WIN. LET EVERY MAN IN ITHACA TRY AND FAIL -- THIS IS ONE CHALLENGE I WON'T LOSE!

GOOD NIGHT!

HM

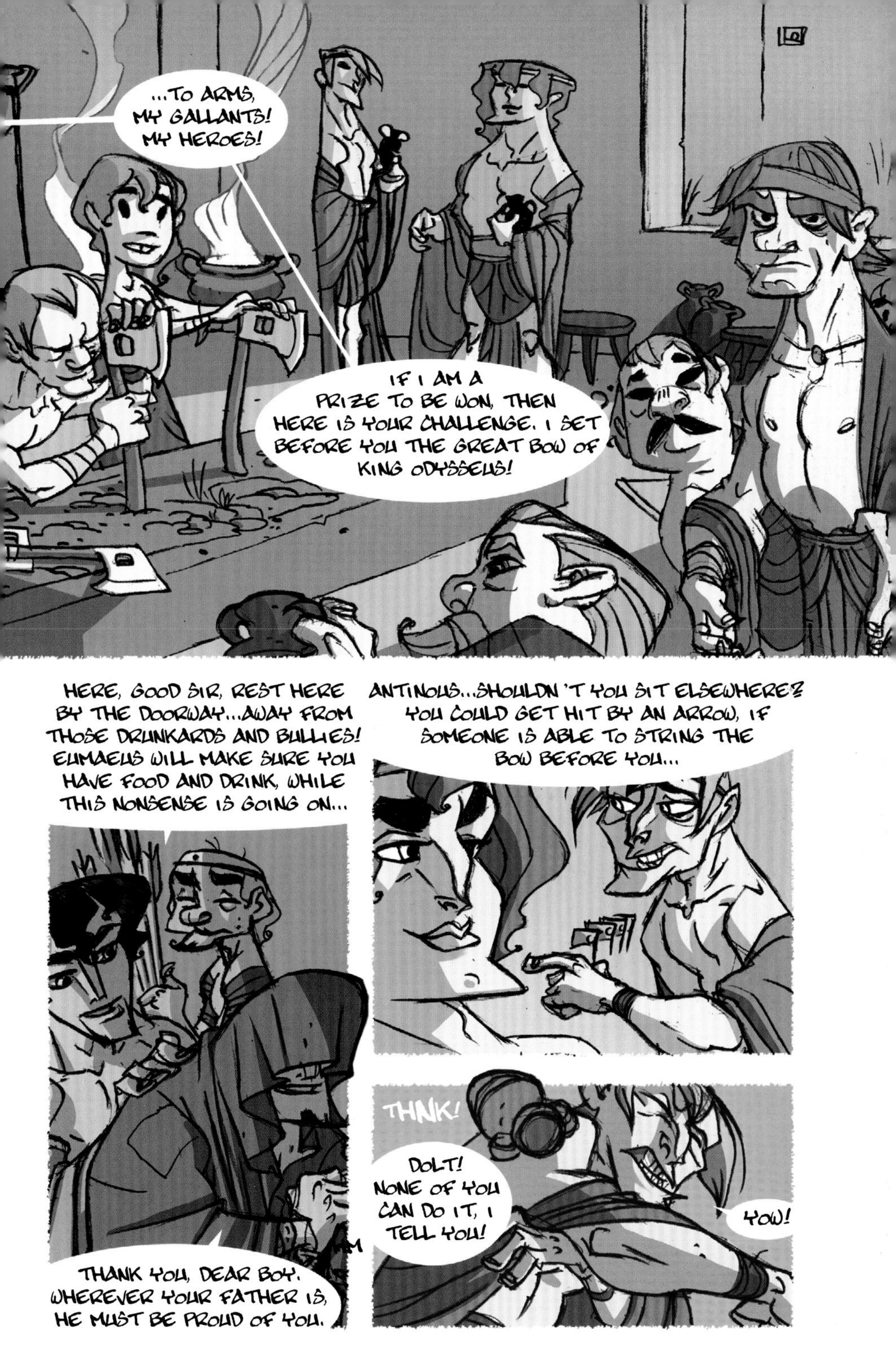
...TO ARMS, MY GALLANTS! MY HEROES!
IF I AM A PRIZE TO BE WON, THEN HERE IS YOUR CHALLENGE. I SET BEFORE YOU THE GREAT BOW OF KING ODYSSEUS!
HERE, GOOD SIR, REST HERE BY THE DOORWAY...AWAY FROM THOSE DRUNKARDS AND BULLIES! EUMAEUS WILL MAKE SURE YOU HAVE FOOD AND DRINK, WHILE THIS NONSENSE IS GOING ON...
THANK YOU, DEAR BOY. WHEREVER YOUR FATHER IS, HE MUST BE PROUD OF YOU.
ANTINOUS...SHOULDN'T YOU SIT ELSEWHERE? YOU COULD GET HIT BY AN ARROW, IF SOMEONE IS ABLE TO STRING THE BOW BEFORE YOU...
THNK!
DOLT! NONE OF YOU CAN DO IT, I TELL YOU!
YOW!

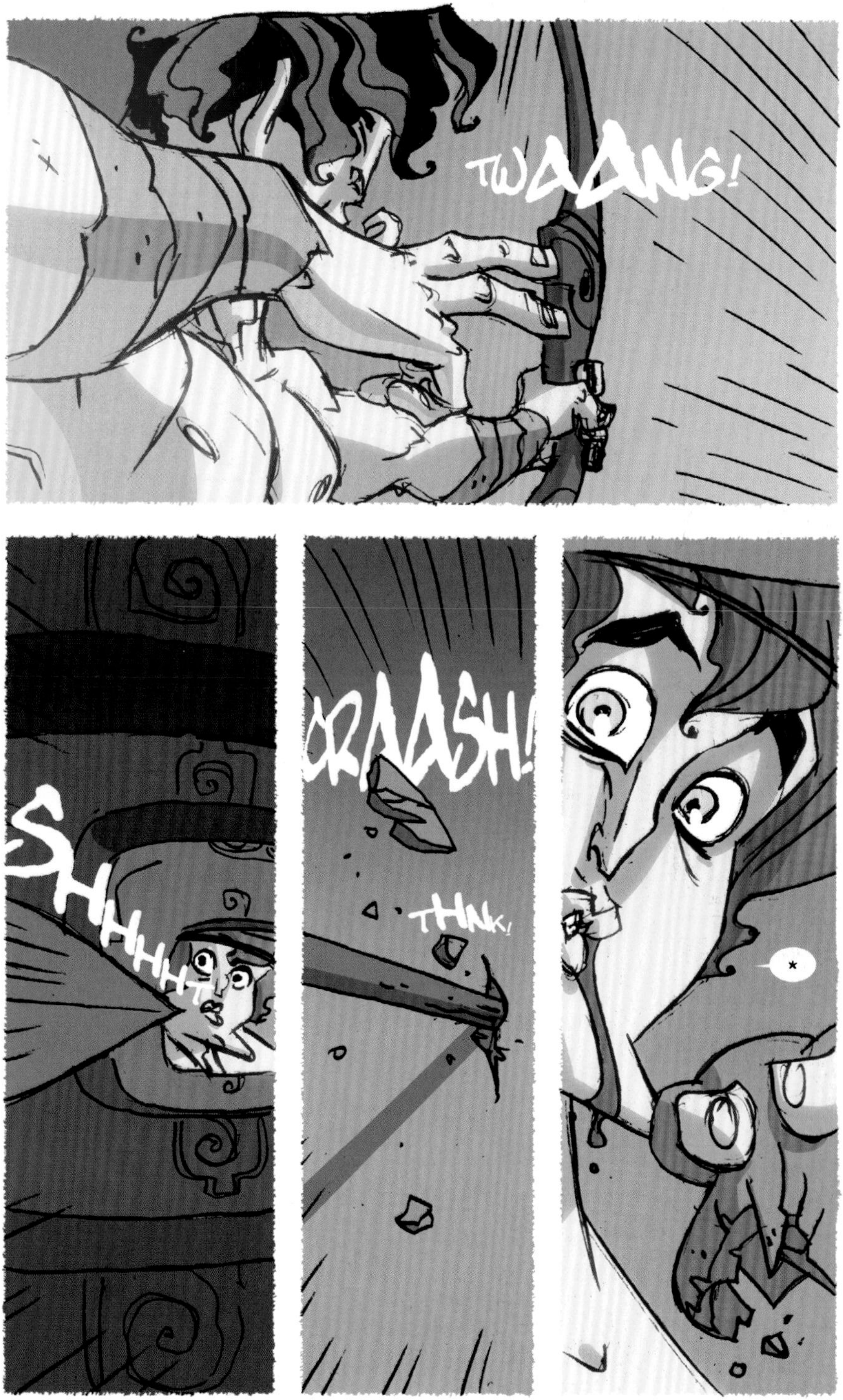
TWAANG!
SHHHHHT
CRAASH!
THNK!
*

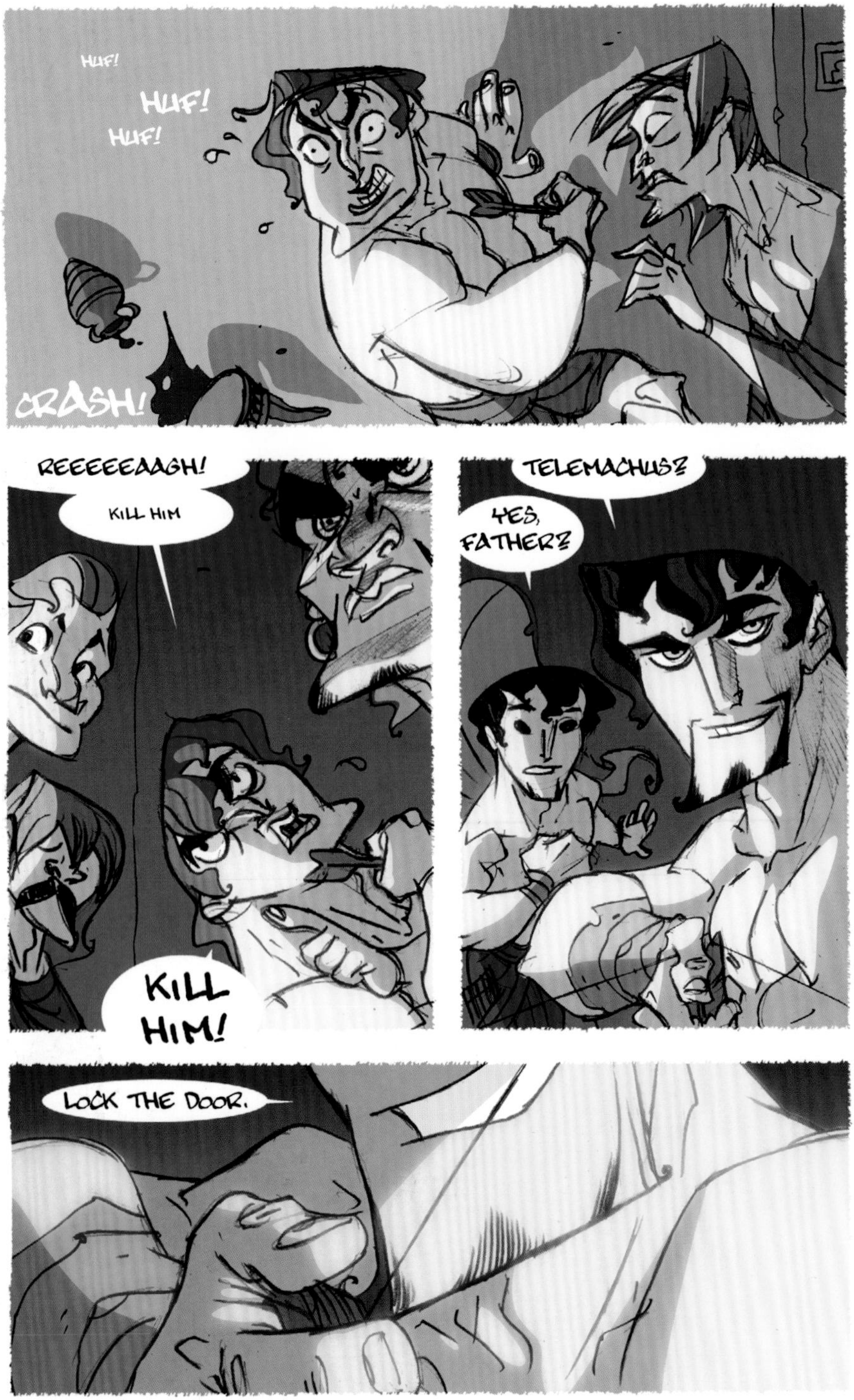
HUF!
HUF!
HUF!
CRASH!
REEEEEEAAGH!
KILL HIM
KILL HIM!
TELEMACHUS?
YES, FATHER?
LOCK THE DOOR.

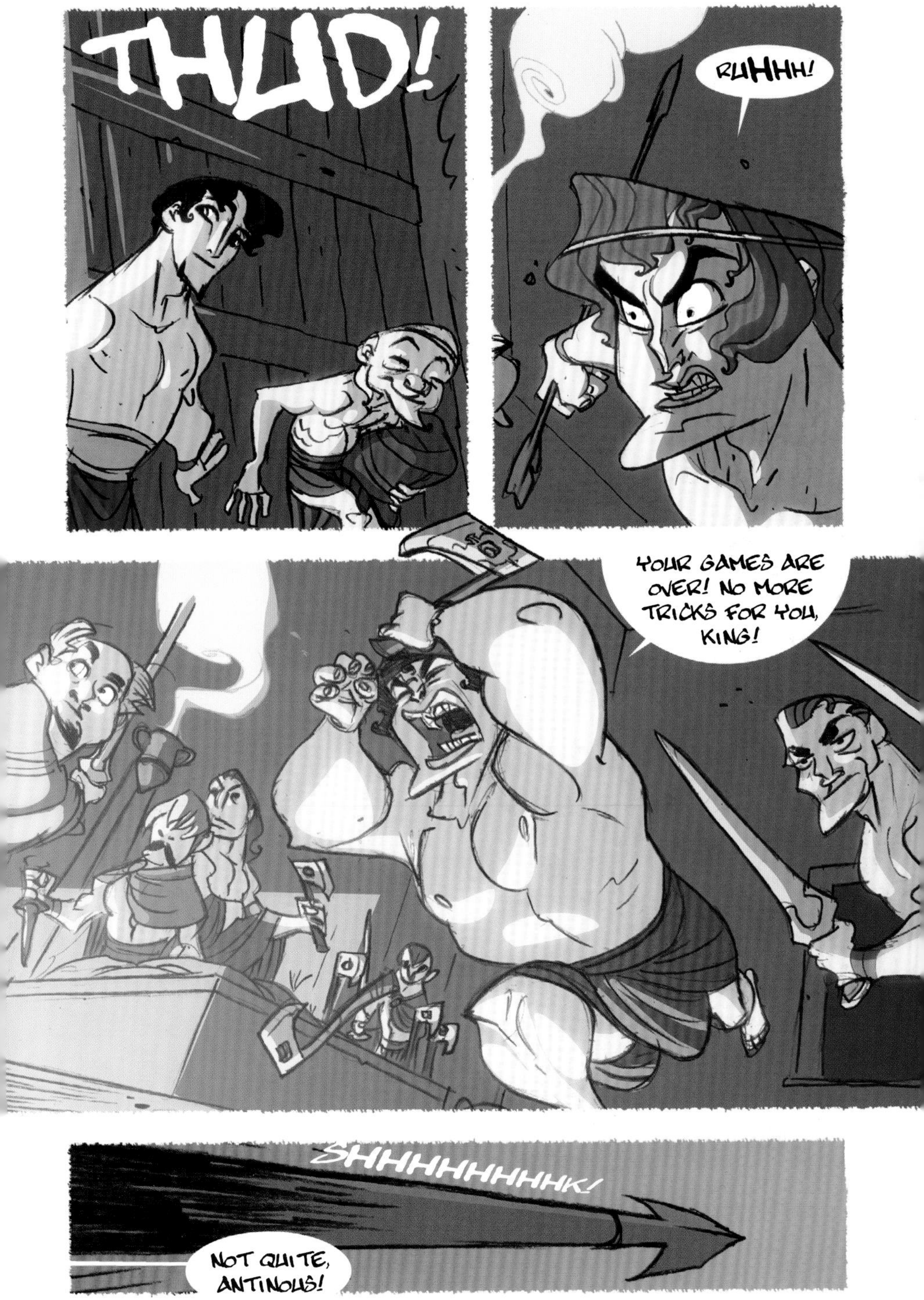
THUD!
RUHHH!
YOUR GAMES ARE OVER! NO MORE TRICKS FOR YOU, KING!
SHHHHHHHHK!
NOT QUITE, ANTINOUS!

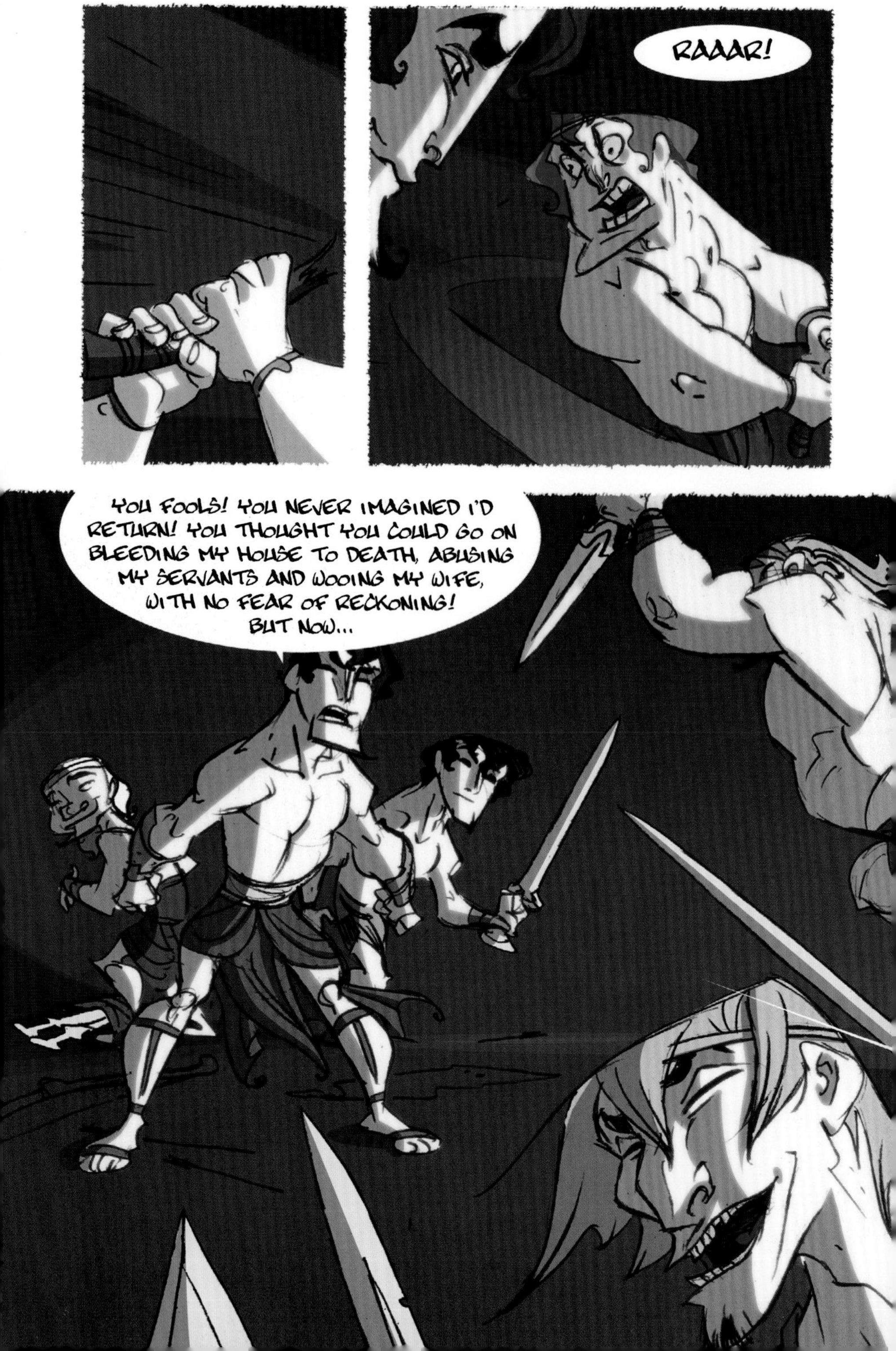
RAAAR!
YOU FOOLS! YOU NEVER IMAGINED I'D RETURN! YOU THOUGHT YOU COULD GO ON BLEEDING MY HOUSE TO DEATH, ABUSING MY SERVANTS AND WOOING MY WIFE, WITH NO FEAR OF RECKONING! BUT NOW...

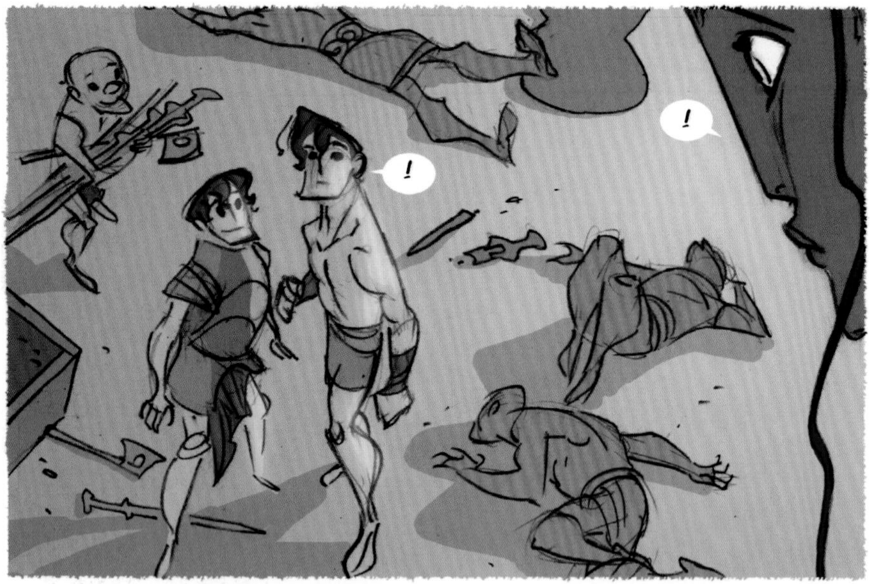
!
!

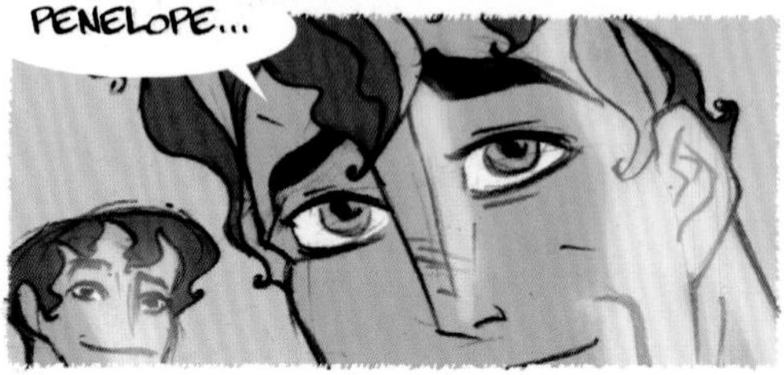
PENELOPE...

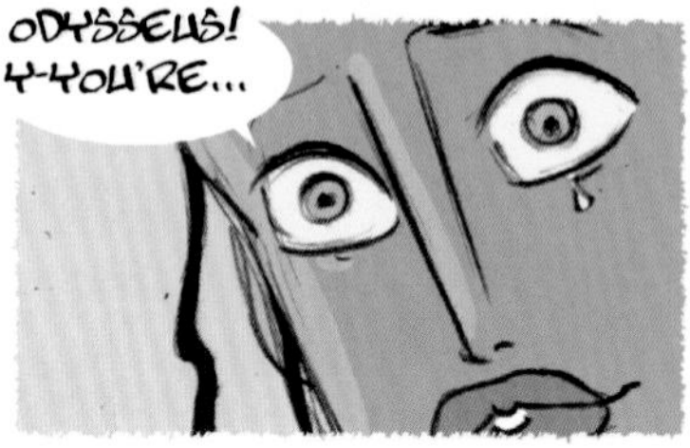
ODYSSEUS!
Y-YOU'RE...

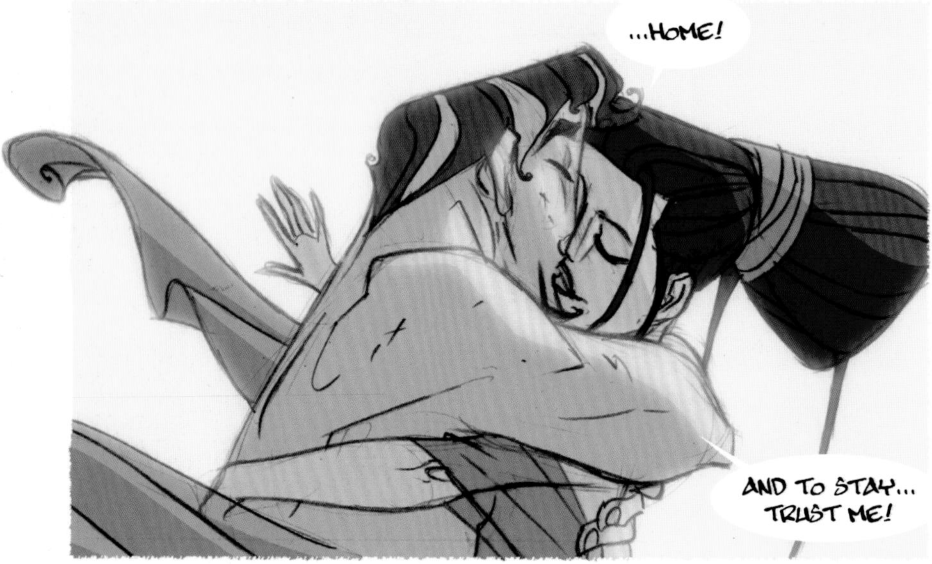
...HOME!
AND TO STAY...
TRUST ME!

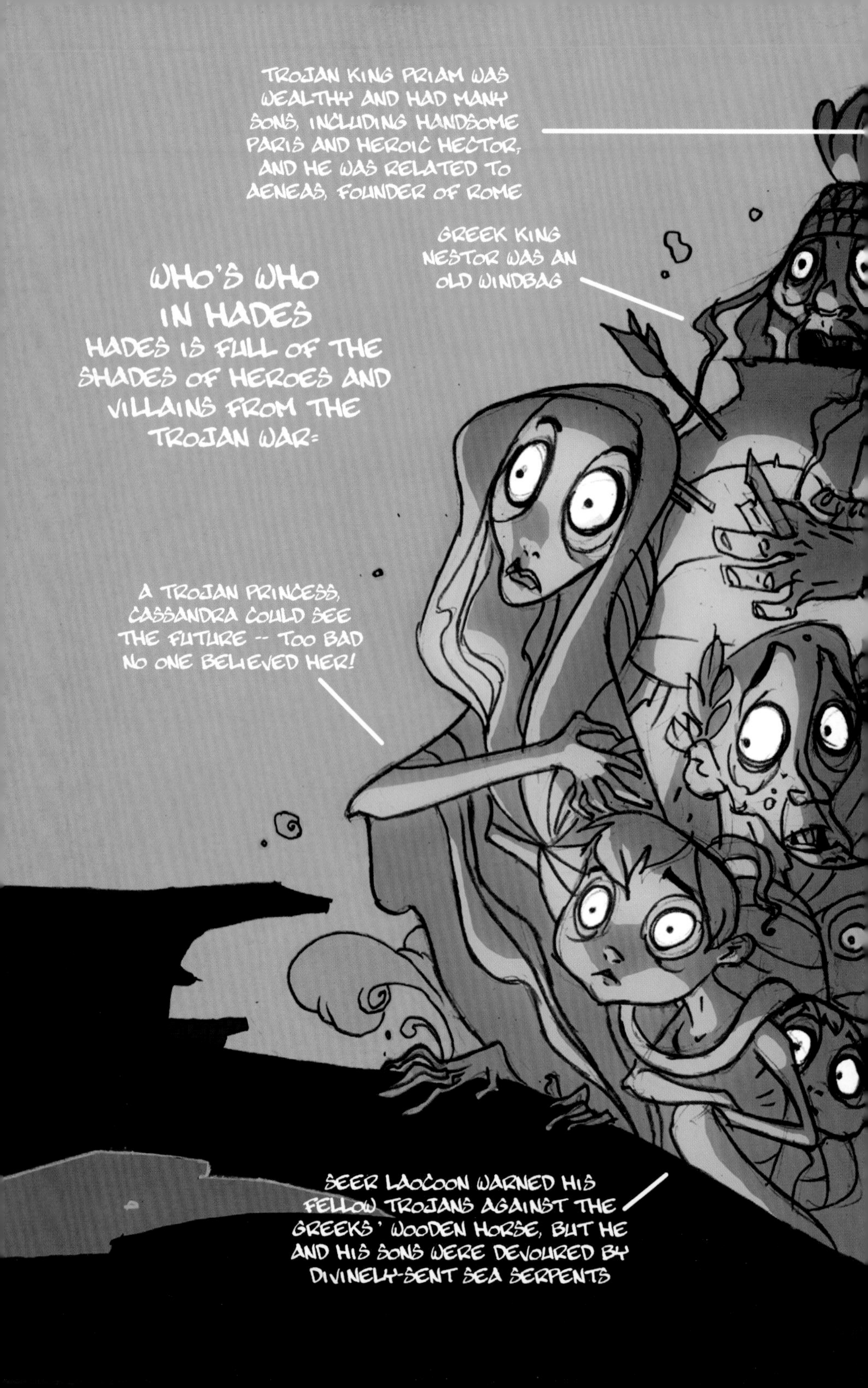
TROJAN KING PRIAM WAS WEALTHY AND HAD MANY SONS, INCLUDING HANDSOME PARIS AND HEROIC HECTOR; AND HE WAS RELATED TO AENEAS, FOUNDER OF ROME
GREEK KING NESTOR WAS AN OLD WINDBAG
WHO'S WHO IN HADES
HADES IS FULL OF THE SHADES OF HEROES AND VILLAINS FROM THE TROJAN WAR:
A TROJAN PRINCESS, CASSANDRA COULD SEE THE FUTURE -- TOO BAD NO ONE BELIEVED HER!
SEER LAOCOON WARNED HIS FELLOW TROJANS AGAINST THE GREEKS' WOODEN HORSE, BUT HE AND HIS SONS WERE DEVOURED BY DIVINELY-SENT SEA SERPENTS

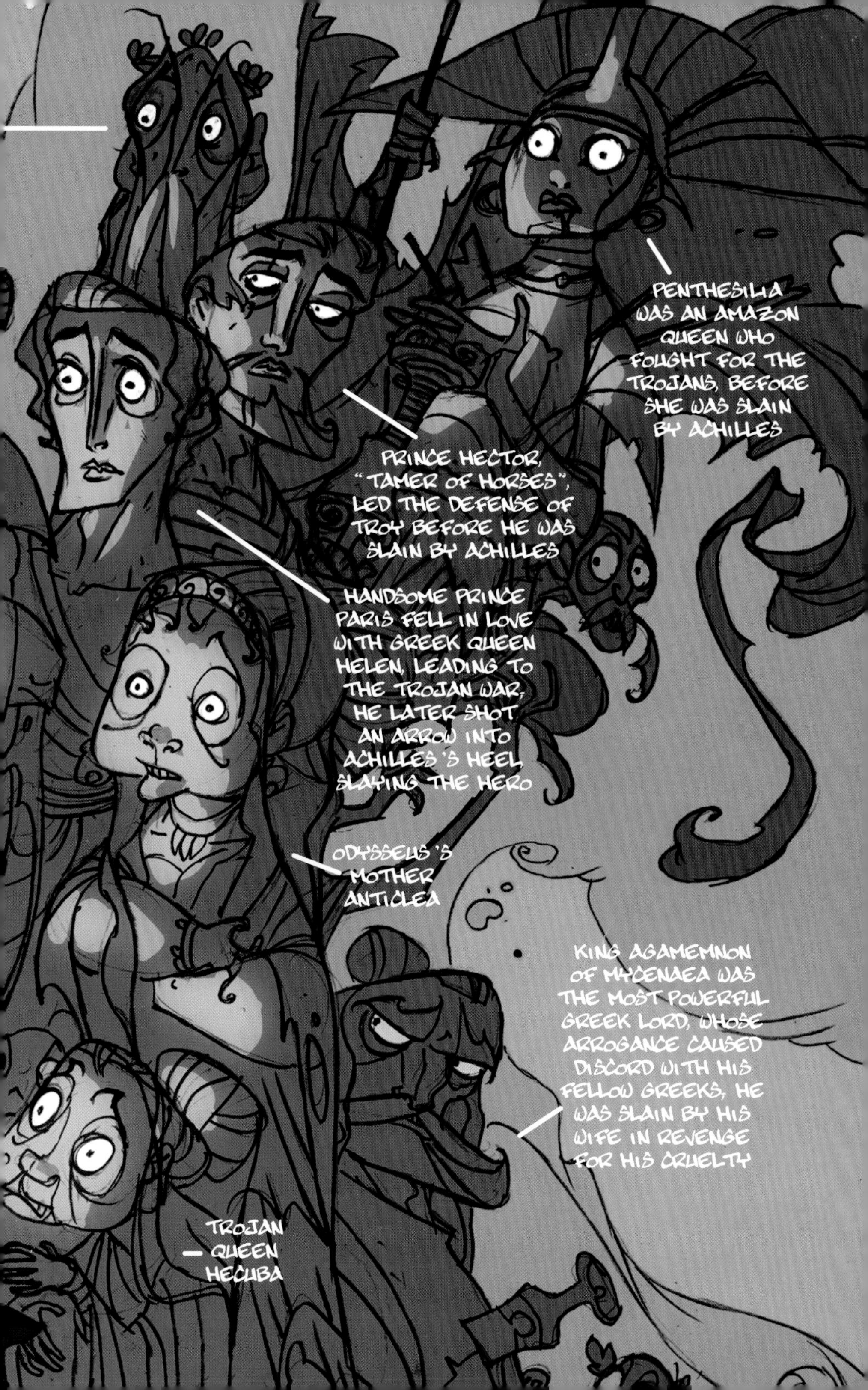
PENTHESILIA WAS AN AMAZON QUEEN WHO FOUGHT FOR THE TROJANS, BEFORE SHE WAS SLAIN BY ACHILLES
PRINCE HECTOR, "TAMER OF HORSES", LED THE DEFENSE OF TROY BEFORE HE WAS SLAIN BY ACHILLES
HANDSOME PRINCE PARIS FELL IN LOVE WITH GREEK QUEEN HELEN, LEADING TO THE TROJAN WAR; HE LATER SHOT AN ARROW INTO ACHILLES'S HEEL, SLAYING THE HERO
ODYSSEUS'S MOTHER ANTICLEA
KING AGAMEMNON OF MYCENAEA WAS THE MOST POWERFUL GREEK LORD, WHOSE ARROGANCE CAUSED DISCORD WITH HIS FELLOW GREEKS. HE WAS SLAIN BY HIS WIFE IN REVENGE FOR HIS CRUELTY
TROJAN QUEEN HECUBA

HOME SWEET HOMER

"THE ODYSSEY" IS THE SEQUEL TO THE EPIC "THE ILIAD," WHICH CHRONICLED THE MASSIVE WAR BETWEEN GREEK KINGS AND THE MIGHTY CITY OF TROY. BOTH POEMS (AMOUNTING TO OVER 25,000 LINES OF ACTION-PACKED POETRY) ARE BELIEVED TO BE THE WORK OF A BLIND BARD FROM THE GREEK ISLANDS, NAMED HOMER. IF SO, HE LIVED LONG BEFORE THE GREEKS HAD A WRITTEN LANGUAGE, AND COMPOSED, MEMORIZED AND RECITED THIS VAST WORK ENTIRELY FROM HIS HEAD!

MODERN HISTORIANS DISMISSED THESE STORIES UNTIL ARCHAEOLOGIST HEINRICH SCHLIEMANN UNCOVERED THE ENORMOUSLY STRONG AND WEALTHY RUINS OF TROY, ON THE TURKISH COAST. ALTHOUGH WE WILL NEVER KNOW ALL THE ANSWERS, THE TROJAN WAR WAS PROBABLY FOUGHT AROUND 1,200BC, WHEN THE CITY WAS CONSUMED BY FLAMES. HOMER HIMSELF LIVED HUNDREDS OF YEARS LATER, AND WHILE HE NOTED MANY ACCURATE DETAILS OF LIFE IN THE TROJAN AGE, HE ALSO ADDED MATERIAL FROM HIS OWN DAY -- MUCH TO THE CONFUSION OF LATER HISTORIANS!

WHILE THEY BELIEVED IN THE SHADOWY AFTERWORLD OF HADES, THE GREEKS WERE MUCH MORE CONCERNED WITH THIS LIFE. HEROES WERE EXPECTED TO SHOW "TIME" (HONOR, OR RESPECT FOR THEIR FRIENDS AND FOES) AND "ARETÉ" (GREATNESS, OR ACHIEVING THIER FULL POTENTIAL).

IN A WORLD WITH FEW LAWS AND LITTLE PROTECTION FOR THE WEAK OR VULNERABLE, GREEKS CHERISHED THE DIVINELY ORDAINED LAWS OF HOSPITALITY AND SANCTUARY. ZEUS WAS SOMETIMES CALLED "ZEUS XENIOS," THE PATRON OF GUESTS. HIS PROTECTION EXTENDED TO TEMPLES AND SHRINES -- VIOLENCE INSIDE A HOME OR TEMPLE WAS CONSIDERED A CRIME AGAINST THE GODS!

ODYSSEUS HIMSELF WAS NEVER WORSHIPPED IN GLORY LIKE ACHILLES OR HERACLES -- HE WAS TOO TRICKY TO BE A ROLE-MODEL. EVEN HIS FELLOW GREEK KINGS WERE SUSPICIOUS OF HIS WILES, ALTHOUGH THEY WERE HAPPY TO TAKE HIS ADVICE! BUT HE PERSONIFIED THE GREEK IDEAL OF THE "VERSATILE MAN" WHO WAS READY FOR ANY CHALLENGE.

BAH!

TO LEARN MORE ABOUT THE ANCIENT WORLD AND THE MISADVENTURES OF ODYSSEUS, AND TO SEE MORE ART FROM THIS STORY, VISIT:

WWW. ACTIONCARTOONING. COM